A Marriage for the Marquess

Barrington's Brigade
Book 1

Ruth A. Casie

Dragonblade Publishing, Inc. is an imprint of Kathryn Le Veque Novels, Inc.
P.O. Box 23
Moreno Valley, CA 92556
ceo@dragonbladepublishing.com

Produced in the United States of America

First Edition January 2025
Trade Paperback Edition

Dearest Reader;

Thank you for your support of a small press. At Dragonblade Publishing, we strive to bring you the highest quality Historical Romance from some of the best authors in the business. Without your support, there is no 'us', so we sincerely hope you adore these stories and find some new favorite authors along the way.

Happy Reading!

CEO, Dragonblade Publishing

Additional Dragonblade books by Author Ruth A. Casie

Barrington's Brigade Series
A Marriage for the Marquess (Book 1)

The Ladies of Sommer-by-the-Sea Series
The Lady and Her Quill (Book 1)
The Lady and the Spy (Book 2)
The Lady and Her Duke (Book 3)
The Duke's Lost Love (Novella)

Pirates of Britannia Series
Donald
Hugh
Graham
The Pirate's Jewel
The Pirate's Redemption

The Lyon's Den Series
The Lyon's Gambit
The Lyon's Alliance

Barrington's Brigade – the Story

From duty to devotion to their King, their Country, and the women that they love.

Against the dramatic backdrop of the Peninsular War, the lives of six courageous retired officers unfold in a world markedly different from the one they knew. These seasoned men soon realize that their most significant challenges extend far beyond the battlefield.

United by an unbreakable bond and led by their revered commander, Lord Barrington, these officers proudly don the title of "Barrington's Brigade." Their commitment transcends the chaos of war as they pledge unwavering support not only to Barrington's service for England but also to each other. Together, they embark on a journey to overcome both the visible and concealed scars of war, navigating a society on the brink of profound social and cultural transformations.

Amidst their quest for peace and normalcy, they uncover a sinister criminal element: the Order of Shadows, a clandestine organization that thrives on manipulation and power. This shadowy group poses a new threat, weaving a web of deceit and danger that these men must unravel to secure justice and protect their king, country, and those they love.

Tied by a loyalty beyond question, these extraordinary comrades stand ready to support each other in times of need. A distinctive gold coin becomes the symbol of their unwavering brotherhood, commemorates their unbreakable bond, and serves as a unique calling card—summoning their assistance whenever it is presented.

Step into a world where honor, loyalty, and love intertwine as the remarkable men of Barrington's Brigade and the women who captivate their hearts traverse the intricacies of Regency society while battling the dark forces of the Order of Shadows, forging their paths to their happily ever afters...

Book 1 – A Match for the Marquess

In a world of secrets, love, and ticking clocks, their alliance of convenience may just become a marriage of the heart.

Ewan, the Marquess of Glenraven, finds himself returning to his home in Belgrave Square, summoned back to London by his former commanding officer, Lord Barrington. Ewan's been entrusted with the task of unraveling a deceitful gambling scheme and uncovering the truth behind the mysterious deaths tied to it. He is also faced with a pressing personal ultimatum: either secure his trust by marrying by his 30th birthday, five weeks hence, or risk losing it all.

In Cavendish Square, a mile north of Belgravia, Lady Juliet Hayward carries the heavy burden of her late brother, Bradley's gambling debts. Her own future teeters on the brink of destitution. Determined to confront the man who has her brother's vowels and control of her survival, she's determined to find him and negotiate a solution.

As Ewan and Juliet are drawn together, they conceal their true intentions, not knowing they both seek the one person who holds the cards. However, time is not on their side. In a bold move, they confess to each other and devise a plan—a marriage of convenience, a calculated business arrangement—to simultaneously fulfill Ewan's inheritance requirement, settle Juliet's brother's debts, and expose the scheming ringleader. As they dig deeper, they uncover a far-reaching conspiracy, orchestrated by a clandestine organization manipulating events from behind the scenes. Yet, a single kiss on their wedding day unleashes a deluge of conflicting emotions within each of them, shattering their carefully constructed façade.

This is a breathtaking Regency tale of love, sacrifice, and the resilience of the human spirit.

*A marriage of convenience,
a game of hearts.*

Chapter One

London, England
March 27, 1820

THE MUFFLED CLOP of horse hooves echoing through the cobblestone streets, merged with the sounds of bustling London and the ever-present fog as Ewan, Marquess Glenraven, stepped from the post-coach at The Golden Cross Inn. He stood by the coach, a layer of dust from Dover Road clinging to his coat.

Tall and broad-shouldered, he carried himself with a military bearing and long titled heritage. An errant breeze tousled his dark hair as it framed his strong chiseled face, but it was his piercing gray eyes that caught attention. They hinted at a depth of emotion hidden beneath a façade of composure and to those that knew him, promised a loyalty and trust like none other.

He took a deep breath. At last, he was almost home.

The bells of St. Paul Cathedral echoed through the narrow alleys. Glenraven glanced at his pocket watch. 12:30 pm. Satisfied he would be on time for his meeting, he tucked the time piece away as the midday sun broke through the fog and cast a warm glow on the inn.

"I'll organize our belongings and secure a carriage." Duncan MacAlister, Glenraven's longtime friend and batman, throughout the turmoil in Paris following the war, didn't wait for a reply. Duncan knew him well.

Their journey began a week ago when Glenraven received a

letter from his father's solicitor, Mr. Hughes. The message directed Glenraven to make every effort to attend a meeting at Lord Barrington's London home at 2:00 p.m. on the 27th of March.

He and Duncan began their trek with a five-day ride from Paris to Calais, followed by a two-and-a-half-hour sail on the paddle steamer *Rob Roy* to Dover. The final leg of their journey was a grueling nine-hour post-coach ride to London. The entire week, Glenraven could not rid himself of the persistent whispers that his return to London was more dangerous than the government affairs he left behind in Paris.

With only ninety minutes to spare before he was to present himself at Barrington Hall, there wasn't any time for him to make himself more presentable and still make it back to the meeting in time. Debating whether to go home and be late or arrive early at Barrington's, he reached into his pocket and took out a gold coin. Skillfully flicking it into the air, the coin spun and captured the light before it fell back into his palm.

"My lord?" Glenraven looked up to see Duncan call to him from a carriage.

"You go on. I'll head to Barrington's." Duncan nodded his agreement and gave the driver instructions.

Not wanting to arrive at Barrington's too early, he went to Covent Garden. He made his way through the busy crowd, following a savory aroma like a field dog tracking a scent trail. He purchased a pasty and searched for a quiet area where he could enjoy his treat before starting out for Grosvenor Square.

Although the area was crowded, he found the last available seat on a bench not far from a puppet stage. As he enjoyed the warm meat-filled pastry, his mind drifted to Hughes. What serious issue could there be that called him back so urgently? Another bite of the pastry brought a sense of certainty that whatever Hughes found could be solved. Besides, it was good to be back in London.

Finishing the pasty, he took out the gold coin. The coin arrived with Hughes' message without any explanation, its presence serving as a silent call to action from his former commander. He mulled over what could be so urgent that Barrington needed him back in London and if it connected in any way to Hughes' need to see him.

"Oh, sir, could you help us, please?" A neatly dressed man called out to him from the puppet stage.

The crowd, which he realized had gathered waiting for the puppet show, turned their attention toward him.

Glenraven scanned the area, unsure if the gentleman was calling out to him. He glanced back at the man.

"Yes, sir, you. You look like a man who would help a lady in distress." A soft chuckle rippled through the onlookers. "It is a simple script that needs to be read."

"Forgive me. I would gladly help a lady in distress." Glenraven glanced at the crowd. "I see some lovely ladies." He nodded to several ladies not too far from him. "But I do not see any ladies in distress."

The man operating the puppet stage peeked under the curtain. "My lady. Are you in distress?" he called out.

"Yes, my lord," came a voice from behind the curtain. As the puppet master opened the curtain, a female puppet was revealed. "I have no Punch."

Glenraven checked his watch. It was ten minutes past one. "Ne'er let it be said that I didn't come to a lady's aid."

Glenraven made his way to the stage to the crowd's chuckling and applauding.

"Thank you, my lord. Thank you." the puppet master whispered to him before turning to address the audience.

"Kind people. I am the puppet master, Percival Thimbleby. You've already met Miss Juliet Hayward, who will be our Judy. She has taken her place. This is," the puppet master turned to Glenraven and waited. He coughed and waited a bit more. "And this is?" He raised his eyebrows at his Punch.

With a good natured smile, he slightly bowed to the audience. "Lord Glenraven at your service."

"My lord." The puppet master doffed his cap and bowed to him. "Ladies and Gents, we have a real hero," he added with a playful eye roll, making everyone laugh. "Lord Glenraven will be playing our Punch. We are fortunate to have found two willing people to help us today. They do not know what has happened in the story so far. It will be very telling how they portray this scene. Be gentle with my actors, my friends. I dare say they are new to this trade. We want to encourage them. Who knows, you may witness the beginning of a most enchanting partnership."

The puppet master turned to Glenraven. "This way, my lord. While you and your Judy say your lines, I will manage the puppets."

He guided Glenraven to his spot, handed him his script, and then returned to address the audience.

Glenraven glanced at the paper and burst into laughter, the sound echoing for all to hear.

"Are you all right, my lord?" the puppet master called out.

"Quite. I see you are also a magician. For us mortals, the script is blank."

The audience laughed along with him, clearly in on the jest.

"Well, my lord. I am a poor puppet master. I only had one script and, as a gallant puppet master, gave it to your Judy as I know you would want me to. After all, you are a gallant hero."

"Yes, I am." Glenraven chuckled. "I accept the challenge. You, my friend, may have to suffer the consequences."

"Very well, my lord. I am certain your quick wit and heroism will come to the fore." Again, the audience chuckled.

The puppet master turned to the audience.

"I will set the stage. Punch has brought back a treasure and must convince his Judy to let him keep it." The puppet master paused. "Punch. You can begin whenever you are ready."

Glenraven took a moment, cleared his throat, and began with a theatrical flair.

"Oh, Judy, my love." Glenraven's voice, a warm whiskey

baritone, rang out. "I have fought hard and long. I've brought back a treasure. It must be protected at all costs." He paused a heartbeat and continued, his voice a bit lower, "I won't let anyone take it from us!"

"But Punch, dear, we must be careful." His Judy's voice was sweet and slightly breathless. "There are those who covet what we have."

"Fear not, my sweet Judy." Glenraven's Punch declared with theatrical bravado. "I'll stand against them all, even if it means facing the darkest of contenders."

He imagined Judy gazing at Punch as she went on, her voice sweet and a touch unsteady, "Then let us be strong together, my Punch. Our love will guide us through."

Glenraven stared at the curtain separating him from his Judy and put the papers down. He focused all his attention on his unseen partner.

"And when the storm clouds gather," Punch continued, his tone filled with anticipation, "and the world around us seems uncertain…" A dramatic pause lingered. "We'll find shelter in each other's arms, and our hearts will be our fortress. But, Judy, my love," Punch's voice softened, "there's one thing you must know. Our journey won't always be easy."

The puppet master skillfully moved Punch to Judy's side, his puppet arm around her.

"I understand, Punch. I'm prepared to face whatever challenges lie ahead."

"Then, my dear Judy, let us embark on this adventure together, hand in hand." The puppet master had Punch take Judy's hand.

"Together, we'll find the strength to conquer all," Judy declared.

"And as we travel through life's mysterious twists and turns…" Punch turned his head and looked around. "We'll uncover the secrets hidden in the shadows, and they shall not hold us back. Judy, my love," Punch's tone deepened with passion, "desire burns within me like an unquenchable fire."

Judy delicately touched Punch's face. "And what of commitment, Punch? Will your flames endure, or will they be snuffed out?"

"Fear not, dear Judy," Even the audience could hear the smile in Punch's voice, "for desire may kindle our passion, but it's a commitment that fuels our eternal flame."

"Then let our love burn brighter than the stars, Punch, for we are bound by both desire and commitment."

This little game excited Glenraven in ways he hadn't anticipated. The essence of sincerity he heard in 'Judy's' voice warmed him. The more he spoke, the more the line between him and his Punch blurred.

Absurd. He gave himself a mental shake. This puppet performance is only a game. Judy isn't the only one capable of playing a believable game.

"So, my love," Punch said tenderly, "let us dance through the pages and write our own story, bound by fate and love."

"Forever entwined, together we'll craft our own destiny. It awaits, Punch, my dearest." There was a pause. "Forever," was Judy's breathless reply.

Glenraven's Punch took Judy in his arms, dipped her backward, and kissed her to the laughter of the crowd. The puppets then parted, each taking a bow as the curtain closed.

The puppet master stepped forward. "Oh, my dear friends, this conclusion has been special. Please, Judy and Punch, come out so we can properly thank you."

The curtain on the left side of the puppet stage parted, and a young woman emerged as Glenraven came out through the drape on the right side.

"Miss Juliet Hayward, you were a wonderful Judy. You are welcome to join our traveling show anytime you like," the puppet master said.

She turned to thank the puppeteer, but her gaze met Glenraven's, causing her to pause.

"Lord Glenraven, thank you again for an interesting reading." Glenraven nodded to the puppeteer and tipped his hat to Miss Hayward, no, Juliet. That is how he would remember her.

"Fare thee well, my dearest. Parting is such sweet sorrow." Glenraven lifted Juliet's hand and kissed her knuckles, mischief in his eyes.

⟫⟪

JULIET FELT THE invitation in his smile and couldn't help but respond with a mischievous smile of her own. "I shall say goodnight till it be morrow." She tried to suppress a smile but lost the battle.

Glenraven escorted her away from the puppet stage. A bump from a passerby caused a small cloud of dust to erupt from his coat. He tipped his hat to the culprit. "Cousin?" The man had already walked on.

"Have you been traveling, my lord?" She glanced behind them at the small cloud from his coat.

"You found me out. I've been abroad. Traveling has its demands, but it is good to be back in London, especially on a day as delightful as today." They stopped at a fork in the pathway. "Regrettably, I must go or be late for an appointment."

She struggled to quickly prevent any shadow of disappointment from passing over her face. Juliet did not believe him. He made no effort to move rapidly through the small thirty-minute performance.

Silly woman. It was a performance. Nothing more. Although, for a moment, it felt so…

"Well then, Punch, off with you," she said with a wave, not giving him a chance to explain himself. "Till it be morrow." She laughed. "You are a good sport, my lord. Mr. Thimbleby approached me in much the same manner as he did you. Thank you for a lovely afternoon diversion." She turned to leave but hesitated. "I do look forward to our next performance."

HER LAUGHTER WAS light and tinkled. He followed her progress as she made her way and was swallowed up by the crowd. He chuckled and shook his head. His step was lighter, and his head filled with thoughts of Punch and Judy as he headed to Barrington Hall. The banter between him and 'Judy' was indeed enjoyable, and she responded to Shakespeare's quote quite nicely. Her quick wit made sparring with her quite enjoyable.

Hayward? He didn't know the name. He made a mental note to ask his father. The man knew everyone in London. She was a beauty with chestnut hair that shimmered in the sunlight and deep hazel eyes filled with mischief. And passion. A smile broadened on his face. Yes, he would like to see them filled with passion.

The thought struck a chord with him. He wasn't some rogue to get excited over a woman's appearance, but there was something appealing about Miss Juliet Hayward that had nothing to do with her slender body or appealing good looks. He let out a sigh. It was, indeed, a lovely way to spend thirty minutes.

Chapter Two

H E TURNED DOWN Grosvenor Square. Barrington Hall was a few steps away.

Glenraven approached the door, raised the brass door knocker, and let it drop. Within moments, the door opened.

"Good afternoon, Lord Glenraven. It is good to see you."

"Good afternoon, Sanderson." Glenraven entered the spacious foyer. The floor was a smooth, glossy chessboard of large black and white marble tiles. To the left of the entrance was a marble fireplace with an oversized gilt-framed picture of the Barrington country estate in Sommer-by-the-Sea. To the right of the entrance was a mahogany console table with a large gilt mirror above it.

Deep green damask wallpaper covered the walls, its subtle pattern lending an understated elegance. The centerpiece of the foyer was an imposing curved staircase with railings crafted from polished mahogany. Tucked into the curve of the stairs was a round mahogany table with a porcelain bowl filled with fresh flowers.

The corridor to the rest of the house was to the right of the grand staircase.

He gave the butler his hat and coat. He couldn't help but spot Sanderson holding his coat at arm's length.

"I came directly from Dover," he said, explaining his dust-covered garment. For a moment, he saw Juliet's expression when she saw his coat and tried not to smile.

"Lord Barrington is expecting you in his study."

Glenraven crossed the foyer, went down the corridor, and entered the first door on the right, Barrington's study.

Mahogany carvings, intricate as the strategies once studied for war, adorned the buttercream walls. Polished mahogany bookshelves lined each wall with volumes of military history and classic literature but stopped short of the lofty ten-foot ceilings. In the generous space above, a gallery of painted landscapes offered windows to the serene countryside, reminiscent of the peace Lord Barrington sought after the tumult of the Peninsula War.

Jade curtains, as rich as the fields he once marched through, draped elegantly from matched cornices framed the grand windows. The room's focal point was the hearth, ever ablaze with a welcoming fire as well as witnessing quiet evenings of reflection. Above it hung a painting of Barrington's parents, the Duke and Duchess of Stirling, flanked by Reese and his older brother, Edward.

A table surrounded by chairs occupied one side of the room. Before the fireplace, a trio of comfortable chairs and a sofa invited conversations. The large bay window housed a pedestal desk and leather chair. Across from the fireplace, a cellarette stood ready to serve refreshments. Underfoot, Turkish carpets, as intricate as the battle plans Barrington once pored over, cushioned the veteran's steps. Across from the bay window were the pocket doors that led to the dining room.

However, the study's best asset was not its décor or furnishings. The room was comfortable and warm, used and enjoyed.

"Barrington," Glenraven called as he entered the room.

His former commanding officer sat at his desk, his head down, reading a document. He looked up and gave Glenraven a large smile.

"I should have taken that bet with Hughes. He doubted you would come today the way you've ignored his messages." Barrington came from behind his desk to greet him.

"I know I'm early. I wanted to return this to you." Glenraven removed the gold coin from his pocket.

Barrington held up his hand. "Please, you keep the coin. Return it to me when the mission is completed.

"Very well." He put the coin in his pocket. "What's this about ignoring Hughes' messages?"

"We can talk about that when he arrives. Come. Sit down." Glenraven sat in one of the chairs by the fireplace while Barrington went to the cellarette and poured each of them a drink.

"I hope the journey was uneventful." Barrington handed him a glass of brandy.

Barrington's bravery was as legendary as the battles he fought. His daring rescue, at great personal risk, had saved him and the other men from defeat. That day, amidst the roar of cannons and the cries of the wounded, Barrington had solidified a bond with his comrades that no force could sever. But their rescue came at a significant cost. It wasn't until every man was accounted for that their commander's severe injury was detected.

Each of them helped with his months of recovery. Glenraven still remembered the day Barrington walked into the drawing room across the hall from where he stood, unassisted with his mother on his arm. His father, Lord Stirling, gave a toast.

"With gratitude and humility, Lady Stirling and I thank you for all you have done. We never thought our son would walk again. He was right when he told me his men perform miracles. Please accept this small token as a remembrance of our gratitude." Lord Stirling signaled the butler, and a small box was presented to each man.

"Every man in our family is given a coin, a talisman of sorts. The custom has been handed down for centuries. It began as a way of identifying the carrier as an emissary from the family. While its use is obsolete, the tradition has continued. This coin has been made especially for you, the men of Barrington's Brigade, and signifies you are part of a unique group of men."

The men opened the small box. Inside, they found a gold coin embossed with a circle of laurel leaves. Inside the circle was the letters BB.

"Gentlemen." Everyone turned to their former commander.

He raised his glass. "To you, the men of Barrington's Brigade."
They toasted together.

Now, in times of need, the simple arrival of a gold coin rekindled that unbreakable bond. The coin, bearing the letters BB, was more than a piece of metal—it was a symbol of their shared history, a reminder of the oath they took to stand by each other. The coin was a silent call to arms, a request for aid that they would never ignore. For them, it was an honor to answer Barrington's summons, repaying the debt of their salvation.

"Glenraven, there is no way to say this gently. Your father has been in a severe mishap." His eyes shot up, the color draining from his face.

Chapter Three

"How severe?" *God's blood.* Glenraven's chest tightened as a hot, swollen lump grew in his throat. He sprung out of his chair, the brandy spilling from his glass. "Is he…"

"No, he is still with us, but we came close to losing him," Barrington assured him, his hand resting on Glenraven's arm to steady him.

Glenraven's mind raced, the news of his father's accident igniting a familiar fear. Paris. "I must go to him." The memory of his past failure drove his need to be present and not let history repeat itself.

Barrington's grip tightened gently. "We've brought him here, to Barrington Hall. It's safer." His eyes met Glenraven's. "The accident, we believe, was no mere mishap."

"Here?" Glenraven's surprise quickly turned to disbelief. His breath came in spurts as flashes of the Parisian street, the flash of a knife, and the chaos that followed rushed through his mind. Life was so fragile, a lesson he'd learned all too well.

"Yes, and there's more," Barrington continued. "Your father's valet and coachman acted swiftly."

"Watts and Pearson are both good men. But tell me the rest."

"I agree. Their quick thinking likely saved his life. It's reminiscent of the night in Paris, isn't it? When quick action was all that stood between life and death of the Duchess."

The chaos and the aftermath haunted his dreams. He had captured the assassin, yes, but at a cost, he still carried with him.

"Your mother is here too, though she's out at the moment. We'll need to discuss security measures, Glenraven. We can't take any chances."

"I must go to him." Glenraven glanced at the door. He had to make certain his father was alive.

"Not just yet. There is more you should know."

Barrington's grim tone made him give his former commander his complete attention.

"Your father slipped into unconsciousness upon his return to London and remains there. Since we have a hospital room here, I offered it to your mother. She decided that he would stay here."

Glenraven sank back into the chair. His face was gray with concern as he stared at the man he trusted with his life. This time, he would be there for his family.

"What happened?" Glenraven searched Barrington's face for an answer.

"Your father and Watts rode into a dreadful storm on his way to Northampton. They were crossing the River Lea at the Harmony Bridge when the bridge gave out. Watts got him safely to shore. He had bumps and bruises, and all seemed well."

"I can't sit here." Glenraven got to his feet. "I must see him now."

Barrington stood. "We'll both go see him." They walked through the hall and climbed the staircase. "Watts is not only a good valet. He took care of your father's wounds until Dr. Manning and I reached them. Somehow, Pearson put the carriage back together and brought your father back. Watts is upstairs with your father."

As they reached the landing at the top of the stairs, Glenraven fixed Barrington with a questioning stare. "Northampton? To see the Quinto family?"

"Yes. Watts said when he got your father to shore, he kept mumbling about Enrico Quinto. I know he was upset with Quinto's sudden passing." Barrington led Glenraven down the hall. "Quinto was a good soldier and a finer man. He often played cards with your father. My brother Edward said fine words about him in Parliament."

"From your tone, I gather you think Quinto may have had some assistance in leaving this world."

Barrington stopped in front of a door and faced him. The importance of the accusation hovered between them. "So did your father. He thought the circumstances surrounding his passing were most irregular."

"As are the circumstances around Father's accident," he said through clenched teeth.

"Which makes me glad, if for no other reason than his protection, that your father is here."

"For his protection? From whom, himself?

"Not at all. Your father can control his demons. He actually has put them to work for him. That's why I sent the coin," he nodded toward Glenraven's pocket. "to you. I will tell you about that but now is not the time. First, you should know the details of what happened on their way to Northampton. I've told you what I can about the accident, but I'd rather you hear the details from Watts."

Barrington opened the door. The curtains were drawn, making it difficult to make anything out. His eyes grew accustomed to the dark, and he saw his father's valet, John Watts, sitting next to him. The room was large. To his left was the large bed and end table cluttered with various items. To his right was a sitting area.

The valet got up and came to him. "It is good to see you, my lord."

The patient turned his head. They all glanced at Lord Aurington.

"Dr. Manning mentioned that His Grace's random movements are to be expected and are nothing to be concerned about."

"Mr. Watts, are you here for Father's protection?" Glenraven walked over to his father's bedside.

"Not at all, my lord." Watts followed him to the bed. "As his valet, I stay with him to ensure he has everything he needs. In his current state, when I am not here, one of the staff or Lady Aurington takes my place. Someone is always with your father so that he will not be alone when he wakes. Dr. Manning says he is making some progress."

Glenraven stood next to his father, trying to collect his thoughts. He took his father's hand. It felt weak. This was not the robust man who arm-wrestled with him.

Glenraven's nature was to make things right, but he could not fix this, which frustrated him. He felt his father's strong pulse and his tension eased. Noticing the beads of sweat on his forehead, Glenraven glanced at the nightstand and reached for the cloth. He also caught sight of a deck of cards, the ace of hearts face up.

Still holding his father's hand, he mopped his forehead. His father squeezed his hand. He didn't care if it was a random movement. Excited at being comforted by his father's small gesture, Glenraven bent close to him. "I'm home, Father. You can rest easy. I will take care of everything. All you need to do is recover." He stood and waited, hoping his father would open his eyes. He took the ace of hearts from the deck of cards. He turned it over and examined the back, expecting to see the Aurington family crest. Instead, he found a black raven with wide-spread wings inside a geometric diamond on a gold background. Many clubs had their crests or initials on the back of playing cards. This one was not familiar to him. He glanced at his father, put it in his pocket, and then bent close to him again. "And, Father, no more cards." In the past, teasing and removing the ace of hearts, his father's signature card, would gall his father, but not today, what he would give for his father to argue with him.

"We should let him rest. We can sit over here," Barrington motioned to the sitting area, "and Mr. Watts can tell you the details of the accident before Hughes arrives."

He, Barrington, and Watts took seats by the fireplace. A polished mahogany table stood in front of them. On it lay a worn leather folio, its edges scuffed from years of use.

"Start at the beginning," Glenraven said to Watts. "And don't leave anything out."

"Of course, my lord." Watts settled himself and began. "We were on our way to Northampton, south of Luton. The weather had taken a turn for the worse. His Grace was in fine spirits. He teased Pearson about using the carriage based on an unusual perfume fragrance, which was distinct and unfamiliar. When we got to the Harmony Bridge, the river was fiercely racing, splashing over the banks onto the roadway. We've crossed that bridge a hundred times and never had to worry about it. So we went on. We were about one-third across when we heard the snap and felt the bridge shake. A board under the carriage had broken, then another, and yet another. With the wind and the noise from the water, we couldn't tell how many more boards were damaged.

"We needed to back the carriage off the bridge. Your father said to hell with the carriage. Take care of the horses. He turned to me and said I was to come with him. He wouldn't lose his best valet because of a little water."

A rustle in the bed had them all turn in anticipation. The movement quieted, and they turned back to Watts.

"Pearson calmed the horses. His lordship and I attempted to leave the carriage when the axle broke, and the carriage tipped. We both slid into the water. I quickly found your father and helped him to shore.

"By this time, Pearson had the team off the bridge and tethered. He came to the shore and helped your father and me up the embankment.

"The carriage was seriously damaged. Even in the poor weather conditions, Pearson was able to see the broken axel. He offered to stay with the carriage while your father and I continued to the inn on horseback.

"Pearson and I prepared the horses, and His Grace and I were soon mounted. Your father established a quick pace as we set off for the Lutin Inn. When we arrived, we sent someone to help

Pearson, and the innkeeper sent his boy to Lord Barrington.

"Pearson joined us before the fireplace, where we dried out and had a good meal. Other than the bruise on His Grace's head, he appeared to be himself. When Lord Barrington and Dr. Manning arrived, the doctor examined him, and we prepared to return to London. We brought His Grace here in Lord Barrington's coach. Pearson followed a day later with His Grace's coach."

"Your father was awake and talking the entire trip back to London," Barrington said. "Thank you, Watts. You did an excellent job."

Watts straightened his posture, his expression firm and determined. "Anything for His Grace. I am honored to serve him and will always do whatever is necessary to ensure his safety."

Glenraven didn't question the man's sincerity. Watts had been with his father since before he was born. "One last question." He took the ace of hearts from his pocket. "Do you know where my father got this card?"

The valet looked at the back of the card, then at Glenraven. "No, Your Grace. I didn't see that deck of cards until I emptied your father's coat pockets. I found a small tin container. Your mother opened it and found the deck of cards."

Glenraven nodded as he stared at the card. His father never carried a deck of cards. No one would trust them. "Thank you, Watts."

Watts quietly left the room.

Glenraven put thoughts about his father's health aside and tried to piece together the puzzles of the accident. "Where is the carriage now?"

"I had it locked up in my mews," Barrington replied, his tone somber and resolute. "The carriage had to be placed in a remote area. It smelled of lemon and smoke. Your father insisted that Watts entertained some doxy, which, of course, he denies."

"Of course." Glenraven relaxed, but only a bit. "You didn't send the coin to me because of my father's accident. But why do I feel that his accident and your coin have some connection?"

Chapter Four

"I THINK YOU are correct." Barrington settled into the chair and set the tone. Glenraven could feel the military edge seep into the conversation.

"Your father's past brush with gamblers and his rehabilitation, with your assistance, went exceedingly well. Everyone thought he was a duke who—"

"Had a bad gambling problem," Glenraven remembered that mission very well. That was a difficult assignment, one that, if he wasn't careful, could have cost his father his life.

"You handled the situation well."

"My father found the scoundrel who preyed on those young men. Once the matter was resolved, Father put his cards away. Although, he plays at White's every so often to keep his hand in the game, to say nothing of his private games with Quinto. In case his skills were needed again." He took the ace of hearts from his pocket and stared at it. "But that was seven years ago before I left for Spain."

"The situation we have is one in which gentlemen of the *ton* are targets, the ones who need blunt and are willing to take great chances. They are drawn into a weekly game with high stakes. They may win at first, but their luck runs out as well as their money."

"And my father answered your call." Glenraven put the card back in his pocket.

"No. I didn't call upon your father. He was the person who

came to me with the problem. An acquaintance of his had lost more than just their money. Determined to get to the bottom of the scheme and find justice for his friend, he decided to intervene. With his reputation, no one would suspect him of being anything other than a wealthy man enticed back into gambling."

"Are you saying that he did this all on his own?" Glenraven raised his voice with each word. What was his father thinking? He rubbed the back of his neck and glanced at his father laying still in bed. "This is my fault."

"Hush. Lower your voice," Barrington cautioned as he glanced in Glenraven's father's direction.

"Or what? I'll wake him up. It would serve him right." Glenraven quieted down. "This is my fault. I should never have involved him in any of my work for you. He must have tried to employ the same tactics we used when he helped me with the situation several years ago." He glanced at Barrington. "We both knew that I was too young, unknown in gambling circles to infiltrate that game. But Father? Everyone knew of his gambling luck and was more than eager to sit at a table with him." Glenraven's fingers tapped on the arm of his chair in a steady rhythm. "He had no idea what you and I did to make that all work. I kept him far away from all that." He let out a short mocking laugh. "If I fully included him then, he would have known he couldn't work this alone." He shook his head in frustration. "How could you let him take such a risk alone?"

"Aurington didn't tell me about this until after Quinto's death. By then, he was deep into it."

Glenraven didn't say anything.

Barrington leaned forward. "I didn't want to get you involved. You had enough to contend with in Paris. We thought we had everything under control. But now, with your father's accident, and another gentleman at the gambling table committing suicide, this has become a priority. It's too reminiscent of the past." Barrington leaned forward. He stared at the carpet seeing another time. "We missed something when we took down that organization. This is all too familiar.

"You know your father's contacts. They will never suspect you. They will only think you are trying to win back what your father lost."

"What do they think about his accident? Does anyone know he is with you here at Barrington Hall? Do they think he's with your brother, a member of Parliament? Or perhaps they believe he's staying with one of Enrico Quinto's acquaintances?"

"Your father's current condition is widely known, as are Manning's visits twice a day."

Sanderson entered quietly and set a decanter of wine and glasses on the table before retiring from the room. Barrington poured them each a glass.

Glenraven swirled his wine, watching the deep red liquid catch the light. "About the deck of cards. Do you know what the symbol is?" Glenraven's tone was more urgent than curious.

Barrington quietly put down his glass and gave him his full attention. "Just an old superstition, some say. But in our world, symbols often have deeper meanings,"

Glenraven's eyes narrowed, his mind racing. "What kind of meanings? And why would my father have such a thing in his possession?"

Barrington hesitated as if choosing his words carefully. "It's often associated with secret societies and organizations that operate in the shadows, wielding power and unseen influence."

Glenraven sat back, his grip tightening on the glass. "So this isn't just some old card deck. It's a message... or a warning."

Barrington nodded slowly. "It could be. We need to tread carefully. This might be connected to much more than we realize."

Glenraven took a deep breath, feeling the gravity of the information. "Then we must find out exactly what it means and who is behind it. For my father's sake."

"For ours," Barrington drained his glass dry.

They sat quietly for several minutes.

At last, Barrington broke the silence. "I'm glad you returned to Paris and got my message."

"Return?" Glenraven looked puzzled. "I haven't left Paris in months. What makes you think I was away?"

Barrington stared at him, his eyebrows knitted together. "Really? That's odd. Hughes sent you several messages and never received an answer."

"That is strange. I received your weekly messages and those from my father. Your last message included the letter from Hughes."

"Good afternoon, gentlemen." George Hughes hurried into the room. He took a seat and placed his folio on the table. "Glenraven. I am glad you are here. I was beginning to think something might have happened to you."

"Barrington was just telling me you were having difficulty reaching me. He has also told me about my father."

"I was giving you up for lost. For six months, I've tried to reach you. If you didn't respond to my request through Barring-ton's message, I was going to Paris myself."

"I'll make a note of that." Glenraven smiled and sipped his wine.

"I wasn't trying to reach you because of your father. At the moment, the issue may seem frivolous. However, in light of your father's condition, it's become an urgent one." Hughes took a document out of his folio. "There is a stipulation set forth in the family trust regarding securing the title and all its holdings. You must marry before your thirtieth birthday to safeguard the family's legacy. I believe that is in five weeks, May 1. It is a provision handed down in your family over the generations and deemed crucial for the continuity of the family and estate."

Glenraven raked his hand through his hair. Of course, he knew about the stipulation. He'd known about it all his life. "I seem to have conveniently forgotten about it with the war and the issue in Paris. Five weeks, you say. That isn't very much time. Is there anything you can do?"

"Lady Gladstone is giving a ball tonight. I took the liberty of seeing her before I came here. When she heard you had returned to London, she immediately gave me an invitation to deliver to you. It would be a great social coup for her if her ball were the first social event you attended after your return. It is just the place to be introduced to eligible women."

"You mean the place for some hungry, title obsessed mother looking for a match for her daughter. Is that what you consider help, Hughes?" Glenraven looked to be in pain.

"Sorry, my lord, but five weeks is not enough time to woo a woman." Hughes shook his head. "I'm not sure that six months would have been adequate."

"Ah, an ally," Glenraven threw his hands in the air. "I'm not sure which news is more dire, my father's illness or having to marry. Whichever it is, I best go home." Glenraven stood.

Barrington and Hughes walked him down the stairs to the foyer, where Sanderson handed him his hat and coat.

"I will be at Lady Gladstone's this evening. To give you moral support, of course." Barrington gave him a mischievous smile.

Glenraven glanced at his very clean coat and then at Sanderson.

"I would never let you leave without your clothes in the proper condition."

"Thank you, Sanderson," he said as the butler helped him with his coat. He turned to Barrington. "I'll see you this evening at Lady Gladstone's event."

"One minute, I'll walk with you." Hughes turned to Barrington. "It is strange that the message I sent in your pouch reached Glenraven while all the ones I sent to you did not."

Barrington's brow furrowed in thought. "Indeed, it is peculiar. If that's the case, something isn't right. We should find out why."

Sanderson stepped forward and opened the door with a respectful nod.

As they descended the steps, Glenraven paused, his gaze

distant. "Hughes, we have much to prepare for. My father's condition and the urgency of the marriage… it all feels overwhelming."

Hughes placed a reassuring hand on Glenraven's shoulder. "We will face it together, my lord. One step at a time."

INSIDE, BARRINGTON WATCHED them depart from the window, his thoughts already turning to the next steps. He turned and made his way back upstairs to Aurington's room.

"Is he gone?" Barrington looked into the eyes of a very awake, very clever Lord Aurington. "You're lucky I didn't start to snore. I hate to deceive the boy."

"We already know that the bridge, as well as your carriage, was tampered with. That is why you are here, and the remains of your carriage are under lock and key. If anyone can get to the bottom of this," Barrington looked at the closed bedroom door, "it is Glenraven."

Chapter Five

J ULIET MADE HER way back to her family's townhouse on Cavendish Square, musing over Glenraven's Punch and their effortless banter—was it his subtle influence, or had she steered their exchange while behind Judy's mask? Whichever it was, the playful banter had been a most welcome delight.

She walked down Cavendish Square and glanced at number fifteen. All thoughts of the afternoon's performance faded, replaced with her family's dire situation. As she approached the door, it opened.

"Good afternoon, Miss Hayward. I hope you had a lovely morning." The butler stood by the door.

"Thank you, Mr. Wilcox. I did have a lovely morning." She removed her gloves and hat.

"Mr. Reynolds is here to see you. He's waiting in the drawing room. Your mother is in her salon with your aunt and asks that you join them there when you are free." The smile in Wilcox's voice was gone.

She let out a deep breath, her thoughts turning to Aunt Geraldine, the Duchess of Rosefield. A paragon of grace and a fount of wisdom, her aunt's laughter was as heartfelt as her counsel was prudent, endearing her to all and making her an invaluable confidante to Juliet. "Inform my mother of my return," she instructed Wilcox, "and that I shall join her and Aunt Geraldine presently. Also, kindly ask Mrs. Murthy to serve tea in the drawing room.

He nodded as she crossed the foyer and entered the drawing room.

"Good afternoon, Mr. Reynolds." Mr. Reynolds stood as she entered the room. "Please, do take a seat." She gestured to the sofa, and he obliged. "I hope I haven't kept you waiting long. I wasn't aware you were coming to see us today."

Mr. Murthy quietly entered with the tea service and set it on the table in front of the sofa.

"Will there be anything else?"

"No, that will be all." Juliet turned to pour tea as Mary quietly left the room. "One sugar and milk?"

"Yes, thank you, Miss Hayward."

Juliet glanced at her family accountant and wondered if his somewhat disheveled appearance was related in any way to her family's dire state of affairs. She handed him his cup and made her own.

"What news do you bring?" She placed a serviette on her lap. News? Her brother Bradley is barely cold in his grave. After his interment, Reynolds told her the ugly details of her brother's debts and their impact on the family. How many times had she argued with her father about giving him free rein with the finances, but he wouldn't listen?

"The creditors are getting most anxious. I've told them that the family is in the midst of grieving, but I do not know how much longer that tactic will work." He paused and seemed a bit nervous.

"Is there something else?"

"Yes. There is. Your brother gave vowels." Reynolds stopped stirring his tea and glanced at her with a pained expression. "Vowels are…"

Her teacup was almost at her lips. "I know that vowels are more than letters in a word but a pledge to pay what is owed. So Bradley lost not only what we had but also what he didn't have." She returned the teacup to the saucer without taking a sip.

"Yes." The room was painfully quiet for several heartbeats.

"Well, then. That is that. Have you found out how much is owed and to whom? You mentioned a ruthless gentleman with whom Bradley played cards. You referred to him as a viper." She was trying to keep her temper. Reynolds didn't deserve her anger.

"I have some idea but need to confirm." The man was sweating. "I cannot go up to someone and accuse him without proof." He took out his handkerchief and mopped his brow. "It would be quicker if I had assistance, a Bow Street runner." He gave her an askant glance.

"I understand, Mr. Reynolds." She glanced out the window. There was no money to hire anyone. Her parents were determined to keep the *ton* from suspecting anything was awry. They wouldn't be able to bear the humiliation and gossip that would run through the *ton* like a pile of dry wood on fire.

What had she said to Punch earlier when he said their work would not be easy? She bit the inside of her lip as she thought. *Yes. I'm prepared to face whatever challenges lie ahead.*

"If you will provide me with a list of Bow Street runners, I will see what I can do." Satisfied she had some direction, she picked up her cup of tea.

"But... You cannot... No one would... Questions were asked. This gentleman we're searching for doesn't take nonpayment of debts lightly. You heard what happened to Lord Aurington. Miss—"

"Oh, dear." She put her cup down. "What you must be thinking." She crossed her fingers under her serviette. "I assure you that I am merely preparing for what I need to discuss with my father."

She uncrossed her fingers. "Lord Aurington had a carriage accident." She should have offered Glenraven her sympathies. A simple wish for his father's swift recovery would have been a thoughtful and kind expression.

"Rumors are swirling through the *ton* about foul play, but nothing has been proven. At one time, His Grace was a heavy gambler." Reynolds took a breath and then gazed at Juliet. "Much like your brother, Bradley." It was two months past when they found Bradley's body in the garden and the note in his room. There was no question as to the cause of death—suicide. It was about that time that Reynolds found the discrepancy with the finances… there wasn't much that remained. Remained. The only thing left was a note from Bradley. She had great doubts it was in his handwriting. *He was distraught*, the coroner said. *'The weight of my transgressions are unbareable. Forgive me. Farewell'*. The spelling error and drama were not Bradley. Or was it that she didn't want to believe he wrote it?

He had an elegant penmanship. She teased him often about how he documented everything: what he ate, what he wore, where he went, and who he spoke to. Scribe. That's what she called him. They would make up names for people and things so they could talk without caring who heard them. A wide smile brightened her face, thinking about him.

She bit the side of her cheek. Where was his diary? She hadn't seen it, but that shouldn't be a surprise. He was always hiding it, afraid Mother would find it. It may be lost forever. She passed his room every day and still hadn't the courage to go inside.

"I really must be going. Thank you for the tea. Let me know how you fare with your father regarding an investigator. Until then, I will do what I can."

"You have been most gentle in not mentioning that the family may be contacted with a demand to pay the debt. I want you to know we are aware of this. I wish we knew who the others were in that card game with my brother."

Reynolds rose from the sofa. "I'll let myself out. Thank you, Miss Hayward. Contact me immediately—"

"I will, Mr. Reynolds. I will." The thought of the scoundrel reaching out to the family for any reason, much less repayment, made her furious.

"Good day." He tilted his head and made his way out.

Juliet sipped the last of her tea. Why hadn't Reynolds spoken up sooner about the family's financial position? She closed her eyes. How many times had she scolded him and yelled at him in her head in the last two months? If he had, Bradley might still be alive, and the disaster avoided. Those were all questions that would never be answered now.

She lingered for a moment to clear her mind. Speaking with Aunt Geraldine would quiet her thoughts. Her aunt always found something to laugh about. As Juliet made her way out of the drawing room and upstairs to her mother's salon, she considered telling her about the Punch and Judy performance and perhaps even Glenraven but quickly thought better of it.

"Mother, Aunt Geraldine," Juliet swept into the salon.

"I saw Reynolds leave. Did he have anything positive to say?" Her mother twisted her handkerchief as if she were wringing out the last of her patience.

"Cecilie, you stop that this minute. Your falling apart is not going to help the situation or Juliet. Victor's information was helpful."

Juliet went to the small cellarette, poured three glasses of wine, and handed them out. "You've a message from Father?"

"Yes, you're correct, Geraldine." Her mother took a healthy drink. "Your father has asked that I join him in Scotland. I'm leaving as soon as the arrangements are made. He believes that I may have a positive influence on the situation. Your Aunt Geraldine will be here with you."

"What information did Father send in his message?" Juliet asked.

Her mother glanced at her sister. She looked more pained than when she first walked in. Without a word, her mother handed her his letter.

"Father's in Edinburgh with Cousin Shane." She read further down the page. "They have been generous. However, he's concerned it will not be enough." She read on. "The family sat together and came to the conclusion..." She turned the page. "What!" She tossed the paper onto the table.

"It is a solution, Juliet," Aunt Geraldine said as if the suggestion weren't devastating.

"A marriage of convenience. What am I to do, look into every man's pocket and pick the one that meets our needs?" She downed her wine.

"Many marriages are arranged that way," her aunt said.

"Yes, but those girls have something with which to bargain. I have nothing. Reynolds told me the creditors are getting anxious about their payment. He anticipates that so will the man holding Bradley's vowels."

Aunt Geraldine got up and pulled Juliet to the window.

"Do you realize what your father is telling you? Think. What does your family have of value? You. If you do not marry now, you could be forced to marry the man who holds those vowels."

Juliet stepped back, her eyes wide with shock as her hand flew to her throat. Fear, cold and icy, ran through her. "No. He wouldn't." Her voice was barely perceptible.

"Let's not give him a choice. Lady Gladstone is a friend of mine. She is having a soiree this evening. You and I will attend. There is no time to lose. Your mother was telling me about the condolence visits she's had from your brother's friends. Some of those young men may be acceptable to you."

A look of horror played across Juliet's face.

Her aunt took her hand and said, "Don't give up hope. I won't let you marry any man other than the right one."

Perhaps she should find the puppet master and join his troupe. She could speak her mind and perhaps find a gentleman who makes her heart stutter, like Glenraven.

Chapter Six

ABOUT A MILE and a half south of Cavendish Square in Belgravia, Glenraven sat in his drawing room with Duncan.

"It was a shock to find out about my father's accident. I'm sure it was the same for you." Glenraven sat in a high back chair, his mind still clouded with a haze of disbelief, staring at the half-full glass of whiskey in his hand.

"Aye. I spoke to Pearson. He told me everything. Did Lord Barrington mention the tampering?"

Glenraven's gaze remained fixed on his glass, the amber liquid reflecting the sunlight that filtered through the window. However, Duncan's mention of tampering sent a jolt through him, quickening his pulse as if he had sprinted around Hyde Park. Without lifting his head, his eyes shifted to Duncan, a silent question in their depths. "Tampering?" he echoed, the word heavy with sudden dread.

"I thought not. It is a lot to take in at one time." Sitting forward with his elbows on his knees, his hands clasped, Duncan gave Glenraven a sobering stare. "Pearson checked the carriage before they left Luton. There were markings on the underside, where the wood had split, which raised his concern."

"What kind of markings?"

"The axles had been partially sawed through. The cuts were artfully concealed by the shadows of the wheel well. He also checked the Harmony Bridge and found the planks were compromised. Unnatural fractures and strategically placed cuts were found that would be invisible at a glance but catastrophic under the weight of a passing carriage."

"That's why Father is staying with Barrington." Glenraven rubbed the back of his neck and shook his head. "He tried to uncover a fraudulent card game by himself. Barrington didn't know about it until it was too late."

"There is more. Your cousin Sebastian has been to see her ladyship, giving her support in these dark hours with His Grace gravely ill, and you, well, no one knew where you were. Sebastian and Fletcher—"

"Robert Fletcher? Father's steward?"

"The same. They have been together in the estate office a great deal. Mr. Flemings, your father's butler, spoke to me in confidence. He reminded Fletcher that the estate office was not for receiving guests. Fletcher told him that with your father gravely ill and you absent, Sebastian, who isn't a stranger but your third cousin, was eager to help. Fletcher told him that Sebastian has been a comfort to your mother."

"You remember Sebastian when we were growing up. He always wanted to help." Glenraven stood and glanced out the window. The afternoon was bright, with the wind sweeping along in gusts. He glanced across Belgravia Square and chuckled.

"Did you say something?" Duncan asked.

"No, no." Glenraven waved away the question. "I was looking at the people sitting in the square. Earlier, I sat by a puppet theater and ate a meat pie before I went to Barrington's. The puppet master conscripted me as if I were a foreign sailor. He needed a Punch." He turned and faced his friend.

"You?" Duncan looked appalled.

"Why are you so surprised? I was quite convincing. So was Judy."

"A puppet? The trip from Paris was worse on you than I thought."

"Don't be silly. The puppet master conscripted a young lady to play Judy. We were quite a team." Glenraven returned to the window, he gazed at nothing with a rapturous smile. "Quite a team, indeed."

"What are you going to tell your cousin?"

His wistful notion burst as quickly as a soap bubble meeting the hard edge of reality. "I will tell Sebastian that I've returned home to take on my duties. And I'll thank him for all he's done." Glenraven returned to his chair. "I'll need my evening wear tonight." He took out the invitation to Lady Gladstone's event.

Duncan glanced towards the door as a footman entered, carrying a garment bag. "Luckily, Flemings just had a footman bring up your freshened clothes."

Glenraven's attention, however, was elsewhere. "The urgency from Hughes was due to a triviality within my trust's terms," he said, his voice betraying a touch of irony. "To be succinct, I must marry by my thirtieth year."

Duncan's grip on the garment bag faltered, the bag swaying perilously for a moment before he steadied it. The significance of the news seemed to momentarily unbalance more than just the bag in his hands.

"Barrington will be introducing me to a flock of beauties." He glanced at Duncan, who was still staring at him. "Close our mouth, man. You look as bad as I feel." He let out a heavy sigh. "I knew about the conditions and conveniently forgot about them. What's more concerning is that Hughes mentioned he's been trying to reach me for the last six months. You didn't see any correspondence from him, did you?"

Duncan's face paled, confusion and concern etching his features. "Not a single letter from Hughes. It's most peculiar. The post has always been reliable."

"Hughes said he gave the letters to Fletcher to put into the weekly pouch he sent us." Glenraven glanced at Duncan. "What is that in your hand?"

Duncan paused, a seriousness taking over his expression as he extended a packet towards Glenraven. "When I opened the safe to store your documents, I found this."

Glenraven's gaze shifted from Duncan to the packet. His heart skipped a beat as he recognized the familiar scrawl of his father's handwriting. The significance of the find was not lost on him. It was rare for his father to pen letters personally. With a steadying breath, he reached out to take the message, his family's crest embossed in wax. He carefully broke the seal and opened the document.

> *"Let no one see this. Burn it if you must. If you are reading this, I have not succeeded in protecting you and your inheritance. You must NEVER let what we've built fall into the viper's hands. Forgive me, but you must marry before your thirtieth birthday or lose everything to your distant cousin. You must secure the title."*

An Ace of Hearts fell from the envelope. His father had an odd habit of leaving cryptic messages or symbols in unexpected places. He recalled a particular instance when he found the playing card, the "ace of hearts," hidden in his father's study. It led to a week-long adventure.

Duncan retrieved the card and handed it to Glenraven, who turned it over. The back showed a picture of winding vines with thorns.

"A shadow quest?" Duncan asked, staring at the back of the card.

"That's what Father called it—a treasure hunt. Father had one next to his bed at Barrington's." He turned the card over. It had the same strange marking. "We need to find the other two matching cards."

WHILE SHE PREPARED for the evening, Juliet stared into the cheval glass and saw a desperate woman. The situation was far past blaming her brother, although he earned that burden. But that wouldn't help now. Her father was doing all he could. He had already spoken to those he trusted in London. They helped, but more was needed. Going to the family in Edinburgh was a final effort.

It was time for her to step up and do what no one else could. No matter what her aunt promised, it was more than likely that hers would not be a love match. That was a childish dream or something found in stories by Miss Austen. She let out a heavy sigh. *It's not easy letting go of dreams.*

"When the storm clouds gather, and the world around us seems uncertain. We'll find shelter in each other's arms, and our hearts will be our fortress. But, Judy, my love, there's one thing you must know. Our journey won't always be easy."

"No, my dear Punch. My journey will not be easy. It's even more difficult facing it alone."

Still gazing into the glass, she shook her shoulders as if that would rid her of the melancholy. *That won't do looking for a husband.*

She went to her dressing table and glanced inside the box that contained all the items Bradley had with him when they found him in the garden: one cufflink, four pounds ten shillings, and a single playing card, an Ace of Hearts.

Chapter Seven

"B ARRINGTON, I THOUGHT by this time you'd be finishing your second drink at Lady Gladstone's Gala," Glenraven called as he stepped down the grand staircase.

Barrington, standing in Glenraven's foyer, glanced at him with a smile. "I'm here—"

"To make certain I attend Lady Gladstone's gala. As you can see," Glenraven gestured at his attire. "I am dressed for the evening's event." He came off the last step, and his face brightened. "Entering with you is a good strategic idea."

Barrington raised a single eyebrow and waited.

Glenraven stifled a smile, knowing his friend recognized his teasing all too well.

"With your usual scowl, you will keep all those hungry mothers at bay. They wouldn't dare approach us."

"Don't be so certain. Mrs. Bainbridge remains in Sommer-by-the-Sea. With her on my arm and her scowl, no eligible woman would dare approach me. I fear this evening, we will both be fair game. You do know that word has gotten out that you are attending the gala. It seems Mrs. Gladstone's drawing room has had more guests than usual this afternoon."

Glenraven muffled a groan.

"Chin up. The faster you choose a wife, the quicker this will all be over."

They stepped out and into Barrington's waiting carriage. As soon as they were settled for the short ride, Glenraven handed

Barrington his father's message.

"It appears my father agrees with my need for a bride post haste." Glenraven leaned his elbow on the carriage ledge and gazed out the window. After a moment, he turned to his friend.

"How can I entertain a marriage, any marriage, when my father's life hangs in the balance? Besides, marriage isn't something to be taken lightly. I've friends who married and had expectations for the future. Months, not even years, but months later, they are disenchanted."

"We've both witnessed marriages that were like a wedding cake, beautiful on the outside but lacking and tasteless on the inside. As I see it, if not love, there must be a mutual connection and respect for each other." Barrington let out a deep breath. "That is how love starts for a woman. It is something to build on. You're a shrewd judge of character. You'll succeed."

"Tonight, if I do not find my soul mate, I could attach myself to someone who can tolerate me and not just for my money and title." Glenraven stared at the coach floor for several heartbeats, then raised his head. "If no one interests me this evening, there is the card room to keep me occupied and work on our project."

The carriage rolled on, the rhythmic clatter of hooves droned in his ears.

"Does Duchess Berry insist on remaining in Paris?" Barrington asked.

Glenraven exhaled deeply, his breath carrying the burden of recent events. "The Duchess is managing, given the circumstances. She's expecting the child in September. Her grief for the Duke is profound—a loss felt deeply and personally. She has others around her to keep her safe. I saw to that before I left."

Barrington nodded, a touch of sympathy in his manner. "And the assassin? I am told you played a key role in his capture."

A bittersweet smile touched Glenraven's lips. "I was involved, yes, but the true hero was a waiter who, by sheer coincidence, subdued the assailant at the café. My part was to secure the villain until the Duke's guards arrived." He paused, his eyes clouding over. "The duchess has compensated the waiter generously. As for the assassin, he now awaits his day in court."

Glenraven's gaze shifted to the passing scenery. "Sometimes, in the quiet of the night, I replay the events, wondering if there was more I could have done. The dreams... they're vivid. It's a failure that haunts me, Barrington. I captured the assassin, yet the Duke... I was there to protect him, and I failed."

Barrington remained quiet, allowing the gravity of Glenraven's confession to settle. "You did what you could. No one bears the blame for the actions of a madman."

Glenraven nodded the acknowledgment, a small comfort against his regrets. "Perhaps. But it's a burden I carry. And I refuse to make the same mistake again, especially now, with so much at stake."

As the carriage continued its journey, the conversation turned to matters at hand, but the shadow of Paris lingered.

Barrington leaned forward with his hands clasped. "Those in the government who need to know are well aware of your part in capturing the villain. You have your King's gratitude."

The king's gratitude belongs to the young French waiter who risked his life, not his failed emissary.

"And now you're back." Barrington settled back in the coach. "You're home."

They drew up to the Gladstone home, one of the more notable houses on Berkeley Square. They stepped out of the carriage in front of an imposing entrance framed with tall, gleaming marble pillars. They went up the wide stairs to the open double doors as if the house itself extended a silent welcome. The foyer was grand but inviting, with a round table in the center. Upon it, a bowl overflowing with greenery and vibrant flowers broke the monotony of space. The artwork filling the walls, tucked between mirrored sconces, watched over the room with quiet approval.

"Good evening, Mr. Jackson," Barrington greeted the butler with a nod, his voice carrying the unmistakable tone of authority. "Allow me to introduce Lord Glenraven."

"Good evening, Lord Barrington, Lord Glenraven," Mr. Jackson nodded. With practiced precision, he pivoted on his heel to address the hostess. "Your Grace, may I present Lord Barrington and Lord Glenraven."

Lady Gladstone looked past her butler. "Lord Barrington, Lord Glenraven, what an honor to have you join us this evening." Her gracious greeting was warm and genuine. "Welcome to our home."

"Thank you for your kind invitation, Your Grace," Glenraven offered. Lady Gladstone's excitement had him grinning. "It is kind of you, especially on such short notice."

"Nonsense, my lord. Your mother and I are good friends. While it pains me to see your father suffer and your mother so distraught, I am pleased that you can join us, especially since you recently returned from Paris. Do go inside and enjoy yourselves."

They moved into the elegant ballroom. The wall in front of them was filled with doors leading to the terrace. An entrance to their right led to the dining room, and a doorway to the left conveniently led to the card room. The evening could easily serve two purposes—become reacquainted with the *ton* and subtly probe the shadows of high-stake card games.

"Barrington," a gentleman called as he came through the crowd.

"Ashfield, it is good to see you." Barrington gestured to Glenraven. "You remember Glenraven. He's recently returned to us from Paris."

Ashfield's expression softened with concern. "Glenraven, it is good to see you again. I was sorry to hear about your father."

"That is kind of you. He is improving."

Ashfield's brow wrinkled with a hint of confusion in his voice. "Then the rumor is wrong?"

Glenraven's smile faltered, replaced by one of puzzlement. "Rumor?"

Ashfield glanced from Barrington back to Glenraven. "I...I don't know how to say this. It was suspected that you had returned because of your father's imminent demise." Ashfield appeared somewhat embarrassed.

Glenraven responded calmly, with a gentle smile softening the difficult situation. "Not at all. We spent time together this afternoon. He was…more quiet than usual. He let me do all the talking."

Barrington let out a chuckle. "Indeed. I've never seen His Grace so quiet. Frankly, I think Glenraven bored him to sleep."

The three chuckled at the very idea of Duke Aurington being silent. Relief washed over Ashfield's face. "That is good news. Very good." Ashfield clapped him on the back with a hearty thump. "Are you back for good?"

Glenraven surveyed the room with a steady gaze. "Yes, I am." His tone was firm.

A spark of delight brightened Ashfield's eyes. "Then I will let my wife know. You are to be added to our guest list." After a moment's pause, he grinned slyly. "Perhaps later this evening, you will join me in the card room."

"Not until you dance with me." The three turned at the sound of Lady Ashfield's voice. Approaching with the grace of the seasoned socialite she was, she presented herself with an air of genteel confidence. Her smile was both inviting and serene. Lady Ashfield was a quiet beauty that complemented the gala's splendor.

"Darling," Ashfield put a protective arm around his wife's waist, "you know Lord Barrington and Lord Glenraven."

"Yes," she tilted her head toward Glenraven, "we spoke of you this afternoon when we called on Lady Gladstone. There was a great deal of speculation about whether you would be here this evening. I was so sorry to hear about your father's… accident."

So, the *ton* has his father dead and buried, and him the new Duke Aurington.

The music started. Lady Ashfield turned to her husband. She didn't say anything. She simply stared at him.

"If you'll excuse me," he smiled at his wife, "she always saves the first dance for me. Glenraven, see you later this evening in the card room?"

"Thank you. I would enjoy that. Until later." Glenraven turned to Lady Ashfield. "It was a pleasure to meet you, my lady." With that, he and Barrington continued around the ballroom.

Chapter Eight

JULIET AND HER Aunt Geraldine stepped into the ballroom with a quiet grace. Juliet paused in the doorway. The soft rustle of her midnight blue gown whispered against the floor. The fabric, a sumptuous silk, accentuated her form. The gown was cut in the latest fashion, with a high waist and short puffed sleeves. The bodice was beautifully made. It wasn't overly ornate or extravagant. The design reflected refinement and sophistication, focusing on details and quality rather than excessive decoration. Around her neck, she wore a simple string of pearls, one of the few pieces left in her mother's collection.

Her hair, a cascade of chestnut curls, was pulled back from her face and secured with a comb that matched the deep blue of her gown. The ensemble spoke of elegance, but the keen observer might detect the tension in her posture and how her striking hazel eyes scanned the room not for a dance partner but a savior. She remained in place as she summoned her courage.

Her aunt leaned in close to her. "We can't stand here all night. Come, put a smile on."

She glanced at her aunt and gave her a smile that didn't reach her eyes. "I'd rather be any place but here."

"Nonsense." Her aunt stepped closer to her. "We're not going to pull an unsuspecting gentleman off the dance floor and drag him to a chapel."

Juliet looked at her aunt, her mouth moving but nothing coming out.

"It would be a waste," her aunt continued with a reassuring smile. "to hide your radiance in a chapel when you could be dazzling the entire room with your charm."

A small giggle escaped Juliet's mouth.

"You must remember that the gentlemen here," her aunt continued, "are more afraid of you than you are of them." She nodded in the direction of the refreshment table. "Look at Sir Haroldson over there. He's been staring at the punch bowl since we walked in. He looks like he is working up his courage to ask for a glass."

Sir Haroldson did indeed seem to be engaged in a silent battle with the beverage table.

"And as for the rest," her aunt continued, leaning in conspiratorially, "they're simply trying to recall whether they've left the hearth burning or their horse tethered. You have nothing to fear. Now brighten up. You look as if you're about to face a firing squad rather than a room full of potential suitors."

The humor in her aunt's voice and the absurdity of her advice eased the tightness in Juliet's chest, and she found herself smiling genuinely for the first time since she began to dress.

Juliet and her aunt ventured out into the room. They wove through the throng of guests. Juliet's smile was practiced and serene, but her heart raced urgently. Her father's desperate attempts to salvage their fortunes had come to naught. Soon, the whispers of scandal would begin and cling to her like shadows dancing along the ballroom walls.

She and her aunt stopped to speak to several people. The gay laughter and music swirled around her, a facade that contradicted what she and her family faced. She knew the role she must play, the sacrifice demanded of her to restore her family's honor. It was a bitter draught to swallow, yet she held her chin high, her eyes blazing with purpose.

"ARE YOU GENTLEMEN enjoying yourselves," Lady Gladstone asked with a flourish. Her silver hair was styled in a fashionable updo, and her gown was made of a rich blue brocade. Her smile was genuine and warm, a detail that didn't escape Glenraven's notice.

"As promised, Lord Glenraven accompanies me this evening." Barrington nodded toward him.

"Ah, indeed, you have kept your word." Lady Gladstone turned her attention to him with a smile that lit up her features. "Lord Glenraven, it is a delight to see you once more."

Glenraven respectfully inclined his head, his expression one of polite gratitude. "The pleasure is mine, Lady Gladstone. Your invitation was most unexpected, yet entirely welcome."

"And it is I who am in your debt, my lord," Lady Gladstone responded, her eyes sparkling triumphantly. "Your presence here tonight bestows a singular honor upon Gladstone Hall. It is a coup indeed to host the first gala graced by your return."

Lady Gladstone offered them both a nod of approval. "Gentlemen, please, do enjoy the evening."

With a tilt of their heads, he and Barrington moved on and continued to mingle among the guests, enjoying the soft hum of conversation and the gentle cadence of music that filled the air.

He navigated the ballroom with the ease of a seasoned diplomat, his recent return to London causing quite the stir among the *ton*. As he made his way through the ballroom, he could feel the calculating gazes of matrons upon him, their eyes appraising him like a coveted trophy, each silently vying to claim him for their daughters.

A trio of gentlemen, old acquaintances from his club, halted him with hearty handshakes and slaps on the back.

"Good heavens, Glenraven, is it truly you?" exclaimed Sir Thomas, his monocle nearly dropping in surprise. "We'd heard you'd taken up permanent residence in Paris!"

He chuckled, deflecting the subtle probing comment with a practiced charm. "Paris could never hold me for long, though it tried with all its might," he quipped, leaving the details to their imaginations.

Before another word could be exchanged, Mrs. Hargrave, a determined matron with matchmaking in her eyes, approached with her daughter in tow. He caught the glint of intent in her gaze and excused himself with a polite nod, "Gentlemen, duty calls elsewhere."

He slipped away just as the woman opened her mouth. He weaved through the crowd with a grace that contradicted his urgency. And then, as if fate had steered his course, he found himself face to face with Miss Juliet Hayward. Her eyes, a calm oasis in the sea of social intensity, met his with a welcoming recognition.

"Miss Hayward," Glenraven greeted, the surprise in his voice genuine but welcome. "It seems destiny has a sense of humor tonight."

"Miss Hayward." Juliet and Glenraven turned to the gentleman who stood next to Juliet. "May I have the honor of this dance?"

Juliet's polite smile did little to mask her hesitation, a subtle shift in her stance that Glenraven caught instantly. Stepping forward with the poise of an experienced gentleman, he interjected smoothly, "My apologies, but I have already claimed the next dance with Miss Hayward."

The gentleman, though disappointed, bowed and retreated, leaving him and Juliet to take their place on the dance floor.

He turned to Juliet with a courteous nod, his eyes betraying a hint of mischief. "Miss Hayward, I must confess, the prospect of this dance has been the sole beacon of light in an otherwise dreary evening."

JULIET'S LIPS CURVED into a smile, her earlier nerves dissolving under his playful banter. "Lord Glenraven, you flatter me. Though I must warn you, my dance card is perilously close to full."

"Then I shall consider myself most fortunate," Glenraven replied, offering her his arm. "Shall we?"

They stepped onto the dance floor. The music, a lilting melody, seemed to echo the change in both of them.

"I trust the evening finds you well?" Glenraven inquired as they began to dance, their movements graceful and harmonious with the music.

"Quite well, thank you," she responded, her gaze steady on his. "And your father? I was grieved to hear of his accident."

Glenraven's expression softened. "He is a resilient man. Your concern is most appreciated, Miss Hayward."

Their conversation flowed as smoothly as their dance steps, from the trivialities of the season's fashions to the latest novels. "Have you read Mrs. Radcliffe's latest?" she asked with genuine interest.

Glenraven smiled, his expression twinkling with interest. "I am fond of Mrs. Radcliffe's works. Her tales of mystery and romance are quite captivating. However, I also enjoy the works of Sir Walter Scott and his vivid historical narratives. And, when I seek a bit of philosophical reflection, I turn to the essays of Mr. Addison. What about you? What captures your imagination?"

Juliet's eyes lit up with interest. "Mrs. Radcliffe's novels are indeed captivating. I find myself lost in her tales of mystery and suspense. As for Sir Walter Scott, his historical narratives are truly engaging. I also enjoy Lord Byron's poetry and Jane Austen's wit. Their works offer such a rich tapestry of emotions and insights. It's wonderful to know we share a love for literature."

As the music ended, Glenraven offered her his arm and escorted her from the dance floor. Their steps were unhurried, which suited her.

"Miss Hayward," Glenraven began, his voice a soft murmur amidst the chatter of the ballroom, "this evening has been a most unexpected pleasure."

Her smile was touched with a hint of melancholy. She was well aware that the moment was fleeting. "Indeed, Lord Glenraven. I shall treasure our dance." Her gaze lingered on his.

A loud announcement from Lady Gladstone abruptly burst their intimate bubble. They both turned to listen.

"Ladies and gentlemen, it is with great pleasure that I present to you a special performance by none other than the esteemed diva of the London opera, Miss Angelica Catalani. Renowned for her unparalleled soprano and captivating stage presence, Miss Catalani will grace us with an operatic solo that promises to be the highlight of our evening. Please join me in welcoming her to Gladstone Hall."

Glenraven's hand tightened briefly on hers before they were separated. "Thank you for the dance, Miss Hayward." Was that a note of regret in his voice? Or was she dreaming?

"The pleasure was mine," Juliet responded, her heart sinking as the current of the crowd surged forward, pulling them apart.

As the performance finished, Aunt Geraldine came up to Juliet. "I saw you dancing with Lord Glenraven. You make a handsome pair. It is common knowledge that he must marry to hold his title and lands."

Aunt Geraldine tilted her head toward her.

"Close your mouth, my dear. It's not becoming."

"Miss Hayward, I believe the next dance is mine." Lord Carter, an impeccably dressed gentleman, stood next to her.

"Of course, my lord." She took his lordships offered arm. They nodded to her aunt as they entered the dance floor.

Lord Carter danced with precision, but his conversation was as dry as the champagne he favored, lacking any hint of passion or wit. He was suitable by society's standards, but he didn't pique her interest.

He returned her to her aunt.

"Thank you, Miss Hayward. You are a wonderful conversationalist. I do hope there will be room on your dance card for me in the future." He nodded to Aunt Geraldine and stepped away.

"Wonderful conversationalist?" her aunt asked.

"Yes. I let him do all the talking."

Aunt Geraldine's laughter rang out. She quickly covered her mouth with a gloved hand, her eyes bright with amusement. "My dear Juliet," she managed, her voice laced with laughter, "you have indeed mastered the art of conversation with such grace that it leaves the gentlemen utterly enchanted."

Juliet shook her head. "Aunt Geraldine, you mustn't laugh so loudly. "You'll give away my secret to surviving these endless dances," her tone a playful scold.

Still smiling, Aunt Geraldine gave her niece a fond look. "If laughter is the key to enduring the season, I shall laugh as heartily as I please. Besides, it seems to me you've found a far more enjoyable diversion tonight." Her gaze shifted meaningfully towards where Glenraven had disappeared into the crowd. "Ah, if I'm not mistaken, here comes your next dance partner."

Juliet nodded to Sir Collingwood, who led her onto the dance floor. The gentleman had a reputation for bravery, but his brashness on the dance floor and the boastful tales of his exploits left Juliet feeling underwhelmed and seeking a retreat. Excusing herself with a practiced grace, she slipped away to the refreshment room, yearning for a moment of tranquility. To the world, she was Miss Hayward, a lady of poise and potential. No one suspected the silent desperation that clung to her like a shadow. How much longer could she keep her family's financial state a secret, or the pressing need for a marriage that could save them from ruin? Yet, in the quiet solitude of the refreshment room, she allowed herself a brief respite from the relentless pursuit of suitors who knew nothing of the urgency behind her smile. She stared blankly at the refreshments.

"Miss Hayward, might I tempt you with a refreshment?" Glenraven approached her with a glass of lemonade and a gentle smile.

Juliet accepted the glass, her fingers brushing against his, sending an unexpected shiver through her. "Thank you, Lord Glenraven." Her voice was soft. "It's quite warm in here, isn't it?"

"Indeed, it is," he agreed, his eyes not leaving hers. "But I find the company more than compensates for the temperature." Their shared laughter was light in the heavy air as they parted. Juliet felt a warmth that lingered, one that seemed to radiate from within rather than from the room itself.

After her refreshing encounter with Lord Glenraven, Juliet again found herself amidst the crowd of dancers. She was led onto the floor by Mr. Harrow, a gentleman of respectable standing whose impeccable manners were marred only by his constant talk of the weather. His attempts at conversation, as predictable as the dance patterns, left Juliet politely nodding but inwardly yearning for the intellectual banter she had shared with Glenraven.

Her next partner, a young Viscount named Mandeville, had a charming smile and a lively step. Yet, as they spun across the floor, his eyes wandered more than Juliet found comfortable, often leaving her words hanging in the air as he greeted acquaintances with a nod or a wink. This dance partner lacked the connection she craved, and as the music ended, Juliet excused herself with a gracious smile.

Unable to stand another dance, Juliet retreated to the library to avoid the next gentleman on her dance card. Closing the door behind her, she took a deep breath, thankful for the quiet haven away from the overwhelming clamor of the gala.

Chapter Nine

L ORD GLENRAVEN HAD scarcely put down his lemonade glass while watching Miss Hayward take to the dance floor with Mr. Harrow when he found himself the target of a determined matriarch.

Lady Wetherby was the first to approach him. With a predatory gleam in her eye, her daughter fluttered beside her like a trapped sparrow. "Lord Glenraven, have you met my Annabelle? A more accomplished pianoforte player you'll not find in all of London." The woman pushed the young lady forward.

"Lady Annabelle, I understand you have quite the talent for the pianoforte." He had no intention of slighting the girl because of her meddlesome mother. Instead, he gave her his full attention. "Music has always been a refuge for me, especially after a long day."

Annabelle's eyes lit up at the mention of her favorite pastime. "Oh, yes, my lord. There's nothing quite like losing oneself in a piece by Chopin or Beethoven." Her voice became steadier as she spoke of her passion.

"I couldn't agree more." Glenraven's expression was one of genuine enthusiasm. "Perhaps you might treat us with a performance at the next gathering? I would be most eager to hear you play."

The young lady nodded, a blush coloring her cheeks. "I would be honored, Lord Glenraven." Her earlier awkwardness was replaced with a newfound confidence.

"I hope you will excuse me, but I believe I'm required elsewhere. It's been a pleasure." He retreated to the safety of the punch bowl across the room in front of the mirrored wall.

No sooner had he taken a sip of punch when Mrs. Bancroft descended upon him, her daughter in tow—a lovely figure who seemed more interested in her reflection than his company. "Lord Glenraven, my daughter has just returned from her Grand Tour. Perhaps you could share your experiences of the Continent with her?"

Before Glenraven could muster a response, a familiar voice came to his rescue. "Glenraven." Barrington clapped him on the shoulder and glanced at Mrs. Bancroft and her daughter. "I beg your pardon, but his lordship is needed."

"Ladies, another time, perhaps." He left the eager mother with a regretful smile.

He walked away with Barrington. "Thank you for that. I hadn't remembered how I hate these events."

"I've been watching…from afar. I've seen you speak to many young ladies but dance with only one. That's good progress."

With a wry smile and an amused glint in his eye, Glenraven offered a subtle shrug, his expression both amusement and resignation.

"Might I suggest a retreat to the library? A moment alone might do you good."

"A splendid idea, Barrington." Grateful for the escape, he nodded. "If you'll excuse me."

Glenraven entered the library and quietly closed the door behind him. He sighed in relief and absorbed the gentle hush that settled around him. He wandered between the bookcases, his fingers tracing the leather spines. Engrossed in a volume of ancient history, it took him a few minutes to realize that the door had opened. Miss Hayward had slipped in. He stood still as she scanned the room, unaware of his presence hidden by a tall bookcase.

"Miss Hayward," he greeted, his voice a low murmur echoing

softly among the shelves as he stepped out from between the bookcase. "Fate seems to have a hand in our encounters this evening."

Juliet turned to face him. He noticed a hint of delight in her eyes. "Indeed, Lord Glenraven. It appears we share a fondness for literature as well as dance." Her words were a soft bridge to common ground, spoken with an ease that contradicted the social whirlwind they each sought to escape.

In the quiet of the library, away from the crowd of suitors and the watchful eyes of matchmaking mothers, they found relief in a display of maps detailing the far reaches of the British Empire. "It's remarkable, isn't it?" Glenraven mused, tracing a line along the coast of India. "Think of the stories these lands could tell."

Juliet leaned in, her finger pointing to a small island. "And yet, for all its vastness, it's the tiny places that often hold the richest tales," she countered with a playful glint in her eye.

He chuckled, meeting her gaze. "True, Miss Hayward. I suppose it's much like a ballroom—a miniature of society where every individual has a story."

"The difference being, in a ballroom, one must wade through a sea of verbal and physical embellishments to find the truth."

His laughter mingled with hers, and for a moment, he wasn't a marquess. They were two kindred spirits delighting in the dance of words. He didn't want their exchange to end. Each comment and retort was richer than the last. And Miss Hayward gave every indication that she was enjoying the banter as well.

Reluctantly, she stepped away from the maps. "I should return to the ballroom." Her voice was barely above a whisper, the unspoken desire to stay unmistakable.

"Perhaps we can continue our exploration of empires and anecdotes at another time." His invitation was genuinely offered.

"I would like that very much, Lord Glenraven." Her smile lingered as she turned to leave.

Juliet went on her way, leaving Glenraven with a more than pleasant impression of their brief connection. He went to the cellarette and poured himself a glass of whiskey, the amber liquid doing little to distract his thoughts from the captivating Miss Hayward.

He remained in the library, the taste of whiskey on his lips and the image of Juliet Hayward in his mind. He savored the quiet, allowing himself to reflect on the evening's unexpected turns. With a final sip, he set the glass down and made his way back to the ballroom.

As he emerged, Barrington approached him with a knowing smile. "Glenraven, I had half a mind you'd taken up residence in the card room." He clapped him on the shoulder.

Glenraven shook his head, a small smile playing on his lips. "No, Barrington, I found myself otherwise engaged." The memory of Juliet's intelligent eyes and quick wit was still fresh.

Barrington raised an eyebrow, his interest piqued. "Oh? And pray tell, with whom did you find such engaging company?"

"It was Miss Hayward," Glenraven confessed, and he couldn't help the warmth that colored his tone. "We shared a rather enlightening conversation."

Barrington's smile broadened, and he gave Glenraven an approving nod. "Miss Hayward, you say? Baron Fairmont's daughter. Excellent choice, my friend. She's a gem among the *ton*—a rare find indeed."

"Indeed, she is." Glenraven smiled at the very thought of her.

"Shall we venture into the card room? I believe it's time you reacquainted yourself with the old guard."

With a nod and the vision of Miss Hayward vanishing, Glenraven followed Barrington.

They entered a room alive with the jingle of coins and the rustle of cards. Familiar faces sat around the table, each absorbed in their game of chance—whist, loo, and faro.

"Seems to be a harmless enough assembly tonight," Barrington remarked, observing the players. "No fortunes lost as of yet, I presume?"

Glenraven leaned against the wall, his arms folded as he observed. "Indeed, it appears to be a friendly game this evening, Though I suspect the night is still young." They studied the game in silence. The tension in the room was apparent, even with the absence of high stakes. Glenraven's gaze drifted, not quite capturing the thrill of the play as his thoughts lingered on Miss Hayward's last smile before she departed the library.

Barrington nudged him gently. "You seem distant, my friend. Perhaps the fresh air on the terrace would clear your mind?"

Glenraven pushed off the wall, left the card room, and stepped into the cool night.

He found her there, gazing at the moonlit gardens below. "Miss Hayward, you've stolen my idea." He joined her by the balustrade.

She turned to him, a soft smile on her lips. "It seems we are of one mind tonight, Lord Glenraven."

Chapter Ten

JULIET'S HEART RACED as she stood with Glenraven on the terrace, the night air cool against her skin. His nearness was both exhilarating and unnerving. Glancing at the sky and its expanse, her mind toyed with infinite possibilities. With a breath, she found the courage to voice a question about her hidden desires. "Do you ever dream of a different life, Lord Glenraven?" Her voice was barely above a whisper. It betrayed her longing for a world beyond her family's misfortunes and her duty.

He didn't respond, and she followed his gaze that had drifted to the distant garden wall and wondered what he was thinking.

"Often," he admitted, at last, his eyes returning to meet hers. His voice carried a rare note of vulnerability that resonated with her hidden yearnings. "I dream of a life where my choices are guided by passion rather than obligation. A life filled with the pursuit of knowledge, the joy of discovery, and perhaps," a playful spark ignited in his eyes, "a touch of adventure in far-off lands."

Juliet smiled at his last remark. She listened, captivated by the way his words echoed her dreams. The earnestness in his voice had her heart fluttering at the thought of such a life where she would be free to explore the depths of her passions alongside someone who understood her.

She stared into his eyes, and a silent understanding passed between them, a shared yearning for a life without the expectations that came with rank or obligation. The feeling spanned beyond the terrace, beyond the night. It was as if he had uncovered her secret wishes—a life where a person could be true to their own heart.

"And you, Miss Hayward?" Glenraven inquired, turning the question to her. "What life do you dream of?"

"A life where laughter is plentiful, and love is the measure of wealth." Those were her innermost desires. As she spoke, her gaze never wavered from his, and she saw a reflection of her dreams in the depths of his eyes. "Where every day is a canvas to be painted with the bright colors of joy and the quiet shades of contentment."

In the silence that followed, Glenraven stepped closer, his presence wrapping her in a warmth she hadn't expected but, oh, so greatly enjoyed. The terrace, the stars above, and the distant sounds of the gala—all faded into the background as the moment between them deepened into something intense and intimate.

Glenraven's hand rose, almost of its own accord, and gently cupped her cheek, his thumb caressing her skin with the softest touch. Their eyes locked, and Juliet's heart pounded with anticipation, as well as a healthy dose of trepidation.

Time seemed to stand still. Glenraven leaned in, his intentions clear in his half-lidded gaze. Juliet's eyes fluttered closed, her body instinctively tilting towards his, her lips parting slightly in a silent invitation.

Her breath hitched as she moved closer to him, drawn by a force she couldn't resist. Their faces were inches apart. The warmth of his breath caressed hers, a tender prelude to a kiss that hovered just out of reach.

But then, laughter spilled from the ballroom, shattering the intimate spell. Juliet stepped back, a blush creeping up her cheeks. "We should return." Though every fiber of her being screamed to stay.

Glenraven nodded, the regret in his eyes mirroring her own. "Yes, we mustn't forget ourselves." As they stood in silence, savoring the moment, a sudden cheer erupted from the open window of the card room. The celebration broke the quiet, drawing their attention to the world inside.

Glenraven glanced toward the source of the commotion, a wry smile forming on his lips. "It seems someone has had a stroke of luck." His gaze returned to Juliet.

"The ace of hearts, perhaps," she uttered impulsively, the words escaping her lips before she could give them any thought. The image of the ace of hearts among her brother's belongings had flashed in front of her.

Glenraven's eyes met hers, a spark of intrigue in their depths. "Are you familiar with the game? A bit of a legend my father shared with me. The shadow quest."

Juliet leaned in, intrigued. "A shadow quest? What is that?"

"It's a game of sorts, a mystery that involves the ace of hearts," Glenraven explained, his voice low. "The card is said to be hidden somewhere in the city along with three others. Finding the cards leads to a hidden secret."

Juliet's eyes widened with interest. "And what does one do if they find this ace of hearts?"

Glenraven's smile turned mysterious. "That, Miss Hayward, is a question only the finder of the matching card can answer. But for me, it's a clue that might lead to justice. There is another explanation of the ace of hearts."

Juliet stood beside Glenraven. The mention of the Ace of Hearts sent a shiver down her spine. It was not just the night's chill that startled her but the sudden connection to the card she had found among her brother's belongings and Lord Glenraven. Her mind raced with questions. Was her brother's Ace of Hearts part of this shadow quest? Did Glenraven hold the matching card that would lead to answers?

"The ace of hearts is said to be a sign of impending change, love, and emotion."

Juliet pushed aside thoughts of her brother, the ace of hearts, and her quest. Tonight was not for dark musings or seeking shadows. Tonight was for the unexpected joy she found in

Glenraven's company. She looked up at him, her eyes reflecting a lovely innocence.

"Lord Glenraven." Her voice was steady despite the turmoil. "Tonight has been a gift," one she didn't know she needed, echoed in her head. "Let us leave the shadow quest and the ace of hearts for another day."

Glenraven nodded. "Indeed, Miss Hayward. I couldn't agree with you more."

They stepped back into the ballroom together, where the music played. The memory of their almost kiss remained their private secret.

"Juliet, there you are. Good evening, my lord." Aunt Geraldine approached them with a graceful stride.

Glenraven respectfully inclined his head. "Lady Rosefield."

He gazed at Juliet, and she saw the same pang of regret in his eyes that she felt in her heart. The easy friendship and peace they had shared on the terrace lingered. "Thank you, Lord Glenraven, for a memorable evening."

"The honor was mine. Until our paths cross again." His gaze held hers a moment longer before he stepped away, leaving her in the care of her aunt.

Aunt Geraldine looped her arm through Juliet's and led her across the ballroom. Juliet's thoughts were a whirlwind. The image of Glenraven bathed in moonlight was imprinted on her heart and mind.

"My dear Juliet," Aunt Geraldine began, her voice low but intense. "You've certainly caught the eye of one of London's most sought-after bachelors. Lord Glenraven's attention is no small triumph."

Juliet felt a flutter of pride at her aunt's words, but it was quickly tempered by the gravity in her tone. "But, my dear, you must tread carefully." Aunt Geraldine's gaze was steady and serious. "Do not set your hopes upon this one encounter. Rumors abound that he may soon return to Paris, and the fancies of men are ever changeable, especially so far from home."

The warning echoed deeply, grounding her soaring spirits. "I understand, Aunt Geraldine. I will remain cautious." Even as her heart held on to the hope that Glenraven was different, Juliet assured her aunt that what they shared was beyond mere fancy.

As they mingled among the guests, Juliet's mind was a whirl of emotions—hope, uncertainty, and a daring wish that, despite the rumors, Glenraven's heart might just be waiting for someone—someone like her.

⟫⟫⟩⟨⟨⟪

AS DAWN'S FIRST light began to chase away the night, Glenraven arrived at his townhouse, the echoes of the Gladstone ball and the card room still ringing in his ears. Yet, Juliet Hayward dominated his thoughts. In the dimly lit foyer, he paused, a hand on the cool banister, lost in his musings.

"Evenin' or should I say mornin'," Duncan greeted him, his voice steady as always. "Was the evening worth the fuss?"

Glenraven offered a half-smile, the memory of the near kiss on the terrace lingering. "The evening was… enlightening. More than I expected." He let out a heavy sigh as he allowed the image of Juliet to fade. He turned to Duncan. "Have you ever found yourself at a crossroads caught between the expectations of your station and the yearnings of your heart?"

Duncan gazed at his friend with a thoughtful expression. "Aye, that I have. It's the bane of every man, noble or not."

Glenraven's fingers tightened around the banister. "I am to marry for the benefit of the family, yet tonight, I found myself questioning that very path." He started up the stairs, Duncan beside him.

"Miss Hayward? She's made you think twice, then?"

A genuine smile tugged at the corners of Glenraven's lips. "She's…remarkable. There's a fire… Indeed, she is unlike any woman I have ever met."

Duncan opened Glenraven's bedroom door and nodded, a knowing look in his eyes. "Well, maybe it's time to follow the fire instead of the cold trail of duty."

Glenraven undressed, giving Duncan his evening clothes while his friend's words echoed in his heart. "Maybe you're right." Saying the words and coming to that decision was both terrifying and exhilarating. He stood at the bed.

"I'll be in my room if you think of anything you need or want to discuss." Duncan quietly left.

Glenraven eased himself onto the mattress, the cool linens a stark contrast to the warm thoughts Juliet brought. He stretched out, his hands behind his head, staring at the canopy overhead. The image of Juliet's smile lingered, as did her laughter. Was she his future? As sleep began to claim him, his last conscious musings were dedicated to thoughts of her.

Chapter Eleven

April 17, 1820

I N THE SOLITUDE of her chamber, Juliet sat before her dressing table, the soft bristles of her hairbrush gliding through her hair. The reflection of the woman who stared back at her was between two worlds—the glittering facade of the *ton* and the stark reality of her family's dire situation. It had been three weeks, and the memory of Lady Gladstone's Gala and Marquess Glenraven were still vivid.

She opened the dressing table drawer and saw the ace of hearts that had been among her brother's effects.

She glanced at the card, now a mocking omen, especially after Glenraven mentioned a shadow quest. Could there be a connection? She toyed with the idea, the corners of her mouth lifting in a wry smile. It was a fanciful notion that belonged to the stories her brother adored.

Three weeks since Lady Gladstone's Gala, and while she attended the season's social events, she had only fleeting encounters with Lord Glenraven. She and Aunt Geraldine had made their daily calls and listened as others spoke of Glenraven's visits, yet he had not once come to Fairmont Abbey. As she sat combing her hair, the image of Lord Glenraven refused to fade— a man who had stirred something deep within her. The gentle pull of her brush was rhythmic and soothing, but it did little to calm the storm in her heart.

The Saturday after they'd met, she attended Lady Worthington's garden tea and stood by the bough, admiring her roses.

"They're lovely this time of year." His voice was warm and familiar. She smiled, relieved that Glenraven was beside her. Had his words concealed a hidden meaning? Though their conversation was brief, his presence lingered with her long after the tea had ended. What if she was mistaken about his interest? The thought left her feeling foolish and vulnerable.

She and Aunt Geraldine made afternoon calls and in the distance saw him leaving before they arrived. The following Wednesday evening at the Bishop's soiree, Juliet was seated across from Glenraven. He was charming, conversational, yet there was a restraint in his manner. His eyes, though kind, held a shadow of something unspoken. As they exchanged pleasantries and discussed lighter topics, Juliet couldn't shake the feeling that he was holding something back, keeping a part of himself at bay. Or was she allowing her own emotions to cloud her judgment?

Their most significant encounter occurred the day after the Bishop's soiree, during a walk in Hyde Park. He approached her, tipping his hat with a warm smile. "May I join you, Miss Hayward?" Unlike the garden tea and the soiree, here they had a secluded moment away from prying eyes and the constraints of social formalities. They strolled together along the path, the cool breeze carrying with it the scent of spring. Their conversation was easy, filled with anecdotes of the previous evening and soft laughter. Yet, there was an unspoken tension between them.

Each encounter with Glenraven left her hopeful one minute and uncertain the next. Her heart fluttered with every kind word and gentle gesture. Yet, the distance between them gnawed at her. She found herself questioning her own feelings and actions.

Slowly, a painful realization began to settle over her—perhaps their budding affection was all in her head. The storm in her heart raged on, but now it was tainted with the bitter taste of doubt.

She closed her eyes. "Bradley, I wish you were here. You'd see this clearly. You always had a way of understanding the heart of the matter."

She placed the brush down and looked at her reflection in the mirror. "Ewan," she said softly, allowing herself to speak his given name. It was a name that felt like a promise, a whisper of potential happiness amidst the tragedy around her.

Her heart ached with the possibility of what might be. As the afternoon sun played across the garden, she conceded the coming days would be difficult.

"'Till it be morrow, Ewan," she murmured, his name a silent vow on her lips as she turned from the window, the new day waiting to begin. She finished dressing and was ready to face the afternoon.

Juliet went downstairs and was drawn to a note addressed to her amidst the correspondence on the salver. It was a stark, plain envelope that stood out against the usual array of letters and invitations. She unfolded the note. Her eyes scanned words that ignited a flare of anger and a tremor of fear. With a swift motion, she tucked the message into her pocket as Mrs. Murthy came down the hall.

"There you are. I was about to go upstairs. You have guests. I've put them in the drawing room."

The Fairmont drawing room was awash with the delicate fragrance of fresh blooms as Mr. Hargrove and Viscount Mandeville presented their floral offerings to Juliet. Mr. Hargrove's bouquet was as predictable as his conversation—neat, orderly, and entirely composed of white roses, much like his views on the weather.

"Miss Hayward, I trust you find the climate agreeable today?" Mr. Hargrove's voice carried the same tone one might use in discussing the prospects of rain.

Juliet accepted the flowers with a practiced smile. "Quite agreeable, Mr. Hargrove. Though, one does long for a breeze of change now and again." Her words included a subtle plea for a new topic.

Viscount Mandeville, not to be outdone, presented a vibrant

array of wildflowers, their arrangement as haphazard as his thoughts. "A token of nature's beauty, much like yourself, Miss Hayward," he declared with a flourish that was meant to be charming.

"Thank you, Viscount. They are… quite spirited." Juliet's gaze flickered to the window, where she half-hoped to see Glenraven approaching.

Ever the gracious hostess, Lady Fairmont directed the gentlemen to their seats. "Tea will be served shortly. Mrs. Murthy, do ensure Mr. Hargrove has his usual spot by the window. He does so enjoy the sunlight," she instructed, her voice carrying the faintest hint of amusement.

Juliet found comfort in the familiar rhythm of afternoon tea, yet her thoughts drifted to Glenraven. Her desk remained barren of letters from him, and despite his attendance at various teas, he had notably avoided hers. His absence was underscored by society's speculative buzz of who had seen him and where they had seen him, all lending a bittersweet note to the otherwise sophisticated clinking of china and polite murmurs that filled the room.

She was putting much into their brief encounter, but it was a welcome diversion from the note she received in the morning post that now haunted her thoughts.

She couldn't help but wonder if whispers of her brother's debts had reached his ears. Such news traveled swiftly through the *ton's* circles, easily tainting reputations. A shiver of apprehension traced her spine as she considered a more disheartening possibility—that the precarious state of her family's finances had come to light.

With these thoughts chilling her heart, she sipped her tea, finding little comfort in its warmth. It was a feeble substitute for her vibrant conversations and undeniable connection with Glenraven. The tea's flavor, once soothing, now seemed as lackluster as the empty chair across from her.

"Miss Hayward, you seem distant. Pray tell, what occupies

your thoughts?" Viscount Mandeville asked, his brow furrowed in a rare moment of perception.

Juliet met his inquiry with a diplomatic tilt of her head. "Merely pondering the complexities of the heart, Viscount. A puzzle, wouldn't you agree?"

The gentlemen exchanged puzzled glances. Their understanding of such matters were as clear as a foggy London morning. Juliet concealed her disappointment with another sip of tea, the delicate china cup hiding her wistful smile. As the afternoon grew late, his absence was felt, but she would not let it cloud the day's pleasantries.

⋙⋘

THAT EVENING, ACROSS Hyde Park in Belgravia, Ewan sat alone at the head of the long dining table, the silverware gleaning in the soft candlelight. The room was silent save for the quiet rustling of papers as he reviewed the estate accounts, something that would never happen at his parent's home. Everything seemed to be in order, a small comfort in the absence of his father's guiding hand.

Duncan entered the room, his steps measured and sure. "Dinner is served," he announced, laying out the dishes with an efficiency born of years of service.

Ewan nodded, his appetite minimal. "Thank you, Duncan. How was the market today?" he asked, more for something to say than genuine interest.

Duncan began to pour the wine, a hint of a smirk playing on his lips. "Oh, the usual hustle and bustle. But I did chance upon Mary Murthy, the Fairmont's housekeeper. She was quite the chatterbox about the comings and goings at their townhouse."

Ewan's hand stilled, the crystal glass catching the light as he set it down a bit too sharply. "And what of Miss Hayward?" he inquired, trying to keep his tone casual.

"Seems she's had quite the parade of suitors since the gala.

Mr. Hargrove and Viscount Mandeville have been particularly persistent," Duncan relayed, oblivious to the tightening of Ewan's jaw.

A swell of irritation touched with jealousy, flooded his senses. "Is that so?" he said, his voice colder than he intended.

Duncan met his gaze, unflinching. "Aye, it is. And what of it? If you've a mind to court the lass, sitting here brooding won't do you any good. For weeks, you've made social calls and returned fretting."

Ewan's eyes narrowed, the truth in Duncan's words stinging. "And what would you have me do, Duncan? Declare my intentions in the middle of the market?"

Duncan chuckled, the sound rich and knowing. "No, but perhaps a call wouldn't go amiss. Or, at the very least, a letter. The lady won't wait forever, and nor will her suitors. It doesn't appear that you or the lady have found anyone in which you're interested. I wonder why that is? If the lass chooses and marries one of those gentlemen, it would serve you right."

Ewan pushed his plate away, his appetite now entirely gone. "You don't understand. It's not that simple." He stood, pacing to the window, the night sky a vast expanse of possibilities. Duncan's words echoed in his mind, a call to action he couldn't ignore.

"What's not simple? You've been moping about like a lost pup. The few, and I mean very few, times you've encountered her, you barely say a word. If you fancy her, do something about it." Duncan's tone took on a serious tone.

His shoulders sagged, the full impact of his fears overwhelming him. "It's not just that. I've gone over that scene in Paris hundreds of times. I was well planted in front of the duke. If I hadn't moved to help the duchess, the bullet would have struck me." He turned to Duncan. "The shooting felt wrong, the bullet was meant for me. How can you put her in jeopardy?"

Duncan's expression softened, realizing the depth of Ewan's turmoil. "Ah, so that's it. You're letting the ghosts of Paris haunt you now, those ghosts, as well as the shades of this criminal order. Remember what the shooter shouted that night? 'For the Duke!' They were targeting Duke Berry, not you."

"I remember what he said, but I looked into the eyes of that assassin. They were not the eyes of a zealot fighting for a cause." Maybe Duncan was correct. Was he seeing ghosts where there were none?

"The *ton* knows you feel strongly for Lady Hayward. To protect her, you need to be with her, not apart. You're stronger than you think. Pushing Juliet away won't protect her or you. As for the Order, we'll face them as we have faced other assignments, head-on."

"And if my father's accident was indeed planned. How can I bring her into all this?"

"You'd rather leave the lass on her own, without any protection?"

Ewan stared out into the night, Duncan's words sinking in. He had been running from his fears, letting them control him. Maybe it was time to stop running.

"Have the carriage ready in the afternoon," Ewan said as he returned to his seat. He lifted his glass of wine, his decision settling over him like a cloak. "I'll call at Fairmont Abbey tomorrow."

Duncan nodded a look of approval in his eyes. "Very good. It's high time you played your hand." Duncan paused, his expression serious. "I haven't wanted to press you, but remember, the weeks are dwindling. Your birthday—and the deadline— is two weeks from today."

The glass paused in mid-air, a symbol of the moment's gravity. Ewan's course of action was clear, even as the significance of Duncan's reminder settled upon him. "I am well aware," he said, his voice steady. "I cannot get her out of my mind. Tomorrow, I shall visit Juliet. It's time I spoke with Baron Fairmont and asked for her hand." He glanced at his close friend. "I haven't come to this conclusion lightly."

Duncan regarded him. "It's a bold move. Are you certain this is the course you wish to take?"

Ewan set the glass down, the clink of crystal against wood punctuating his decision. "I've never been more certain of anything. Juliet is… she's unlike any other, Duncan. Her grace under pressure, her strength—she's the partner I desire."

Duncan nodded. "I understand. I'll make sure everything is in order for your call. And Ewan," he added, "I believe the Baron and his wife will see the honor in your intentions."

After Duncan departed, Ewan remained at the table, sipping his wine, his thoughts as turbulent as the North Sea storm. The prospect of seeing Juliet again sent a thrill through him, along with a healthy dose of concern. After barely speaking to her these weeks, would she decline his offer? Setting that fear aside, he was determined he would not lose her.

Chapter Twelve

April 18, 1820

THE AFTERNOON SUNLIGHT streamed through the curtains into the Fairmont drawing room, where Juliet sat in a soft blue muslin dress, her hair neatly coiffed into a chignon. The room was fragrant with the scent of fresh-cut flowers, vibrant gifts from Mr. Hargrove and Viscount Mandeville, who were once again expected for tea.

The clock chimed the hour, echoing through the house with a resonance that normally would have set Juliet's heart to fluttering in anticipation. Yet today, the sound that signaled suitors would soon arrive felt more like a tolling bell, a reminder of the duty that awaited her. Other gentlemen had shown interest, yet none seemed inclined to step forward with the urgency her situation demanded. All except Mr. Hargrove and Viscount Mandeville. They alone had been persistent in their attentions, their visits becoming as regular as the clock's chimes, each visit echoing the pressing need for Juliet to secure her family's future. She sat, poised and elegant, but her mind wandered, lost in the memory of a moonlit terrace.

Her thoughts were interrupted by a knock on the door, bringing her back to the present. Juliet quickly settled herself, straightening her skirt and smoothing out the wrinkles. She took a deep breath and put on a practiced smile, ready to receive her callers. When the door opened, Lord Glenraven stood in front of her. Neither Mr. Hargrove nor Viscount Mandeville were anywhere in sight. Her heart skipped a beat.

He stood in the doorway, a vision of charm, holding a bouquet so vibrant and alive it seemed to bring the very garden into the room. The flowers in his hands were a stark contrast to the polite, predictable arrangements that usually graced such visits. His was an elegant bouquet with a touch of the unexpected, much like their encounters. Rare blue roses were the centerpiece of the bouquet, symbolizing the mystery and intrigue of their relationship. Delicate white lilies surrounded the roses implying purity and modesty. Interspersed among the flowers were sprigs of heather from Scotland, signifying admiration and protection, and lastly, sprigs of rosemary for remembrance, which hinted at their shared moments and conversations. The bouquet was tied with a simple ribbon.

Juliet stood to meet him, her heart beating faster with sudden excitement. "Lord Glenraven," she greeted, her voice steady despite the surprise that danced in her eyes. "To what do I owe the pleasure of this unexpected visit?"

He stepped forward and offered her the flowers. "I saw these and thought of you." His voice carried the warmth of their shared moments. "They reflect the beauty and depth I've come to associate with you, Miss Hayward."

Juliet's fingers brushed against his as she took the bouquet, reigniting their connection at the ball. The room, with its fine furnishings and portraits of ancestors long past, seemed to fade away, leaving only the two of them standing amidst the quiet of their undeniable bond.

Before they could settle into a conversation, Mr. Hargrove and Viscount Mandeville were announced. The two gentlemen entered, each bearing floral tributes, but the atmosphere they were accustomed to had shifted substantially with Glenraven's commanding presence. Mr. Hargrove's usual prattle about the weather fell flat, and even Viscount Mandeville's attempts at charm seemed to falter under Glenraven's silent, discerning gaze.

The tension was such that Hargrove's and Mandeville's visit, which would usually extend well past an hour, was cut short. With awkward excuses, the gentlemen took their leave, their departure as hurried as it was unceremonious.

Once alone, Juliet turned to Glenraven, her eyes alight with amusement. "Well, that was rather surprising," she said, a laugh escaping her lips.

His response was a slight shrug, the corner of his mouth lifting in a half-smile. "I merely came to see you, Juliet. Their timing was… unfortunate."

When he tenderly uttered her given name and did not address her as 'Miss Hayward,' she felt a flutter in her chest, a warmth that spread to her cheeks. It was an intimacy she had not expected.

"Juliet," he said again, and this time it sounded like a caress, a secret only they shared. She looked up at him, her eyes wide with surprise and delight.

He met her gaze, a gentle affirmation in his eyes. "Forgive me for taking the liberty, Miss Hayward. But Juliet suits you far better," he corrected himself.

A soft smile played on her lips. "It's quite all right, Lord Glenraven—"

"Please, Ewan. It seems only right, considering you've allowed me to use your given name."

Juliet glanced at the bouquet in her hands, a playful smile tugging at her lips. "These flowers are lovely. Are you trying to outshine the garden outside?"

He leaned back, his smile broadening. "I merely wished to bring a small part of the garden's beauty indoors. Though I must admit, even the finest blossoms pale in comparison to you."

Juliet laughed. "Flattery, my lord, will get you everywhere, or at least into the good graces of Mrs. Murthy." She found herself laughing more freely than she had the last weeks, her earlier disappointment forgotten.

"Ah, but it is not your housekeeper I seek to impress." He leaned in slightly, his gaze holding hers with an intensity that made her heart race.

In the quiet of the drawing room, Juliet's mind was a whirl-wind of thoughts. Her heart waged a silent war as they spoke about favored places and hidden gems in London. Ewan's reassuring and solid presence was also a mirror reflecting the truth she had yet to share. The guilt of withholding the reality of her family's plight clawed at her, but fear whispered caution—fear that revealing the depths of her troubles might drive him away, severing the fragile connection they'd just begun to create.

She stole a glance at him, his expression open and inviting. How would it change once he knew everything? The obligation of her brother's looming debts and the shadow of scandal were burdens she bore. She had no right to ask him to shoulder them, too.

As she wrestled with her thoughts, a stronger voice urged her to be honest. He needed to know the truth if there were to be any hope for them. Once she did, Ewan could decide. And perhaps, just perhaps, he would see beyond her family's troubles and see the woman who stood before him—imperfect but loyal.

"Ewan," she began, her voice barely above a whisper, "I find myself at a crossroads, and I believe it is something you should know." She paused. Telling him everything seemed so easy in her thoughts, but now that she had to voice them, the words eluded her. She took a deep breath and gathered the courage. *Just say it.* "My family… we are facing difficulties since my brother's passing." She paused with her hands folded tightly in her lap as if holding the pieces of her story together.

The confession hung in the air like a rain cloud waiting to burst. Yet, she felt relieved knowing she had done the honorable thing. She couldn't bear the thought of Ewan hearing whispers from others—gossip that would inevitably spread as the two of them became closer. The *ton* loved a disaster.

Ewan reached across the small space between them and gently touched her hand, anchoring her in the moment. "Juliet, whatever challenges you face," his voice was steady and sure, "know that you are not alone."

Juliet continued, but the words were coming with more difficulty now. "Since Bradley... since we lost him, things have been... challenging." The last word understated the turmoil that followed her brother's death.

Ewan's expression softened. "Juliet, whatever it is, you can tell me," he urged gently.

She couldn't stop now, but the horror made her want to. She might as well simply ask him to leave. Juliet lifted her head and was taken aback by the encouragement she found in his eyes.

Chapter Thirteen

"**B**RADLEY LEFT BEHIND more than just grief... there were debts, ones we can't possibly settle." Her voice trembled with the admission, the facade of the composed lady crumbling to reveal the scared young woman beneath. "We're facing ruin, Ewan."

Ewan tightened his grasp on her hand, a wordless vow of solidarity. He leaned in. "Juliet," his voice was low and confident, "we'll navigate this together."

As they sat there, she took another deep breath, the pain evident in her eyes. "Bradley... he took his own life. The shame of his gambling debts was too much for him to bear." A single tear escaped, tracing a path down her cheek.

Ewan put a reassuring arm around her. "I am so sorry for your loss," he said softly, his thumb gently wiping the tear away.

Juliet's heart ached with the telling, but Ewan's warmth provided a small comfort. "Thank you, Ewan. Your kindness means more than you can know." Her voice was steadied by his touch.

He gazed at her, and she felt a bit uncomfortable. She could see his mind working, putting some pieces together.

"Bradley," she stared at the carpet. She couldn't look into Ewan's face where he'd see her embarrassment. "He was a poor card player. He thought he could win his losses back."

Ewan's back straightened, but he never let go of her hand.

After several heartbeats, she faced him. The warmth in his eyes caught her off guard, prompting an involuntary deep breath.

Ewan spoke softly. "Your father's finances have been compromised as well."

She glanced at his hand holding hers as a tear, her unwanted, uncontrollable tear splashed on his hand. She nodded. "And there are vowels."

He held her close, blocking out the world for a moment. She would never forget his support. She gently moved out of his embrace and wiped away the tears that dared to fall. "I mustn't weep," her voice firm despite the tremor she couldn't conceal. "There is still hope. We Fairmonts are made of sterner stuff."

"I am aware of what a strong woman you are. I'll return tomorrow to speak with your father," he said as he stood to leave.

"You can't," she blurted out. He stopped in his tracks. "Father is away in Scotland speaking with the family," she said, a bit panicked. She didn't know what else to say.

Ewan stared at her. She could see his mind working. Finally, he asked, "Can he count on the family's help?"

Another response she couldn't answer. Juliet's heart clenched, fearing what her father's visit might lead to. She looked away.

Ewan gently reached around and turned her head toward him. "Juliet, whatever assistance your father seeks from kin, know you have an ally in me."

Ewan's declaration and intent were clear, but her pride bristled at the thought of entangling him in her family's misfortunes. "This is not your battle," she protested, her voice fortified with stubborn purpose. "I told you because... because you deserved to know the truth from me and not some gossip. I am not asking you for assistance but for your understanding. And allow you to decide whether you wish to continue our association, knowing the full extent of my family's circumstances."

His smile was gentle yet unwavering. "Juliet, knowing the truth only deepens why I love you," he confessed. The word 'love' slipped into the conversation with an ease that startled them both. "Your strength, your honesty, and your loyalty are what I admire most about you. I am devoted to you, not just in the good times but through every challenge we may face together."

Juliet's eyes grew wide, and a flutter of astonishment seized her chest. She stood up, needing some space between them. "You can't mean that," she whispered, the word echoing in her mind. "I cannot allow you to be drawn into this mess. Everything has been quiet so far, but it will not last long. That is when the financial instability of my family, as well as the scandal of Bradley's passing and what he left behind, could taint your family as well. I wouldn't be able to live with myself if that happened."

"Juliet, you've shared much with me, and I'm grateful for your trust." His voice was calm and insistent. "But there's something more, something you're not telling me. Please, whatever it is, tell me. I cannot help you unless I know everything."

Juliet hesitated. She hadn't told anyone of the threats. It would only worry them. As she met his gaze, she recognized not only his concern but also his unyielding strength. "There have been threats, Ewan. Anonymous notes warning of dire consequences if my brother's debts aren't settled."

His expression hardened. "Show me these notes," he demanded gently, his hand outstretched.

She pulled a note she had just received from her pocket, handed it to him, and stood by as he read it.

Miss Hayward,

Consider this a friendly warning. The debts of the past have a way of reaching into the present. It would be a shame if the beauty of Fairmont were marred by misfortune. The consequences unbareble if actions are not taken. I trust you'll find a way to settle accounts before matters take an unfortunate turn.

A Concerned Observer

"No one threatens you without facing my retribution." Ewan's firm determination was evident in the set of his jaw, a silent pledge of his protection.

Juliet's breath caught as the air between them became charged with a tension that was both thrilling and terrifying. She heard his declaration spoken with purpose and sincerity.

"I cannot let you be drawn into my family problems." She shook her head and took a step back. But he took her by the shoulders. She could not turn away.

"You have no say in what I allow myself to be drawn into," Ewan said, his voice low and unwavering. "I refuse to stand idly by when I can help."

He drew her in closer, close enough for her to feel the warmth radiating from him. Juliet's earlier decision melted under the intensity of his gaze. She knew she should maintain a distance and protect both their hearts from the potential pain of a future denied. Yet, as she looked up at him, all thoughts of caution vanished.

"Ewan," she whispered. "You mustn't—"

But her protest was silenced as he leaned down. His lips captured hers in a gentle kiss. The kiss spoke of support, shared burdens, and a growing affection that refused to be ignored.

Juliet's hands found their way to his chest, clutching at the fabric of his coat as she returned his kiss, her mind a frenzy of emotion. She felt a surge of hope, a daring belief that perhaps they could face the future together, no matter the obstacles.

Their kiss deepened, and little by little, the excuses Juliet used to protect her heart began to crumble. Ewan's touch was tender, his kiss a comfort to the silent fears that had haunted her. In his embrace, she found strength and a sense of safety she hadn't known she craved. The world outside, with its expectations and judgments, faded into insignificance. In this moment, there was only Ewan, his kiss, and the promise of a love that might conquer all.

As the intensity of their embrace waned, Ewan became acutely aware of the propriety they challenged. With great reluctance, he eased back, his hands sliding from her back to grasp her hands gently. "I should leave," he whispered, his words heavy with unspoken longing.

He led her by the hand to the drawing room door. When they finally parted, breathless and wanting more, Juliet looked up into Ewan's eyes, seeing not just the marquess but the man who was kind and brave.

His gaze held a silent vow that this was only the beginning. He released her hands as if letting go of a treasured possession and stepped back toward the threshold. "I must go. 'Till it be morrow," he murmured, a tender echo of their farewell at Covent Garden.

And with that, he turned and stepped through the doorway, leaving her with a heart full of hope.

In the quiet that followed Ewan's departure, Juliet grappled with a whirlwind of emotions. His offer to help and declaration of affection were a quiet reassurance against her persistent worries. A sharp rap at the door jolted Juliet back to reality. Her heart leaped with the hope that Ewan had returned. She quickly made her way to the foyer, her bearing poised, her expression serene. Mr. Wilcox opened the door and found Mr. Wickham, whose insistent rap on the door was more demanding than polite, on her doorstep.

"Miss Hayward," he began, his voice carrying an edge of impatience, "this is the third time I've called regarding the debt owed. I trust you understand the gravity of the situation."

"I am fully aware, Mr. Wickham," Juliet replied, her voice steady despite the tension knotting her stomach. "My family is working diligently to address the matter. I ask for your patience." Her gaze was unwavering, meeting his with a quiet defiance that contradicted her refined appearance.

Mr. Wickham's eyes narrowed. His behavior was unyielding as he took a step closer. "Patience is a luxury I can no longer afford. If the debts are not settled, I will be forced to take what is due to me." His gaze dropped to the pearl earrings Juliet wore, a gift from her late grandmother. "Those will do nicely." He pointed to her earrings. "They'll look fine on my wife."

Juliet's hand instinctively rose to her earlobes. The pearls were a family treasure worth ten times the cost of a suite for Bradley that Mr. Wickham swore he made, but Mr. Wilcox nor Mrs. Murthy were able to locate. "You will not have my earrings, sir," she declared, her voice cold, her verdict final. "We will settle our accounts, but not through such means."

"Now, see here," he wagged his finger at her.

"No, sir. You see here." The command in her voice had him step back.

"Our accountant has instructed me not to pay your bill until he completes his investigation of those charges. Do I make myself clear, sir?" She spit out each word to make certain Mr. Wickham thoroughly understood her meaning.

The hate she saw in his eyes was nothing compared to her anger. "I believe that will be all for today, Mr. Wickham."

Juliet closed the door behind a retreating Mr. Wickham. Her heart raced, but her spirit was unbroken as she leaned against the door. The cool wood contrasted with the heat of her flushed cheeks. Her breaths were sharp and quick. "Compose yourself, Juliet," she whispered, her voice a soft command in the silent foyer.

The echo of Mr. Wickham's fading footsteps was a bleak reminder of the delicate balance she now had to maintain between her family's honor and their impending ruin. Her hands, though trembling from anger and fear, were not weak. They were the hands of a woman preparing to fight for her and her family's future.

The thought of Ewan and the support he had offered was a comfort to her frayed nerves. He could shield the family from the scandal, but the mention of love, a bond that might deepen into something profound, was enticing. Ewan had offered her a lifeline, not out of obligation, but from a place of genuine caring. With Ewan, there was the promise of more than just a marriage of convenience; there was the possibility of true companionship and love.

Chapter Fourteen

April 19, 1820

T HE MORNING LIGHT spilled across the breakfast table, casting long shadows over the fine china and silver. Across from Juliet, her mother sat in silence, the morning paper a crisp rectangle beside her. She placed her cup onto the saucer, the sound sharp and solitary, magnified by the room's hush.

"Juliet, my dear." Her mother's voice carried the flourish as if she just played the winning card in a high-stakes game. "I have done what you could not. I found a suitor for you." Her mother's eyes lit with the thrill of triumph.

Juliet's spoon paused mid-air, a droplet of honey suspended like amber. "A suitor, Mother?" Her voice was controlled, but her mind raced with implications.

"Yes, and not just any suitor," her mother continued, leaning forward as if to emphasize the grandness of her achievement. "He will soon inherit a marquessate, and he is fully aware of our… difficulties, and still, he is willing to help, to stand by us. He is suggesting several years in India, away from the scandal."

Her mother studied her for a moment before nodding slowly. "Juliet, remaining in London, in England, is out of the question. The scandal would be unbearable. We'd be shunned by the very people we know."

Juliet felt a pang of anxiety but remained resolute. "I appreciate your efforts, Mother, but…" Her voice faded.

"You're upset, Juliet." Her mother sighed, a thoughtful expression on her face. "Very well. I will say nothing about the suitor until you hear from your father."

The rest of the breakfast passed with Juliet's thoughts in turmoil. A suitor. A marquess. A journey to India. Each piece of news was a strategic move in a game that Juliet only realized she was playing.

Her heart, once caught in a tempest of hope and despair, now steadied itself firmly on hope. There was no choice but to leap. A future with Ewan, where love could blossom from the ruins, was a risk she was willing to take.

After breakfast, Juliet excused herself, feeling the dining room walls closing in with every word her mother spoke. She needed a place to think and to breathe, so she headed to her room.

She slid open her dressing table drawer. There it was—the ace of hearts, lying innocently among Bradley's effects along with various trinkets and baubles. It was as if the card was waiting for her, a silent ally in her time of need.

She couldn't help but think of Ewan, his declaration of love, and the possibility that she might lose him to circumstances she could not control. The card, a symbol of love and emotion, now represented a chance to clear her brother's name, save her family from ruin, and perhaps secure a future with the man who had captured her heart.

The shadow challenge Ewan had spoken of, with its elusive prize, suddenly seemed like the answer for which she had been searching. If there was indeed a prize to be won, it was the key to their salvation. The money would pay off all of Bradley's gambling debts, freeing her family from ruin. Her tenacity hardened. She would not wait for fate to decide her path. She would take this card to Ewan, and together, they would uncover its secrets.

Her reflection in the mirror now showed a woman of action, ready to face whatever challenges lay ahead. With the ace of hearts in hand, Juliet felt a renewed sense of hope. This was more than a card. It was a promise of possibility, and she was ready to seize it.

The voices outside Juliet's chamber grew louder, Aunt Geraldine's voice unmistakable as it competed with her mother's. The door opened, and the two women entered, their expressions indicative of their concern and tenacity.

"What marquessate is this man set to inherit, exactly?" Aunt Geraldine's voice cut through the tension, her eyes sharp with skepticism. "And what if his expectations are misplaced?"

Juliet's mother, her usual composure shaken, faltered for a moment. "He is of good stock, and his intentions are... honorable," she insisted, though her voice lacked conviction.

Aunt Geraldine turned to Juliet, her gaze conveying a silent message of caution. "We must be vigilant, Juliet. This suitor, whom you have not yet met, may have designs beyond a simple marriage proposal."

The room seemed to close in on Juliet as she considered the implications. To be promised to a man she did not know, a man who might seek to control her fate, was a prospect that left her feeling uneasy and uncertain.

A soft knock interrupted their conversation, and Mrs. Murthy peeked her head through the door, her expression apologetic. "Begging your pardon, Lady Fairmont, but there's been a bit of a mishap in the kitchen, and your guidance is needed."

Juliet's mother sighed, a frown creasing her brow. "Very well, I shall attend to it." She rose from her seat with a resigned air. "I'm leaving for Scotland this afternoon. Aunt Geraldine has reminded me that the issue of your marriage is too important and must be discussed with him directly. Your aunt will take my place and stay here until your father and I return." She exited the room with a swish of her skirt.

Once her mother closed the door behind her, Aunt Geraldine's manner shifted from concern to a glimmer of hope. "We need a plan, and it must be one that ensures your happiness. I have it on good authority that Lord Glenraven was quite the gallant gentleman yesterday when he called."

Juliet responded with a nod, her mind already racing with the implications of Ewan's intentions. "I must speak with him. He planned to speak to Father. Ewan should be aware of what mother has done."

"Indeed." A smile broke through Aunt Geraldine's earlier apprehension. "And we'll seek Mrs. Murthy's assistance. Her discreet ways could prove invaluable now." Her aunt tugged on the bell pull.

Moments later, Mrs. Murthy entered, a questioning look on her face.

"Mrs. Murthy," Aunt Geraldine began, "Do you know any of the staff at Lord Glenraven's home?"

"I do, my lady," Mrs. Murthy replied.

"Duncan, his lordship's batman, is a fine Scotsman and the son of Baron Blair. He is loyal to his lordship. I understand he and Lord Glenraven grew up together at his lordship's home near Sommer-by-the-Sea and the River Tweed." Mrs. Murthy stopped, a blush painting her cheeks. She continued, her voice filled with pride and a touch of mischief. "Duncan and I struck up a conversation at the market. He has a secret passion, you see. He's quite the connoisseur of rare books, always looking for hidden gems."

Aunt Geraldine's eyes sparkled with intrigue. "Books, you say? How fascinating. And does Duncan know of the... situation here?"

Mrs. Murthy nodded, her keen eyes reflecting a shrewd understanding. "He inquired when Baron Fairmont is expected to return. His lordship requires an important meeting. He's not one to stand idly by. If there's another suitor in the picture, Duncan would want his lordship to know, to... hasten his decision."

Juliet felt a surge of gratitude for Mrs. Murthy's perceptiveness. "Could you, perhaps, mention this to Duncan?" she asked, her voice hopeful. "Without revealing too much, of course."

"Leave it to me, my lady," Mrs. Murthy assured her with a confident nod. "A word here, a hint there, and Duncan will understand. He'll ensure Lord Glenraven receives the information."

As Mrs. Murthy excused herself, Juliet turned to her aunt. "We must act quickly. Before Mother does something that will seal my fate."

Aunt Geraldine placed a reassuring hand on Juliet's shoulder. "We will, my dear. We will." Her gaze was a silent vow.

Chapter Fifteen

T HAT EVENING, GLENRAVEN paused at the wrought iron gates. The address he'd been given etched in elegant script on the card in his hand led him to this secluded place on St. James Place. The once majestic home, now cloaked in the shadows of the evening, loomed with an air of silent stories and faded glory. Its stone facade, etched by time, whispered of a nobility long past. Above, the distinct silhouette of the turret cut a stark figure against the twilight sky.

He stepped through the gates and walked up the stone path to the heavy oak door, which swung open before he could knock. The entryway was a cavernous space, the grandeur of its high ceilings and sweeping staircase evidence of its former glory. A dimly lit chandelier cast shadows that danced across the portraits of stern ancestors that lined the walls.

The modest octagonal turret room was perfect for this evening's entertainment. It was elegantly appointed, with high ceilings and mirrored sconces on each of the eight walls. The grand turret, in its roundish form, rose above the room and added an architectural touch. The space was rich with the scent of polished wood and tobacco. The wood panel walls bore witness to countless games of chance. A round mahogany table dominated the center of the room, where men of varying degrees of wealth and desperation waited to begin. Their faces were etched with concentration, their eyes flickering with greed, or was that fear?

At the table sat Lord Thornfield, his eyes sharp and calculating behind round spectacles had a hawkish gaze. His fingers deftly handled his cards as if they were an extension of his will. Lord Whitby, his cuff frayed, a subtle sign of his dwindling fortune. Sir Charles Bentley, a young baronet whose laughter rang out with the carelessness of youth. His eyes betrayed the naivety not yet tarnished by loss of any kind. Across from him sat Lord Gray, a man of few words, his silence a stark contrast to the clink of chips and the soft drop of cards. His eyes, however, followed the hands of every player with a calculated intensity. And there was Viscount Drake, who had a face that was a map of experience and weathered hands that moved with the precision of a man who had seen many such games.

Servants in crisp livery moved as silently as shadows, navigating the room with trays of spirits and glasses. Their presence was unobtrusive.

The game had been one of many Ewan had attended since his father's warning, but none revealed the gambling den he sought. Each visit left him with more questions and the answers as elusive as the turn of a card.

As the door to the room swung open, a hush fell over the table. Every player paused, and those standing turned in unison to the person who entered. Sebastian Morgrave's arrival was a performance. His confidence bordered on arrogance, his smile a challenge to the room. He glanced around as if he dared anyone to question his presence. When his gaze settled on Glenraven, the surprise was mutual. Sebastian appeared to relish the moment of unexpected recognition.

"Glenraven, what a pleasant surprise. I was certain you'd be back in Paris by now."

Unfazed, he acknowledged his cousin with a nod. "Sebastian."

Sebastian's eyes narrowed slightly as he gestured towards the empty chair. "Please, have a seat. Gentry will not be joining us this evening," Everyone caught the sly edge of Sebastian's words.

Glenraven sat in the empty chair, his stature, head and shoulders above the rest, cast a long shadow across the table. The candlelight flickering from the sconces behind him only accentuated his imposing figure. His broad shoulders squared as he settled into the chair, an unspoken assertion of his place at the table.

"I trust you'll find this game more… stimulating than the others you've attended recently. Word does get around. Do be careful here, though. You see, fortunes can change as quickly as the cards are dealt." Sebastian's warning filled the silence, a challenge that went beyond the green baize of the card table.

"I'll keep that in mind." Glenraven motioned for another whisky as the game began. Glenraven won hand after hand. His winnings mounted up. But as the night progressed, he allowed his luck to fade, and his cousin's winnings grew. Sebastian's overconfidence was blatant, his smug smile widening with each hand Glenraven lost.

Yet Ewan was not easily bested. With a calm focus, and when he saw fit, he turned the tide, his winnings again mounting until his victories overshadowed the table. Sebastian barely concealed his rage. His veneer of civility thinned with each loss.

"You may think you have the upper hand now, Glenraven," Sebastian sneered, "but the night is long, and fortunes change."

Ewan met his cousin's gaze, his response carefully considered but firm. "Indeed, they do. And I intend to see this game through to the end." His expression remained composed, a slight smirk playing at the corner of his mouth as he collected his winnings with a calm assurance that contradicted the intensity of the game. He was the picture of confidence, leaning back in his chair with one arm casually draped over the back of the empty chair beside him. The subtle challenge in his attitude, the unspoken assertion of control, was enough to unsettle his cousin, whose confidence hinged on the intimidation of others.

The tension in the room continued to mount as the game progressed. Glenraven's gaze remained fixed on Sebastian.

"Sebastian," he interjected smoothly just as the next hand was about to be dealt. "I must thank you for overseeing the estate in my absence. Your efforts were... noted."

Sebastian's smile faltered, a flicker of uncertainty crossing his face. "Of course, Ewan. It was my pleasure to assist."

Glenraven's expression remained impassive as he continued, "Now that I've returned, I'll be resuming full control of the estate affairs during Father's recovery. Your services, while appreciated, are no longer required."

His words echoed in the room, a subtle yet unmistakable dismissal that sent a ripple of murmurs through the onlookers. Sebastian's composure cracked, his veneer of civility giving way to a flash of anger before he regained control.

Leaning back in his chair, Glenraven let a small, victorious smile stretch over his lips. He took pleasure in Sebastian's grappling with the implications. As the power dynamics shifted, he turned to the game, his confidence unshaken. "Now, shall we continue?" he asked, his voice filled with a challenge as he met Sebastian's gaze.

Pulling out his pocket watch, Ewan noted that it had been over an hour since the first cards were dealt. He leaned forward, his eyes locking with Sebastian's. "Let's make this interesting." His voice was steady and clear. "I'll raise the stakes." With a flick of his wrist, he pushed all his chips into the center of the table, effectively doubling the bet and heightening the tension in the room even more.

THE SOFT RAP at the servants' entrance at Fairmont Abbey broke the evening's stillness. Mrs. Murthy opened the door and found Duncan standing there, a bottle of homemade punch cradled in his arm, a peace offering or, perhaps, an overture to more candid conversations to come.

"Come in, Duncan." She stepped aside to let the cool night air sweep him into the warm kitchen. "That looks like a fine brew you've got there."

Duncan offered a small, appreciative smile as he entered, placing the bottle on the sturdy wooden table. "Aye, it's from my mother's own recipe. Thought it might sweeten our talk."

Mrs. Murthy fetched two glasses and a plate of biscuits, the clink of crystal against wood interrupting the silence. She poured the punch and inhaled the rich aroma that mingled with the lingering scents of the day's cooking. "So, what treasure did you find at the market today?" Even though her tone was light and her eyes keen, she asked not only to fill the space but also because she was truly interested.

"A rare find indeed," Duncan's Scottish accent thickened with pride. "An old volume of Burns' poetry. It's for his lordship, but I'll admit, I'll be enjoying it myself before it finds its way to his library."

Their laughter filled the room as they tipped up their glasses. "To his lordship's new edition." But as the joy faded, Mrs. Murthy's expression grew serious, and she leaned in closer. "Duncan, there's talk of another suitor for Miss Juliet." Her voice dropped to a conspiratorial whisper.

Duncan's face clouded with concern. "And what does the lass think of this?"

"She's none too pleased," Mrs. Murthy sat back, her Scottish lilt wrapping around her words like a comforting shawl. "It's a marriage of convenience, nae more. To pay off the family's debts."

Duncan's hand tightened around his glass. "And Lord Glenraven? Does he ken about this?"

Mrs. Murthy's gaze held a shadow of sorrow. "She's afraid to tell him. Afraid he'll see it as a betrayal, that she tricked him. But she willnae marry him without being honest."

The room grew quiet, save for the soft crackling of the fire. Duncan nodded slowly, his respect for Miss Hayward deepening. "Aye, the lass told him all. And brave she was. It's not easy to admit such a downfall. We must do something. We cannae let her be trapped in a loveless marriage."

"Aye, not when the lass loves Glenraven," Mrs. Murthy agreed. "She was mooning over him for weeks until he came calling. We'll need to be clever about it. A bit of Scottish cunning might just turn the tide."

"Mrs. Murthy, get us paper and pen. We need to send Glenraven an anonymous message about what is happening, although I wouldn't be surprised if he deduces the source."

Mrs. Murthy nodded at Duncan's request, her movements swift as she gathered the necessary materials. "We must be cautious with our words," she said, dipping the quill into the inkwell. "The message must be clear yet discreet."

Duncan leaned over her shoulder, reading as the letter began to take shape on the paper. "Start with 'A matter of urgency has arisen,'" he suggested, his voice low.

Mrs. Murthy's hand moved across the page, the words flowing smoothly. "And mention 'a suitor with intentions not of the heart,'" she added, her brow furrowed in concentration.

Duncan read over the line, his lips pursed. "Perhaps we should say 'intentions that are more monetary than affectionate,'" he corrected, seeking precision in their message.

"Good," Mrs. Murthy agreed, scratching out the previous words and replacing them with Duncan's suggestion. "Now, we need to hint at the pressure she's under without revealing too much."

"'The lady finds herself in a delicate situation, one that may lead to an unwanted union,'" Duncan offered, his eyes fixed on the letter.

Mrs. Murthy wrote it down, then paused, considering. "Let's add 'Her heart belongs to another, whose declaration has already been made,'" she said, a hint of urgency in her voice.

Duncan nodded, satisfied with the addition. "End it with 'Time is of the essence, and discretion is paramount,'" he said, knowing the power those words carried.

Mrs. Murthy finished the letter with a flourish, setting the quill aside. They both reviewed the message, their heads close together, the tension of their task hanging in the air.

"A matter of urgency has arisen. A suitor with intentions that are more financial than affectionate threatens to bind a lady in a delicate situation, one that may lead to an unwanted union. Her heart belongs to another whose declaration has already been made. Time is of the essence, and discretion is paramount."

"Perfect," Mrs. Murthy whispered, her eyes meeting Duncan's.

"Seal it if you will, Mrs. Murthy. I will see that Glenraven reads it. He will understand that this letter, left unsigned and sealed, is a silent plea for action, a call for him to step forward before it is too late.

"One last glass before I leave." With the letter safely tucked in his pocket and Mrs. Murthy clearing away any signs of their secret plot, Duncan poured them each a glass of punch.

He raised his glass, the amber liquid catching the light as he nodded to Mrs. Murthy. "To clever plots and honest hearts," he declared, his Scottish brogue coloring the words.

Chapter Sixteen

April 20, 1820

L ATE MORNING FOUND Glenraven in his study, the light filtering through the windows catching the letter on the salver on his desk. He read it carefully, recognizing the handiwork. He couldn't help but smile. "Duncan," he murmured, appreciating the man's forthrightness and meddling. The letter confirmed his intentions. He would ask for Juliet's hand and celebrate their union with a gala to announce their engagement.

Before he could muse further, Duncan and Hughes came through the door. The solicitor entered with the air of a man bearing a heavy responsibility. "A threat has been made," Hughes announced and handed Ewan the note.

Ewan's mind raced as he turned the letter over in his hands. The words in the spidery scrawl warned him.

"Marquess, the misfortune that fell upon your father now looms over those you cherish. Their well-being hangs in the balance, much like he did. Consider this a caution: the legacy of Glenraven is not immune to being reduced to mere echoes and dust. The consequences will be unbareable if you do not heed this warning."

Sebastian's face flashed before him—the easy smile, the casual toss of the cards the night before. It would be easy to cast him as the villain. Yet, Ewan's thoughts drifted to Whitby, lurking in the shadows, his eyes darting greedily toward the pile of coins. And there was always the mysterious Gray, whose fortunes had turned as dark as his name suggested. No, it wasn't just Sebastian who left the table with his pockets less than he desired.

"With your birthday on the horizon, less than a fortnight away," Duncan added, "One can't help but wonder if this isn't a ploy to keep you from the altar."

Ewan paced the room, his mind in an uproar. "Marriage? Now?" His temper flared. The idea that had warmed him moments ago seemed more absurd by the second. "With this shadow upon my house?" He shook the paper at Hughes and Duncan.

"It seems the law cares a great deal about timing but not for threats." Hughes reminded him. "Your title, your estate—it all depends upon you marrying."

Ewan reconsidered his plans as the reality of his predicament sank in. He handed Hughes the letter regarding Juliet, his confession of love for her a whisper in the quiet room. "I can't put Juliet in danger, Hughes. I won't."

"This marriage could be the perfect answer. It secures your title. Marrying Miss Hayward gives her the protection she requires."

The suggestion ignited a fire in Ewan. The thought of Juliet in harm's way was unbearable. His jaw tightened, and his fists clenched at his sides. The idea of anyone threatening her safety made his blood boil. He took a deep breath, trying to steady his emotions, but the intensity of his feelings was undeniable.

"Ewan." Hughes and Glenraven turned to Duncan. "Do you remember when my father arranged for my sister Mary Rose to marry—"

"Pardon me, Duncan," Glenraven interrupted his man. "I am not interested in Mary Rose at the moment."

"You should be. She holds the answer for you." He stood by the door, confident and knowing.

"Go on, Duncan," Hughes gave Glenraven a quick glance,

then focused on Duncan. "I'll listen."

Duncan nodded and glanced at Glenraven, who waved his hand, signaling him to continue.

"My father arranged for Mary Rose to marry Laird Alasdair MacGregor without her consent, unaware she loved another—Liam Fraser. In defiance, they married in secret and kept it hidden for months."

Glenraven's gaze sharpened. "And you believe this is the path I should take with Juliet?"

Duncan's eyes met his friend's. "Aye. Keep your marriage a secret. Keep her safe. Until we've dealt with the threat."

Glenraven had made many difficult decisions, but none with as much to lose as this one. The thought of Juliet in harm's way was unbearable. But Mary Rose's secret defiance brought a glimmer of hope.

"So, my friend," Duncan's voice broke through his thoughts, a hint of lightness in his tone, "shall we venture to the archbishop and secure a special license?"

Once heavy with dread, the room now echoed with the possibility of a brighter future. Ewan nodded, his heart buoyed by the thought of marrying Juliet, of facing their challenges together.

"We'll both join you." Duncan glanced at Hughes, who nodded with a smile. "You may need someone to vouch for you."

Ewan shook his head with a silent chuckle. "Your company would be appreciated." As they prepared to leave, Ewan's attention was caught by an unfamiliar invoice on his desk. "What's this?" he asked, holding the document from Mr. Wickham's tailor shop.

"Ah, I meant to mention that earlier." Duncan scratched his head. "Found it among your father's things. Odd, isn't it?"

Ewan's eyes narrowed as he scanned the document. "My father never patronized Wickham's. Why would this be in his possessions?"

"This is one of the items in question. Fletcher had asked me if you purchased the goods. I assured him you had better taste."

Glenraven studied the bill further, his mind racing. "You're correct. These items are neither mine nor my father's transactions.

"Fletcher and I concluded." Duncan took a breath. "Someone's been using your father's account."

"Who would dare?" Glenraven's voice filled the room, a roar of anger that sent papers fluttering from his desk.

"Someone who thinks he is immune to any consequences." Duncan's eyes darkened. "Perhaps someone who already thinks the accounts are his."

"Surely, you don't mean…" Hughes took a step forward but was unable to finish his sentence.

"Wickham was evasive until Fletcher mentioned the magistrate. Then he suggested speaking to Sebastian Morgrave," Duncan said, his stance rigid with anger.

Frustration and realization mingled into one as Glenraven's hand swept through his hair. "Sebastian's behavior last night… it's all starting to make sense.

"Arrange a meeting with Sebastian," Glenraven instructed Hughes, his voice commanding. "We need answers."

As the three opened the door to leave, they found Mr. Fleming, his butler, about to enter. "You have a caller, my lord. I've put her in the drawing room."

"Her?" Glenraven was too startled to say anything further.

"Yes, my lord. Miss Juliet Hayward."

⤜⤛⤜⫷⫸

"JULIET," EWAN CALLED out as he entered the drawing room. His voice, though quiet, carried across the room. There she was, a silhouette against the window, haloed by the light.

She turned, her eyes wide, with a tumult of emotion that was easy for him to see.

"Ewan, there's something I must tell you." Her voice was

steady, but her hands betrayed her nerves.

He moved closer, reaching out to offer her comfort.

"No. Please." Her voice was a whisper as she stepped away from him, her hand raised in a silent plea that he not come closer.

He stopped, his arms falling to his sides.

"My mother… she's found a suitor." She stared at the blue Aubusson carpet. "She believes it's the answer to our family's problems, so you see, I can't—"

"Yes, you can. You don't have to marry your mother's suitor." His voice was firm. "I already know, and I have a plan."

Her gaze snapped up to meet his. "You do?"

"Before I tell you more, there is something you must know." He drew in a breath, the air seemingly heavier with the gravity of his admission. "Juliet, the Aurington name is not merely a title— it's a legacy with a centuries-old edict. The heir must marry before his thirtieth birthday to secure the lineage and estate's future. As my father's oldest son and Marquess of Glenraven, I am bound by this duty, a charge that ensures the continuity of our line and the preservation of our estate." He paused to give her a moment. "I sought a wife at Lady Gladstone's gala, but fate presented me with an unforeseen treasure. Instead, I found… my soul mate."

Juliet's eyes widened with realization. "Aunt Geraldine told me about the edict at Lady Gladstone's Gala. You were concerned that I would think you were manipulative and devious." Her laughter was touched with irony and softened with understanding. "What a pair we are. We're both afraid to disappoint the other. But I don't see how your situation solves my problem."

"Marry me." He stepped forward and cradled her hands with his own. "Now. Hughes and Duncan are in the library, prepared to accompany us to the Archbishop of Canterbury and secure—"

"A special license?" Her words were barely above a whisper, and her eyes were wide in disbelief.

Glenraven's expression grew somber, a jovial marquess replaced by a man bearing the gravity of an untold secret. "Yes. But there is more to our story, a complication. Someone has threatened my family and implied my father's mishap wasn't accidental." He moved closer, her presence a refuge. "We'll need to marry secretly and live apart until the threat ends. But more importantly, you must understand that marrying me means you may be in danger, too."

In the silence that followed, Juliet's eyes met his, with a storm of consideration churned behind them. After a moment, she nodded, her decision made. "Together, then," she said, her voice a whisper of courage.

His relief was unmistakable. "Together," he confirmed, their fates now irrevocably intertwined. He closed the distance between them, his gaze locked with Juliet's. The air seemed still, heavy with their undeclared promise. His hands gently cradled her face as he leaned down, his lips finding hers in a kiss that was tender proof of their unspoken vows.

The world outside faded, leaving only the sensation of Juliet's soft and yielding lips against his. The kiss deepened, a slow dance of intimacy that spoke of shared secrets and the promise of a future together. It was a kiss that sealed their fate, binding them with a passion that whispered of love and a defiance of the dangers ahead.

"Together," he murmured against her lips, "we will create our own destiny."

Juliet's response was immediate. Her lips sought his with an enthusiasm that she didn't try to contain. She answered his declaration not with words but with action.

Her hands rose to frame his face, pulling him closer and deepening their embrace. She was wholly devoted, her heart and soul entwined with his in the silent language of love that needed no words to be understood.

"Come with me. Duncan and Hughes are in the library." Glenraven, still holding Juliet's hand, led her to where they waited. The door swung open to reveal the two men standing amidst the rows of leather-bound books. Their faces turned in unison towards them.

Duncan beamed as he came forward to greet them. "It seems congratulations are due," he said warmly. "The days ahead look all the brighter with you two at the helm."

Hughes stepped forward, offering a respectful nod. "Indeed, Miss Hayward, you have our best wishes. This is a cause for celebration."

The library, a sanctuary of silent musings, now buzzed with a pleasant warmth, its air charged with the profound excitement of shared anticipation and fellowship. Glenraven's fingers tenderly entwined with Juliet's, a soft caress of the promising romance between them, and his profound gratitude for her bravery and trust.

"We need to go to the archbishop." Hughes removed his watch from his pocket. "It's close to noon. We want to see His Excellency before he goes out for the afternoon."

With the matter settled and their course set, they made their way to the carriage. As they settled into their seats, Juliet felt the ace of hearts in her pocket, a reminder of Bradley and the shadow quest. Her curiosity surfaced.

"Ewan, what is the shadow quest you mentioned?" she asked, her voice filled with intrigue.

Ewan's gaze lingered on her, noting her interest. "The shadow quest is akin to a scavenger hunt. It's a series of clues that lead to… something of significance. My cousin and I played the game as boys, racing through Aurington Manor's halls and the grounds, deciphering each clue."

Juliet listened intently, her mind already turning over the possibilities. "And the ace of hearts?" Her question was casual yet pointed.

"It's a pivotal piece in the game. It's not an ordinary card. It leads to the next clue."

He studied her for a moment, a question dawning. "Juliet, why all these questions about the shadow quest and the ace of hearts?"

With a deep breath, Juliet reached into her reticule and withdrew a worn playing card—the ace of hearts. "My brother had it when he…" Her voice was steady, but her hands betrayed a slight tremor. "… when he died. I can't help but wonder if there's a connection."

Chapter Seventeen

G LENRAVEN HELD THE worn card between his fingers, turning it over. As his eyes fell upon the back, his breath hitched. There, faint but unmistakable, was the shadowy raven symbol of the Order of Shadows.

He ran a thumb over the symbol, a chill creeping up his spine. His mind raced with questions and half-formed fears. What does this mean? How deeply is the Order involved in our lives? If Juliet's brother had a card, what had he uncovered before his death?

Juliet leaned closer, her eyes searching his face for answers. "Ewan, what is it?"

"This card." He showed it to her, his voice was low, barely more than a whisper. "It's identical to one I found among my father's belongings. It can't be a coincidence."

Juliet's eyes locked onto the card in Ewan's hands, a frown creasing her brow. "What could it possibly signify?"

He met her gaze, the mystery urging them to take action. "It means there's a connection we've yet to understand. The shadow quest my father devised is more than a game. And this card," he said, holding it up to the light, "it's a clue, one that we must decipher."

For a moment, he considered telling her about the Order of Shadows. The words hovered on his lips, but he held them back. The implications were too dangerous, and he didn't want to alarm her without information and proof.

Duncan, sitting across from them, cleared his throat, breaking the momentary silence. "If it's a clue, it's the start of our hunt. We need to follow where it leads."

Glenraven spotted Hughes' nod of agreement. It was clear to him that Hughes saw the urgency of their situation. "Securing the marriage is paramount." Hughes echoed Glenraven's priority. "It's the shield that will guard you both."

Juliet leaned close so only he could hear. "I can hear your thoughts. No, I haven't changed my mind."

Ewan took her hand and squeezed it gently. "I am the most fortunate of men. The most fortunate."

With everyone in agreement, they temporarily cast aside the puzzle. He took command, his mind already turning over their immediate concerns as they continued on to Lambeth Palace.

"We'll need to be careful about how we proceed." Ewan's gaze moved between Hughes and Juliet. "We must time our marriage announcement perfectly and arrange to settle your debts."

"Ewan, even if we keep our marriage secret, my mother will question the sudden clearing of our debts." Juliet didn't hide the distress in her words. "She'll suspect something is amiss."

Ewan nodded. "It's a delicate situation. We'll tell her an anonymous benefactor has come forward, moved by your family's situation."

A flicker of alarm crossed Juliet's features, her eyes widening at the realization. "But that would imply I'm engaged to a stranger. She'll never consent to such an arrangement without meeting the man first."

"We can assist you with that," Duncan interjected, his voice steady. "Hughes and I can corroborate the story. We'll say the benefactor is a reclusive nobleman who values his privacy above all else."

Hughes folded his arms, his mind working through the legalities. "We can draft a document, a settlement of sorts, detailing the arrangement. It will lend credibility to our tale as well as explain the financial commitment."

"And what of the benefactor's identity?" She pressed, seeking holes in their plan.

"We'll be vague," Ewan assured her. "We'll say he's a distant relation, perhaps from abroad, who wishes to remain unnamed."

He could see her processing the plan. Her contemplative silence spoke volumes. "And when the time comes for this benefactor to appear?" Ewan understood the importance of that question, knowing the answer would require all their cunning.

"We'll have eliminated the threat by then," Ewan said with conviction. "And we can reveal the truth—that I am your benefactor and your husband."

Juliet glanced at Duncan and then at Ewan. "We could say the benefactor is a Scotsman?"

Ewan considered Juliet's suggestion, the idea fitting seamlessly into their story. "That could work," he agreed, his excitement growing. "A distant cousin of my family, currently residing in Scotland. It's plausible and close enough to be believable."

Juliet nodded, a small smile playing on her lips. "And it explains your involvement without raising too many questions."

Duncan spoke up. His eyes sparkled with mischief. "Ach, no, Ewan, not a distant cousin, the Viscount of Ardoch. I'll vouch for the scoundrel Scottish viscount. After all, who better to confirm his existence than another Scot?"

Juliet's gaze flitted between Duncan and Glenraven. "We cannot use someone's name without asking him. Surely, you understand why."

"Viscount Ardoch, it is," Glenraven announced. He leaned over to Juliet. "I am the Viscount Ardoch. It is one of my lesser Scottish titles. Few know of it. Using that title, you'd be telling your parents the truth."

A laugh escaped Juliet. "Brilliant and genuine. It is a clever plan."

"I'll draft a document to formalize the arrangement." Hughes glanced at Glenraven and Juliet. "It will state all the terms, of course, and that the benefactor wishes to remain anonymous for personal reasons but is fully committed to supporting Miss Hayward."

"What shall we tell my mother when she inquires about the plans with my Scottish benefactor? A wedding date? She and Father may be in Scotland now, but they will return." Her voice carried a hint of mischief. "What should I tell her?"

The suggestion caught Glenraven, Hughes, and Duncan unaware. Their shared look betrayed a momentary lapse. The thought had never crossed their mind. It was evident that such particulars had not escaped Juliet's keen foresight. While their plan was painted with broad strokes, Juliet had meticulously attended to the finer details that would complete the picture and turn it into a masterpiece.

From the corner of his eye, Glenraven caught Juliet's almost imperceptible smile. She inhaled deeply, poised with a suggestion. "Perhaps I could tell her he wishes for the wedding to be soon, within the next four weeks, May 17th? That is when she and Father planned to return to London." she proposed. "We can also mention that he's a man of solitude, preferring a ceremony that reflects his private nature. He values discretion above all in these matters." Her eyes sought theirs, silently questioning their consensus. "Would this meet with your plans?"

Ewan felt a surge of admiration for Juliet's initiative. "That's a prudent course. It will give your mother peace of mind while preserving the secrecy vital to us." His voice carried a newfound respect, the admiration clear as he witnessed Juliet's deft handling of the delicate issue. It was an enlightening moment for him, one that not only provoked pride but also deepened his respect... and desire. He saw she possessed all the qualities necessary to stand by his side, whether as his Viscountess, Marchioness, or the Duchess of Aurington.

"One last item. How did this benefactor propose this solution? Was it a chance meeting in Hyde Park?" Juliet's eyes were wide with a guileless curiosity, a stark contrast to the sharp mind behind her question.

Ewan reclined into the coach seat. He couldn't suppress a chuckle. His betrothed was indeed a woman of subtly, wit, and wisdom.

"With my mother away, a letter from Aunt Geraldine about the Viscount and his petition might do the trick," she mused. "A message from someone Mother trusts and holds dear would surely ease her mind."

Straightening, Ewan's eyes shone with genuine esteem. "Your ingenuity amazes me." He looked to his companions, their affirming smiles and nods solidifying their collective decision.

Juliet gently placed her hand on Glenraven's arm, an unspoken understanding passing between them. "It appears we have a plan, my lord."

"Yes." Glenraven's tone was soft and sincere. "A delicate web of half-truths designed to protect you and keep our secret safe."

As the carriage approached Lambeth Palace, Juliet's gaze was drawn to the imposing Tudor gatehouse, its red-brick façade, and ornate Tudor arches a vivid indication of its past. The carriage passed beneath the gate's shadow, drawing up to the grand steps that led to the towering door, an entryway that promised both welcome and majesty.

Glenraven's pulse quickened as they stepped into the Archbishop's office, each man silently bearing the urgency of their mission, yet the unexpected warmth in His Grace's eyes as he greeted him provided a reassuring counterpoint. Ewan felt a quiet strength settle over him as he crossed the room, ready to put their plan into action.

"Lord Glenraven, I've been expecting you as your birthday draws near," the Archbishop greeted, his voice a gentle rumble.

"Yes, it does, Your Excellency. How kind of you to remember." Ewan smiled, remembering the archbishop joining him and his family for dinner before he left for France on the eve of his nineteenth birthday.

"I suppose this is not an invitation to a dinner celebration."

His Excellency did enjoy banter… and teasing.

"No, sir, not to dinner but a wedding, with your assistance."

The Archbishop's eyes widened for a heartbeat or two before he nodded. "Continue."

Ewan cleared his throat, steadying himself. "Your Excellency, I come before you to request a special license for marriage." His words were carefully thought out and deliberate.

"Ah," the Archbishop turned to Juliet. "It took your intended time to decide. Will it be a grand affair?"

Ewan shook his head. "For reasons most grave, I must ask that this union remains confidential."

The Archbishop looked over Glenraven and then at Juliet. "There are several reasons that can be grave…"

"Begging your pardon, Your Excellency." Everyone turned to Juliet, who stood with her hands clasped respectfully in front of her. "Our reasons are like none you have heard before."

"You've come with no one to vouch for you. What am I to think?"

Juliet continued, her demeanor composed. "I stand before you on my own behalf. At twenty-three, my conduct has been such that it would withstand the scrutiny of the highest circles." Her gaze was steady, her voice unwavering. "I assure you, there is no cause for scandal or concern that would bring dishonor to our names."

The Archbishop paused, nodded, and made a note on the document in front of him: "Very well, Miss Hayward. Your self-sponsorship is noted. Yet, I require further details." His gaze shifted to Glenraven: "Pray tell me, what are these reasons that are most grave?"

Glenraven's hand hovered over the letter, the entire endeavor resting on the Archbishop's decision. Disclosing the threat to his family was a last resort. "We have reason to believe my father's recent misfortune was no mere accident." With a firm hand, he passed the parchment to His Grace.

The Archbishop read it quickly and turned to Juliet with a

troubled glance. "Are you fully aware of the danger this union brings?"

Juliet's gaze was unwavering, her decision etched in her features. "Yes, Your Excellency. I've received my own share of ominous threats." Glenraven couldn't be prouder of her. Her voice was steady despite the undercurrent of fear. "It appears Lord Glenraven and I are both targets of this person."

"How did you arrive at that conclusion?"

Ewan and Juliet, visibly tense, laid out the evidence before the archbishop. Letters, notes, and cards were spread across the desk, each containing threats and warnings.

Ewan pointed to a particularly chilling note. "This was found among my father's belongings after his accident. It warns of dire consequences if I continue my investigations."

Juliet nodded, holding up the Ace of Hearts. "And this card was found with my brother when he died under mysterious circumstances. It seems to be a signature or calling card of sorts."

The Archbishop evaluated their situation. He glanced once again at the threatening letter and other documents and items.

"Your circumstances are as you say, I concede, but..." His voice trailed off, leaving the sentence hanging.

"Your Excellency," Juliet stepped forward. "Did I mention why I want to marry Lord Glenraven?"

A nod came, indicating he already knew the reason. "To shield yourself from this threat?"

"While many seek to marry for such reasons, mine lie elsewhere." Her response was gentle yet firm.

All attention returned to Juliet.

"Fate brought me to a puppet theater, where I, as Judy, found myself in a twist of drama only to be saved by a gallant Punch, played by Lord Glenraven." Her eyes met Glenraven's, a shared memory sparking a soft smile between them. "And just as fate had scripted for our puppets, it guided me to my true hero, my destined partner." She turned back to the Archbishop, her expression earnest. "That, Your Excellency, is the heart of why I accepted Lord Glenraven's proposal. Lord Glenraven is my heart's desire."

Glenraven waited as understanding dawned on the Archbishop's features, his concern deepening. "Then we shall be discreet in our proceedings. Your courage is to be commended, and the church will offer its sanctuary," he declared. The Archbishop's gaze lingered on Juliet, clearly moved by her sincerity. "Is tomorrow too soon for the ceremony?" he proposed, a hint of compassion emerging amidst his stately manner. "I leave London tomorrow in the early afternoon. If you need secrecy, come at ten, and I shall be honored to marry you in my private chapel. When you're able to reveal your marriage, few will argue about the ceremony." Glenraven clasped Juliet's hand as a silent message passed between them. Words were unnecessary, given the Archbishop's understanding and promise of protection. A ripple of excitement passed through the room, and with a flourish of his quill, the Archbishop signed the paperwork, sealing their fate with the church's blessing.

"You haven't changed your mind, have you?" The Archbishop's eyes twinkled with a delight he could scarcely conceal.

"Not at all, Your Excellency," Ewan replied with conviction. Juliet's grip on his hand tightened in silent affirmation.

"Good. Congratulations," the archbishop handed Juliet the license. "Now, if you will excuse me." He crossed the room with the air of having done a great deed.

Glenraven, still holding her hand, found his voice. "Your Excellency, we are profoundly grateful. We are indebted to your kindness and discretion."

The Archbishop paused at the threshold, turning back with a reflective gaze. "Don't thank me," he said, his voice carrying a note of respect. "It is Miss Hayward's eloquence and conviction that swayed me. I could find no fault in her argument. I look forward to seeing you both tomorrow at ten." With a final nod, he stepped out the door.

Chapter Eighteen

A s THEIR CARRIAGE rolled away from the archbishop's residence, Juliet's voice cut through the clatter of hooves. "I would like my aunt, Mrs. Murthy, and Mr. Wilcox to attend our wedding."

Glenraven caught the subtle longing in her request and understood her wish for the comfort of someone close when her family could not be there. "Is there anyone else you would like to attend?"

Juliet's eyes met his. With a nod and glance across the carriage, he followed her meaning.

"That is a fine idea," Glenraven agreed, turning to Hughes and Duncan. "Gentlemen, Miss Hayward and I would be honored by your presence at our nuptials tomorrow."

"I would be most honored," Hughes said as he nodded, accompanied by a deep, appreciative smile.

"Aye, and I'll give the groom away," Duncan declared with a wink at Juliet.

They all settled back for a quiet carriage ride. Glenraven reached in his pocket for his watch and felt the slick surface of the playing card. The Ace of Hearts. He understood the urgency the card played other than it was part of a mystery that had brought them all together.

He pulled out the card, breaking the silence. "We won't be able to ignore this much longer." He glanced at Juliet. The others nodded with as much conviction as his. "I fear the clearance of your debts will not stop the villain's attempts. We must be prepared."

"This is the playing card Juliet found among her brother's effects." He handed it to Duncan, rested his back against the seat, and glanced out the window as if the answer was there. "It's identical to one I found among my father's belongings."

"That can't be a coincidence." Hughes took the card from Duncan and studied it.

"My brother…" Juliet paused and took a breath. "He had it with him the night he fell from the balcony. I didn't think much of the card until Glenraven mentioned it." She turned to him. "What do we do now?"

Hughes nodded, his mind already at work as he handed the card to Juliet. "We'll investigate this matter thoroughly. For now, let's focus on securing your marriage. We must prepare the settlement and letter for your aunt. This is the first step in protecting you both. Tomorrow afternoon, with the documents signed and secured, we can dwell on this puzzle."

"I've instructed the coachman to take us back to Belgravia." Glenraven turned to Juliet. "If you prefer, we can bring you home—"

"No, not at all." Juliet's fingers twisted the delicate lace of her handkerchief, the fine threads straining against the pull. "I will go to Belgravia with you." The handkerchief tightened in her grip, betraying her attempt at composure. "I don't think I can keep all this inside me until you return with the documents, and I wouldn't want to spoil the surprise for Mrs. Murthy or Aunt Geraldine."

Glenraven's gaze lingered on Juliet. With a nod to Hughes, he added, "Hughes, you and I will work on the settlement document. Your expertise is unparalleled. Duncan and Juliet will draft a letter for Aunt Geraldine to send to your mother."

"Is that necessary? Aunt Geraldine is very capable with a quill and parchment." Juliet glanced at him. He could easily see the question on her face.

"You are quite correct." Ewan took a breath, his eyes softening as he looked at her. "But preparing a draft for her to edit will speed things along. It's a three to four-day ride to Edinburgh. The quicker the rider leaves, the faster your parents have the information."

Juliet considered his words, then gave a decisive nod, recognizing the soundness of his plan. "Very well. It shouldn't take Duncan and I long to draft a letter for her to use."

Moments later, the carriage rolled up to Glenraven's home. With time of the essence, they hurried out of the carriage, rushed past a somewhat perplexed butler, and followed Glenraven, who led them to the library. Fleming brought in refreshments.

"Good man," Glenraven looked up from retrieving paper, ink, and quills from his desk. "See that we're not disturbed."

Fleming finished setting out the refreshments and silently left the room.

Within minutes, Hughes, quill in hand, was bent over a piece of parchment, writing furiously. Every so often, he handed the document to Glenraven. He read what the solicitor had written while he walked to the hearth, the firelight dancing in his eyes. He would return to Hughes and discuss the text and figures in hushed tones.

While Hughes and Glenraven engaged in a low-voiced discussion across the table, Juliet and Duncan had their heads together as they crafted the letter to Aunt Geraldine. The scratch of the quill and the soft murmur of their voices filled the library with a sense of purpose and anticipation.

"You've been very tactful in requesting your marriage remain a secret. I think that is the finishing touch." Duncan handed Juliet the letter.

She sat close to Duncan and quietly read the letter to him.

"My dearest Cecily,"

"Mother spells her name C-e-c-i-l-i-e. It's a common error."

She handed the parchment back to Duncan and he made the correction.

> *"My dearest Cecilie,*
>
> *As you and Victor enjoy the Scottish countryside and our family, I trust they bring peace and a respite from your worries. How do you find our ancestral lands? I hope they are as enchanting as ever.*
>
> *I write with urgent news that demands your attention. Cease your search for suitors, for a husband has been found for our dear Juliet. A man of respectable title, the Viscount of Ardoch, has agreed to marry our Juliet, the details of which must remain within the family for now.*
>
> *The wedding will be a private affair, and while I know this may come as a surprise, it is imperative for reasons I shall explain in due time. Though shrouded in secrecy, it will be arranged with all due haste and propriety under my careful supervision. Trust in my judgment, as you have so often before, and know that Juliet's happiness and well-being are at the heart of this decision.*
>
> *Additionally, The Groom had agreed to discharge in full all outstanding debts and financial obligations incurred by the family.*
>
> *With love and anticipation of our families' joy, your loving sister,*
> *Geraldine"*

She sat back. "I think it is quite well written and that Aunt Geraldine will approve."

Glenraven cleared his throat, drawing Juliet's attention. He stood beside her with a parchment in hand.

"Duncan and I have finished the letter to Aunt Geraldine. Would you like to read it?" She offered him the parchment.

He took it from her and read it. "Excellent. I am certain this will allay your mother's concerns. Hughes and I have completed the contact."

He gestured towards the paper, inviting her to read it. "This document will be prepared by both of us, for both of us. Every clause, every term, is a reflection of our mutual understanding and respect."

Juliet took the document from him. Her eyes scanned the words that would shape not just her life but the lives of those yet to come. Glenraven's expression was solemn. "Remember, anything here can be changed. This is our foundation, and it must be built on trust and unity."

> *This Agreement made this day the twenty-fifth of April, in the year of our Lord eighteen hundred and twenty, between The Most Honorable Ewan Danford, The Marquess of Glenraven, son of His Grace, The Duke of Aurington, herein referred to as "The Groom," and The Honorable Juliet Hayward, daughter of The Baron of Fairmont, herein referred to as "The Bride."*
>
> *Whereas The Groom and The Bride are to be lawfully wed under the auspices of the Church of England, and whereas The Groom has agreed to settle the outstanding debts and financial obligations of The Bride's family as a gesture of goodwill and commitment to their forthcoming union.*
>
> *Now, therefore, it is agreed as follows:*
>
> *1. The Groom shall assume responsibility for the payment and satisfaction of all known debts and financial obligations incurred by The Bride's family up to and including the date of this Agreement.*
>
> *2. Upon the event of the Groom's demise, The Bride shall receive a jointure of £2,000 per annum for her maintenance.*
>
> *3. The Bride shall be allotted a monthly allowance of £200 for her personal use, known as pin money.*
>
> *4. Trustee, Mr. George Hughes of Hughes, Swift, and Lacey shall be appointed to oversee the execution of this Agreement and the management of the properties and funds described herein.*
>
> *5. This Agreement shall be binding upon and inure to the benefit of the heirs, executors, administrators, and assigns of*

both The Groom and The Bride.

In witness whereof, the parties hereto have set their hands and seals the day and year first above written.

Signed:

The Most Honorable Ewan Danford, The Marquess of Glenraven

The Honorable Juliet Hayward, daughter of The Baron of Fairmont

Witnessed by:

Her Grace, The Duchess of Rosefield

George Hughes as attorney for Richard Danford, The Duke of Aurington

Duncan MacAlister, The Master of Blair

Glenraven continued as Juliet absorbed the gravity of the words, "This will impact not only us but also our children and their children after them. It is the legacy we professed to the archbishop today and the promise of our future."

A tear slipped down Juliet's cheek, a silent witness to the importance of their decisions. Glenraven reached out, his hand gently catching the tear. "Do not fear what we've created. For in this, as in all things, we shall stand together."

Juliet's gaze lifted from the settlement to meet Glenraven's. "You've done more than just listen; you've heard me," she said, her voice steady and sincere. "You've anticipated my every wish... and more. There is no need to change a single word."

Glenraven's lips curved into a smile, a mixture of relief and joy evident in his expression. "Then we are agreed," he said, extending his hand to her.

"Let's get you back home. We've yet to discuss our plans with Mrs. Murthy and Aunt Geraldine. I'm sure they'll understand the benefits of our plans."

They gathered their prepared documents and made their way

to the carriage. They rattled along the cobblestone streets, each bump and jolt mirroring the tumultuous thoughts swirling in their minds. Ewan sat beside Juliet, their hands almost touching but not quite, a silent promise of solidarity. Across from them, Hughes and Duncan sat in quiet contemplation, each absorbed in their own thoughts.

Juliet broke the silence, her voice steady but tinged with anxiety. "I hope Aunt Geraldine understands the urgency. Everything hinges on her swift action."

Ewan nodded, his gaze fixed on the road ahead. "She will. We've explained the stakes, and she's always been astute and decisive."

The carriage rolled to a gentle stop before Juliet's home, a comforting sight amidst the whirlwind of recent events. Juliet's heart fluttered like a caged bird with anticipation and anxiety. Glenraven's hand was reassuring as he helped her down from the carriage.

Inside, Mrs. Murthy's warm greeting was a stark contrast to Aunt Geraldine's cool face as she greeted them from her armchair.

Chapter Nineteen

GLENRAVEN CLEARED HIS throat, the sound slicing through the tense silence. "Lady Rosefield, Juliet and I have an understanding, yet she declined to marry me." He squeezed her hand. "If she declined because she found me wanting, while I would be crestfallen, I would step away. But that was not the reason. You, and now I, know her reason." He gazed at Juliet. "It is all the more reason I want to marry her."

Aunt Geraldine softened as she stared at her niece.

"Now, we come bearing good news. The archbishop has granted us a special license, and we are to be wed tomorrow at ten."

Juliet almost laughed when her aunt's eyebrows arched in surprise, and her lips parted slightly. "Such haste," Aunt Geraldine murmured.

"It is a matter of protecting our families," Juliet interjected, her hands clasped tightly in front of her. "Threats loom over us. This… this is the only way."

Aunt Geraldine's gaze shifted between Juliet and Glenraven, searching, probing. Mrs. Murthy's hand found Juliet's, a silent pillar of support.

"Lady Rosefield," Hughes came forward. "I have drafted a marriage settlement with the help of both Glenraven and Miss Hayward. As her parents are in Scotland, they asked that you witness them sign the document after, of course, you review it."

Hughes handed her the parchment. Aunt Geraldine's eyes

scanned the document, her finger tracing the lines of text. "No dowry?" she finally said, her tone incredulous.

"Under the family's circumstances, there is no need for a dowry," Glenraven assured her, his hand finding Juliet's shoulder.

Yet Aunt Geraldine was resolute. "Mr. Hughes, the following is to be added." Hughes sat at the table. Mrs. Murthy provided ink and a quill.

"I'm ready, Your Grace," he said, poised with the quill.

Aunt Geraldine bent close to Hughes and gave him the words to write.

"I've made the change. The document is ready to sign." Hughes stood and held out the quill. Juliet scanned over the document, looking for whatever changes her aunt had requested. Everything remained the same except for the addition of another stipulation after the first:

2. The Bride, being the sole surviving child and heir to her father, the Baron Fairmont, shall bring forth a dowry amounting to £1,500. This sum shall encompass the land and all appertaining valuables, which shall be held in trust for the benefit of the couple and their issue.

"Aunt Geraldine," Juliet knelt at her aunt's side. "Father cannot provide—"

"No, he cannot." Her aunt softly touched Juliet's cheek. "You have worked hard to protect your family. Consider this my wedding gift to you. Now, if Mr. Hughes will surrender the quill, I will gladly sign the document and make it official."

Hughes passed the quill to each of them, sanded the parchment, and handed the document to Juliet. "Keep it safe."

"What do you intend to tell your mother?" Aunt Geraldine had a gleam in her eye as she faced Juliet. "Knowing you well, I suspect you have a plan."

Juliet handed her aunt the drafted letter she and Duncan had created. "I thought the information would be best coming from you."

"Did you now?" Aunt Geraldine read the letter and nodded. "Well done." She glanced at Juliet and Duncan, who came up beside her. "It almost sounds like something I would write. I will add my wedding gift and have a rider off to Scotland in the morning. Is there anything else?"

"Mr. Wilcox, Mrs. Murthy," Juliet began, her hands clasped before her, "you have both been important in this house, and it would bring me great joy if you would attend my wedding to Lord Glenraven."

Mr. Wilcox, an outwardly stoic man, allowed a rare smile, his eyes crinkling at the corners. "It would be my utmost honor."

Mrs. Murthy's response was eyes glistening with unshed tears. She nodded, her lips curving into a smile that spoke volumes.

"A moment, if you please," Aunt Geraldine beckoned Juliet and Glenraven and brought them to a quiet corner of the room, away from the others. "Tomorrow's vows will make you man and wife, soon after, in the eyes of the world," she began, her words measured. "Yet, until the time is ripe for such an announcement, no one can know.

"Not even a wedding night You must walk separately in public."

"My lord, court Juliet under the prying eyes of the *ton*, and none will be the wiser until you deem it prudent to announce your marriage."

"I agree with all that you've shared, Your Grace." Glenraven glanced at Juliet. They both gave a nod of understanding. "I don't know how to thank you for your understanding and your wisdom."

She led them through the doorway to the sitting room. Glenraven stood with his arm cradled around Juliet's waist while Aunt Geraldine placed herself in front of them. "You can thank me by loving my Juliet with all your heart. But under these circumstances there will be challenges, more precarious than you can imagine. Being in love and separated is not easy, but being in love and seeing each other with other people and not being included is, well, it will take great courage." She paused. "After the ceremony, we can give you one afternoon and evening together, but that is all until your marriage is announced publicly."

"I will make the arrangements, Lady Rosefield. I will protect Juliet with my life." Glenraven's gaze never left Juliet's.

Aunt Geraldine smiled a knowledgeable older woman's smile. "I do not doubt that you will." She stepped back. "Enough said. You both will do the right thing. We should return to the others."

Aunt Geraldine caught the butler's eye. "Mr. Wilcox, would you be so kind as to pour us a small sherry?"

"With pleasure, Your Grace." Mr. Wilcox's movements deft as he handed served everyone the rich, golden liquid.

Once everyone had a glass, Aunt Geraldine lifted hers, prompting the others to do the same. "Tomorrow," she said, her gaze touching each face in turn, "and to the union it shall bring."

"Hear, hear," Hughes, Duncan, Mr. Wilcox, and Mrs. Murthy said in unison.

The sherry was savored, and there was a quiet moment of whispered good wishes before Mr. Wilcox and Mrs. Murthy excused themselves.

"Now, my dears," Aunt Geraldine turned to the remaining gentlemen, her hands folded together with finality, "we must all find our rest. The morning will be exciting, and we shall meet it with clear eyes."

Juliet escorted her guests to the door. Duncan and Hughes, with nods of gratitude, stepped into the evening, leaving Juliet, her hand on the doorframe, and Glenraven in the quiet of the foyer.

Glenraven lingered behind. Juliet's pulse quickened. A fluttering rush of anticipation, a thrilling sensation that reached every part of her.

"Juliet," he whispered, his words a tender caress. Her heartbeat, a rhythmic dance, grows more pronounced, echoing the excitement of the moment and the promise of what's to come. "I feel tomorrow cannot come soon enough."

Juliet's breath caught—a soft gasp held at the edge of a whispered, "As do I." The delicate pause, a silent acknowledgment of the intimacy and significance of their connection.

As he leaned in closer, Juliet's fingers trembled as she leaned against the doorframe, a delicate quiver as she anticipated his closeness and desired his kiss.

In the seclusion of the moment, his lips met hers in a kiss that spoke of promises and shared dreams. It was a kiss that lingered, a sweet prelude to their life together.

He stepped back, but the warmth of his kiss remained. "Sleep well," he whispered. He stepped out into the night. She remained at the door as he climbed into the carriage and drove away.

She closed the door and went upstairs. Juliet stood before her open wardrobe in her room, her Aunt Geraldine and Mrs. Murthy at her side.

"Something special for you, my dear," Aunt Geraldine said, pulling a delicate lace handkerchief edged with the finest thread from a small ornate box. "It belonged to your grandmother. Carry it with you as a token of her love."

Juliet accepted the heirloom, her fingers brushing over the intricate embroidery. "Thank you," she whispered and placed the treasure on her dressing table.

"Which gown will you wear?" Aunt Geraldine browsed the dresses as if she were at the modiste. "One is more beautiful than the other."

Juliet did not hesitate. She selected the dark green silk and soft muslin gown. Its high waist and long sleeves made it modest yet elegant. The fabric rustled as she lifted it out of the wardrobe.

Mrs. Murthy stepped forward and hung it on the hook so the creases would fall out. "You will be the most radiant bride." With a knowing smile, the housekeeper, Mrs. Murthy, helped Juliet pack a few essentials for the overnight stay after the ceremony.

With her gown ready, Juliet turned to the two women who

had been her steadfast guides. "Thank you," she whispered, her voice thick with emotion.

After they left, Juliet gazed out the window at the evening sky, but the promise of tomorrow held a joy that outshone the stars themselves.

Chapter Twenty

April 21, 1820

GLENRAVEN'S BREAKFAST WAS usually a solitary affair, but this morning, he daydreamed of the delightful prospect of sharing mornings like this with his wife, his Juliet. Lost in these pleasant thoughts, he was brought abruptly back to reality when the disheveled figure of Sebastian barged into the room. The man's appearance was as untidy as the pungent mix of last night's revelry that clung to him, a combination of smoke, spirits, and a heavy, smoky lemon scented perfume used in a vain attempt to mask the evidence of his indulgence. The scent clashed with the clean morning air of the breakfast room, an unwelcome reminder of the world beyond.

"Good God, Sebastian, do you ever sleep?" Glenraven criticized his cousin with a voice that echoed through the hall.

Sebastian, with a roguish grin that didn't quite reach his bleary eyes, slumped into a chair across from him. "Sleep is for those without cards in their hand," he slurred, pouring himself a generous glass of what remained in the bottle of Glenraven's wine he had taken from the sideboard on his way to the table. "When are you going to let me win back my blunt?"

Glenraven sighed, pushing his plate away. "You lost fair and square, Sebastian. I owe you no chance at redemption."

Sebastian's gaze wandered, taking in the room as if seeing it for the first time. "But you do, cousin. I insist we play tonight." The tone of his demand was insistent.

"I have already made arrangements for this evening." Glenraven drummed his fingers on the table. "Perhaps next week."

A sly look crept into Sebastian's eyes as he leaned forward. A conspiratorial whisper colored his words. "On your birthday, then?"

Glenraven paused, considering, then nodded in resignation. "Very well, on my birthday. I had no idea you were so eager to give me another gift."

With a satisfied smirk, Sebastian drained his glass and rose, his departure as unceremonious as his arrival, leaving Glenraven to speculate on what the visit was all about.

"Was that Sebastian stumbling out of the door?" Duncan appeared in the doorway, his eyebrows raised. "Did you ask him about Wickham?"

"No. It slipped my mind." Glenraven stared at his friend as a wide grin spread across his face. "You do me a big honor. I can't recall the last time I saw you in your kilt with your sporran, kilt hose, and ghillie brogues. I must admit, you are a handsome highlander lad."

Duncan made his way over to him. "Ach, I sport my kilt for the wee lass. Not you. And while I wear my plaid, I have laid out your clothes for this morning. I'll have you all cleaned up and looking like a prize by the time you say your vows." Duncan clapped him on his back a bit more forcefully than usual and sat beside him. "So, what was Sebastian doing here?" the playfulness out of his tone.

"He didn't like that I haven't given him time to win back his money. I told him we'll have a go of it next week. He suggested on my birthday."

"You know he intends to press you about the inheritance." Duncan spit out the words.

"Yes, and hopefully, I will have a present of my own to give him. Enough about him." Glenraven got to his feet. "I need to clean up, at least according to you."

"I don't know." Duncan stood up. Next to Glenraven, the tall

Scotsman was only a touch taller. "It will take me days to get you ready."

Glenraven raised an elegant eyebrow and glanced at his pocket watch. "I'm afraid you'll have to work fast. You only have an hour before we leave."

The two friends laughed as they left the room and headed upstairs.

⊱✦⊰

NINETY MINUTES LATER, a hush fell over the small gathering in the Archbishop's chapel. Light from the stained-glass window cast a glow on the intimate setting. Glenraven and Duncan waited with the archbishop. Mr. Wilcox and Mrs. Murthy sat facing them.

Glenraven stood next to Duncan in his bottle-green coat, his cravat two shades lighter, and buff trousers and waistcoat. On his lapel, he wore a pin with his family crest.

"Did you bring the flowers?" Glenraven asked Duncan, a slight fear evident that they had been overlooked.

"Yes. Do you have—" Duncan replied.

"I gave it to the archbishop when we arrived." Glenraven nodded toward the table to his side and paused. Juliet and Aunt Geraldine entered the chapel. A subtle smile played on her lips when Juliet's gaze met his. The archbishop's voice filled the hushed chapel as he held a platter draped with velvet cloth embroidered with the Glenraven crest. "As we gather in the presence of this sacred union, it is with great joy that we witness the Marquess bestow upon his bride a gift, a cherished tradition of the House of Glenraven."

He turned to Glenraven, who stepped forward and removed the cloth from the small table that stood close to him, revealing a delicate circlet of diamonds set in gold vines. He lifted the heirloom and turned toward Juliet.

"This coronet symbolizes my family's past, which we welcome you into. You and I will add our mark on the family history. May this circlet rest upon your brow as a sign of our shared future and all that binds us. As each stone has been carefully set into place, so too are our lives now intricately intertwined." He held the coronet over her head. "I crown you my wife, my partner, and the new matriarch of the Glenraven lineage."

With steady hands, he placed the circlet on her head, the diamonds catching the light. Juliet's eyes met his, a silent affection reflected in their depths.

Glenraven gently adjusted the circlet, then leaned closer, his voice a hushed echo of the solemn chapel around them. "With this circlet, I vow to honor the legacy of the Glenravens who came before us," he whispered. "To cherish you as they cherished their beloveds, with a heart steadfast and true. Our union shall be as unyielding as my love for you, enduring through all our days."

"I had no idea." A soft blush painted her cheeks, and the corners of her lips curved into a smile that radiated the surprise and joy of the moment.

"This bride gift is part of an ancient ceremony and is traditionally bestowed upon the new marchioness at the discretion of the marquess. Are you ready for the archbishop?"

Juliet nodded. "Yes, I am."

They both turned and stood before the archbishop. In a gentle voice that resonated through the chamber, he began, "We are gathered here to join this man and this woman in matrimony, witnessed by those they hold dear."

As the archbishop's words echoed through the stillness, vows were exchanged. Glenraven turned to Duncan, who placed an etched gold band in his hand. He faced Juliet and took her hand. He placed the ring on her finger and stared into her bright hazel eyes. "With this ring I thee wed, with my body I thee worship, and with all my worldly goods I thee endow."

AS THEY STOOD before the archbishop, their eyes remained locked on each other, a silent conversation between them. The archbishop cleared his throat softly, a smile dancing on his lips as he drew the couple's attention. "By the sacred trust placed in me, I declare you husband and wife. May your journey be rich with love, steeped in understanding, and abundant in joy."

Aunt Geraldine, Mrs. Murthy, Mr. Wilcox, Hughes, and Duncan moved closer, each competing for the biggest smile. Duncan's hearty slap on Glenraven's back and wide beaming grin clearly reflected his genuine happiness for them. Hughes gave a subtle nod. A man of few words, the small gesture confirmed he was happy for them.

Aunt Geraldine whispered her congratulations before pulling Juliet into a warm embrace with tears in her eyes. Mr. Wilcox and Mrs. Murthy exchanged knowing smiles, their affection for Juliet clear and from their hearts.

"Thank you," Glenraven said to everyone, his voice filled with gratitude. "Your presence here today means more than words can express."

Juliet nodded in agreement, her voice soft but filled with emotion. "You have all been a part of our journey, and we are happy to share this moment with you."

"May your journey together be filled with love that deepens, challenges that strengthen, and joy that endures," the archbishop said, his voice warm and sincere.

"Together, we will create—" Glenraven began.

"Our own destiny," Juliet whispered, finishing the phrase. A smile touched her lips. "I didn't think you'd remember the lines from our Punch and Judy performance."

"How could I forget? That's when I found you." Glenraven's eyes reflected the truth of his words. "Come, we don't want to keep the others waiting."

"There is one last formality." The archbishop stood before them. "Come into the vestry. You must enter your marriage lines. You and your witnesses need to sign the marriage registry,"

Standing before the registry book with Glenraven looking on and the archbishop at her side, Juliet took the quill in hand, her signature flowing across the page—Juliet Anne Hayward.

There was a sad sense of farewell to her maiden name, a name that connected her to her family's history. Yet, along with the bittersweet farewell was the thrill of beginning a new chapter, the excitement of adopting the Glenraven title and all it signified. And as she handed the quill to her husband, her heart skipped a beat. Her husband. She was a Glenraven, ready to step forward as the Marchioness and face the future with whatever it would bring.

Chapter Twenty-One

GLENRAVEN TOOK THE quill from his wife. The excitement rolled over him like a wave in the great North Sea as he realized his new responsibility. He glanced at Juliet, and his pulse settled. With his work for Barrington and his brigade, he had laid down his life for others. But at this moment, Juliet and her well-being were paramount to him. He leaned over the registry and clearly, proudly wrote Ewan James Alasdair Danford, Marquess of Glenraven.

"Well done, Lord and Lady Glenraven. Now," the archbishop rubbed his hands together, "we celebrate."

The small wedding party gathered in the refined elegance of the Archbishop's Private Chamber. The room was filled with the soft clinking of fine china and the low murmur of pleasant conversation. Glenraven and Juliet, now man and wife, sat side by side, their hands occasionally brushing beneath the table—a silent language of shared joy.

The archbishop's steward ensured that their guest's glasses remained full while the archbishop kept the conversation light. Yet, amidst the pleasantries, his gaze often lingered on Ewan, sensing the unspoken concerns that lay beneath his composed exterior.

"Lord Glenraven," the Archbishop began, his voice carrying a gentle authority that quieted the room, "how fares your father these days? I've heard of his accident and have kept him in my prayers."

Glenraven met the Archbishop's kind eyes, gratitude warming him. "Thank you, Your Excellency. He is recovering, though it's been a trying time for us all."

"Would it be amiss if I were to visit him? Offer some solace, perhaps?" the Archbishop offered, his concern genuine.

Ewan considered the offer, the idea of such a visit bringing a sense of comfort. "That would be most welcome, Your Excellency. I believe he would find great comfort in your visit."

The Archbishop nodded, pleased to be of service. "Then it shall be arranged. It is the least I can do for a family that has contributed so much to our community."

The morning was getting late. Glenraven discreetly nodded to Duncan and Hughes. "Duncan, there are other legal matters that need my attention." Hughes tapped the Scotsman on the shoulder.

"Of course, Mr. Hughes." As Duncan rose to take his leave and raised his glass, "Friends, raise your glass and join me." He turned to the newlyweds with a warm smile. "May the love that binds ye be strong as the oak and gentle as the heather. May yer joys be as deep as the lochs and yer sorrows as light as the thistle's down. And in all yer days together, may ye find peace as enduring as the highland stones." He downed the last of his drink.

Juliet met the archbishop's gaze, her expression one of heartfelt gratitude. "Before you leave, Your Excellency, I am truly thankful for all you've done for us."

"Lady Glenraven, you stand beside a man of rare quality," the archbishop gave her a gentle nod. With a final, respectful bow, he left the chamber as unobtrusive as possible.

Moments later, they emerged into the forecourt, where their carriages waited. Aunt Geraldine reached for Juliet's hands, holding them between her own. "Juliet, my dear," she said, her voice warm with affection, "cherish this day no matter how fleeting they may seem."

Juliet's eyes met her aunt's. "I will." She embraced her aunt, a gentle strength in her hold. "Thank you for everything. Your wisdom has been my guiding star."

Aunt Geraldine returned the embrace, a soft sigh escaping her. "It takes time to adjust to a husband. Be patient. You'll have some challenges until you publicly announce your marriage. Remember, I'll always be here. We'll navigate tomorrow's soiree and all that follows."

"Lady Glenraven," her husband called to her as he waited by the coach door with his hand extended to her. After a tender embrace with her aunt, he handed her into the carriage, and they both waved goodbye.

She turned and stared at her husband. In the privacy of the carriage, with the steady rhythm of hooves against cobblestone, she deeply understood and felt the importance of the promises they made to each other at the ceremony. These vows were a profound connection to the moment, to each other, and to the future they were creating.

"Lady Glenraven." He hadn't let go of her hand. "I am taking you to a very special place. One that no one knows about. It is my secret and a place I've never shared with anyone."

The carriage rolled smoothly out of Lambeth Palace's fore-court, subtly shifting as it crossed the cobbled streets to a softer path. The route took them through a lesser-known gate, discreetly positioned along the palace's perimeter wall, which opened onto a secluded lane obscured by overhanging trees.

The lane meandered, its bends shielding the newlyweds from the city's eyes, and continued across the Thames to a place enclosed by tall hedges and the remnants of an old stone wall. The garden was a green oasis, a breath of tranquility amidst the bustle of London. The carriage came to a simple wrought-iron gate that stood at the threshold of the garden's entrance. The coachman stopped, unlocked the gate, returned to the carriage, and carried on.

The carriage wheels came to rest on the gravel of the hidden garden's path. Glenraven assisted Juliet from the carriage, their hands lingering in each other's grasp.

They walked side by side, each step on the garden's winding paths a step further into their own private area. As they strolled, they were accompanied by silent sentinels—statues and fountains that stood as quiet witnesses to their promenade.

"This is a remote part of our estate." Glenraven's voice was a quiet echo amidst the rustling leaves. "Only a few know of this summerhouse, hidden by ivy and ancient walls. It is here where one can escape the clamor of London."

Juliet's fingers gently pressed his in acknowledgment, her steps beside him unhurried. "To think such a treasure has been kept from view. Do you find this secret garden the same as our situation? We cannot tell anyone about our wedding. We must keep it from view as well."

As he passed a bush, he carefully picked a violet-blue bloom and handed it to Juliet. "It's not what I want. But there is little choice."

"I understand the necessity. We don't have to like it."

"No, we don't." They moved on.

"The bouquet," Juliet sniffed the bloom he gave her, "was thoughtful of you, to say nothing of its beauty. Duncan mentioned you selected each bloom."

A smile found its way to Glenraven's face. "There was so much you gave up for your wedding. I hoped that the flowers might brighten the day. Yet, it was you who were the most breathtaking flower. And I will say we made a handsome couple in our matched attire, you in your dark green gown and me in my bottle-green coat."

"We both chose the same color. Does that mean we are 'well suited.'"

A soft chuckle escaped Glenraven as he caught the playful twinkle in Juliet's eye. "Indeed, we are 'well suited' in more ways than one." The delight in his voice mingled with the afternoon air. They continued their stroll, the shared humor drawing them closer together.

As they neared the summerhouse, he halted beside a venerable stone statue of Artemis, goddess of the hunt, which stood sentinel at the entrance. With a conspiratorial wink, he reached behind the quiver slung over the deity's shoulder, his fingers brushing against the hidden niche to the divine huntress. He pulled out a small, aged, and ornate key and unlocked the door. At the threshold Juliet could see it was a place untouched by time, where the outside world could not intrude.

"The summerhouse was built by my great-great-great grand-father as a gift to his new bride. It has sturdy stone walls that have weathered over time."

Juliet's gaze swept across the summerhouse, her eyes landing on the small, lattice-paned windows. She took a deep breath, her fingers absentmindedly tracing the delicate pattern on her wedding ring.

She glanced out of it and was rewarded with a view of the garden. "It's beautiful." Her voice, full of awe and nervousness, was barely audible. "Almost like a dream."

The walls painted a soft buttery yellow with crisp white wainscoting, created a cozy warmth. She ran her fingers over the antique wooden furniture—a sturdy table set in the center of the room, flanked by matching chairs, and a sideboard resting against the far wall, all polished to a gentle sheen. Along one side of the room was a modest bed draped with handmade quilts. The scent of aged wood, enriched by the delicate fragrance of dried herbs hanging from the beams, filled the air, creating a room steeped in history and charm. A comfortable armchair and a plush sofa were positioned by the hearth, promising warmth and hearthside cooking. Behind the sofa was a small table with a chess set, ready to play, with two chairs placed on either side.

Glenraven gently closed the door behind them, the soft click a final pause to the world outside. They moved toward the sofa, their steps in quiet harmony. He paused a moment for the stillness of the summerhouse to settle around them.

"I hoped you'd like the cottage. This place," he spoke softly, "is where we can speak freely, away from prying eyes. I want you to feel as much at home here as I do."

Juliet turned to him, her eyes searching his face. "You're correct. This isn't what either of us planned." Her voice trembled slightly. "But I'm glad we're here together." She picked up the queen and placed it back on the chess board.

"Shall we play?" Ewan asked with a smile, as he held out the chair for her.

Juliet nodded, her fingers delicately placing the knights and bishops. "It's been too long since our last match. Let's see if I can still outmaneuver you."

Ewan chuckled, his eyes twinkling. "I doubt I've improved much. But let's talk as we play. There are important matters we need to discuss."

Juliet mirrored his move, her eyes focused on the board. "Agreed. Where shall we start?"

Chapter Twenty-Two

E WAN PAUSED, CONSIDERING his next move. "First, the matter of our residences. We'll maintain separate households but engage in public courting to uphold appearances."

Juliet considered this, her fingers absently tracing the delicate pattern on a chess piece. "Yes, I think that will keep the gossip at bay. It will also give us time to get to know each other better."

Ewan nodded, capturing one of her pawns. "For our communication, I suggest Duncan assists us. He can relay messages and ensure discretion."

Juliet smiled, appreciating his foresight. "Duncan is trustworthy. That arrangement works well for me."

She moved her bishop, capturing his knight. Ewan nodded, impressed. "Regarding our finances, the terms of our marriage contract will be enacted today. Hughes will oversee the process and ensure everything is in order."

Juliet looked up, her eyes meeting his. "I trust Hughes to handle it efficiently. It's a relief to have that settled."

Ewan studied the board, then moved his rook. "We should also respect each other's privacy. Our separate lives will give us the space we need."

Juliet's fingers traced the edge of a pawn as she considered her move. "Privacy is important. It will help us adjust to this new arrangement without feeling overwhelmed."

She advanced her queen, creating a strategic threat. Ewan raised an eyebrow, a smile playing on his lips. "Lastly, any future decisions, including potential children or changes to our living arrangements, will be discussed and mutually agreed upon."

Juliet leaned back, her gaze thoughtful. "Communication will be key. We need to ensure we both feel heard and respected."

Ewan moved his king defensively, buying time. "Agreed."

Juliet smiled, appreciating the shift in conversation. "I hope your brother Edward is well. He's taken to his duties as a member of Parliament with great enthusiasm. "That he does. It fits him well. He likes to boss people around." Ewan moved his bishop.

As Juliet moved her queen for the final strike, she looked at Ewan with a confident smile. "Checkmate."

Ewan nodded in genuine admiration, a warm smile crossing his face. "Your strategic mind is as sharp as ever, Juliet. You play as ruthlessly as your brother Bradley." He glanced at her. "He was always a worthy opponent." He remembered the few times he had played him at the gaming hells.

Juliet returned his smile, feeling a warmth in the shared moment. "And you, Ewan, have always been a worthy opponent and a good friend." She let out a deep breath. "Bradley was a worthy opponent. He wouldn't let me beat him at chess. He made me earn it." She stopped resetting her pieces and stared at nothing. "We had our own aliases." She shook her head. "I still find it difficult to believe." She gave herself a shake and went back to setting her board.

With a glint of mischief in her eyes, she began to reset the board. "Shall we make it best two out of three?"

Ewan smirked, accepting the challenge. "Indeed, I accept."

He rose and crossed the room to retrieve a hamper that Mrs. Murthy had thoughtfully prepared, filled with refreshments. Returning to the table, Ewan set out the contents: a selection of cheeses, fresh bread, and a bottle of fine wine. "We might as well enjoy ourselves while we play," he remarked, pouring them each a glass.

Juliet laughed softly, appreciating the gesture. "Agreed. Let's see if your strategic prowess extends to our next game."

As they settled in for another match, the atmosphere grew warmer, filled with laughter and playful banter. Juliet's competitive spirit shone through with each move, her eyes sparking with determination as she plotted her next strategy.

Ewan moved his rook with a confident flourish, positioning it strategically on the board. "You know, Juliet, this rook isn't just a piece. He is Sir Punch, the steadfast guardian."

Juliet raised an eyebrow, intrigued. "Sir Punch, you say? And who does he protect?" He was making a story about them.

Ewan smiled, his eyes twinkling. "He stands watch over the castle, ensuring safety for his lady love while they navigate threats."

Juliet chuckled, moving her bishop.

"And your bishop, Lady Judy, a daring profession for a woman, but bear with me. Lady Judy is wise and strategic," he leaned in toward her. "Even if she is a bit stubborn at times."

"And then we have the pawns, loyal and brave. This one here," he moved a pawn, "is young Percy, eager to prove himself. Everyone must prove who and what they are to the world."

Juliet's fingers traced the edge of her queen, her gaze thoughtful. "And the king, she is resourceful and resilient." Barrington perhaps.

He gazed at her. "Much like how we must be. She relies on Sir Punch and Lady Judy, but she also must make her own decisions."

Ewan moved his king, aligning it with Sir Punch. "Together, they face their challenges, balancing duty and personal desire. United is a single purpose."

The game progressed, the chess pieces coming to life with each turn. Ewan's eyes sparkled as he moved his knight. "This knight, Sir Alden, had a claymore. He's a friend and ally we rely on."

"Like Duncan." Juliet couldn't help but smile as Ewan's eyes twinkled with mischief, weaving whimsical tales with each move on the chessboard.

The game continued, their conversation flowing easily. By the end of the afternoon, they had played seven games, with Juliet ahead. Ewan leaned back with a playful smile. "I must request a rematch soon."

Juliet grinned, her eyes twinkling with mischief. "I look forward to it."

With their time drawing to a close, Ewan leaned in and kissed her tenderly, his lips lingering with a promise of more. Juliet felt a flutter in her chest, the beginning of something new and sweet between them.

Reluctantly, they left the warmth of the cottage and headed back to the carriage. As they traveled towards Juliet's home in Cavendish Square, the initial contentment began to wane, replaced by the reality they faced. Juliet found herself completely drawn in by Ewan's charm and humor, which turned their chess game into a magical escape. Their time together was a cherished reprieve, a tender interlude filled with warmth and growing affection.

Juliet glanced out the window, the familiar streets of London coming into view. "Ewan," she began, her voice tentative, "our arrangement… will it truly be enough?"

Ewan sighed, his gaze fixed ahead. "It will have to be, for now. While marrying me protects you from being forced into another marriage, it also puts you at risk from those who are after me. For your safety, it is best that we remain apart." He let the thought set for a few heartbeats. "Besides, I can court you and we can get to know each other properly."

The carriage pulled to a stop in front of Juliet's home. Ewan stepped out, offering his hand to help her down. They walked to the door in silence, the earlier ease replaced by unspoken worries.

As they reached the door, Ewan turned to Juliet, his expression earnest. "Goodnight, Juliet. We will make this work."

Juliet nodded, a small smile playing on her lips. "'Till it be morrow, my Punch."

With that, she stepped inside, the door closing softly behind her. Ewan stood there for a moment longer, contemplating the challenges ahead. The evening had shown them a glimpse of what could be, this plan may just work.

✦ ━━━◦⧼⋄⧽◦━━━ ✦

Chapter Twenty-Three

April 22, 1820

IN THE DRAWING room of Barrington Hall, Lady Aurington paced in front of the hearth. "Are you certain he will be here?"

"I sent him the message this morning." Hughes was sitting at the writing desk, papers in hand. "Ewan will be here,"

Lord Aurington had not raised his head. He sat on the sofa, continuing to read the London Chronicle. "Pacing like that will not make him arrive any faster. And you will wear a hole in Barrington's fine carpet."

"One would find it difficult to believe that only hours ago, you were at *death's door.*" Lady Aurington had stopped pacing long enough to admonish her husband. "How do you plan on explaining that to Ewan?"

The clatter of coach wheels drew Lady Aurington to the window. "He's here." She hurried and sat beside her husband, picked up her embroidery, took a deep breath, and created a casual scene.

The rapid footsteps across the marble floor echoed through the entrance hall. Sanderson, the butler, called out just a beat behind them, "Good morning, my lord. They're in the drawing room."

Glenraven's stride faltered as he entered the drawing room. "Father!" his eyes locked on his father, sitting comfortably reading a newspaper. The initial relief that he was alive and well swiftly turned into a surge of anger. It was obvious the man had not been as gravely injured as he was led to believe. His chest was on fire with the urge to confront him, to demand answers.

"It's obvious you're on your deathbed. Why the deception?" Glenraven challenged him, his thoughts a tumultuous storm against the calm façade he struggled to maintain.

Lord Aurington looked up, his eyes meeting Glenraven's. "Ewan," he said, with a calmness that contradicted the gravity of the situation. "It is good to have you home."

"And when Barrington brought me into your room," Glenraven fought to control his voice, but his fists were clenched at his sides. "Letting me believe you were at death's door." The hurt was obvious by the tremor that ran along his clenched jaw. "How could you not tell me?" he whispered.

His mother, her embroidery forgotten, stepped forward, her presence a steady force. "We feared for you." Her voice broke through his anger. "I know you well." She reached out and lightly touched his arm. Her fingers rested there, warm and reassuring. "You would have charged into danger, and you wouldn't have rested until you found what or who you were looking for, just like you did on your quest to find the oldest oak tree in our woods. Nothing stood in your way."

Glenraven's breath caught, his anger fading like mist in the morning sun. He turned to look into his mother's eyes. *She was right.* The realization settled in him with the heaviness of a stone in his stomach, but it dulled the edge of his frustration.

He let out his breath slowly. "I should have been told," he insisted, though the fire behind his words had reduced to a smolder.

Lord Aurington's composure was as steadfast as ever, yet there was a certain depth to his gaze, quiet evidence of the past week's strain. Trembling hands folded the newspaper, and there was a new deliberateness to his movements.

Glenraven detected these minute changes, the quiet signs of a man who had faced his mortality and carried the responsibility of his family's safety on his shoulders.

"It was to protect you," His father said as he set aside the newspaper and rose. "Barrington shared a great deal with you. There is more."

The words hung between them as Glenraven's anger ebbed away, replaced by the undeniable truth of his father's love and the lengths to which he would go to safeguard his family. Glenraven's resistance crumbled, and he stepped forward, embracing his parents.

"It was your news last night that had me out of bed. Congratulations."

"Yes. I have married," Ewan announced, his voice echoing in the high-ceilinged room.

Curiosity danced in his parents' eyes. "To whom, my boy?" There was excitement and concern in his father's voice.

"I cannot say. As with you, Father, there's been a threat. For now, her identity must remain a secret from you and her family."

The room fell into a hushed silence, the gravity of his words settling like dust over the family portraits. His mother's hand fluttered to her chest, her eyes wide with worry. "A threat? But why—"

"It's a matter we're handling," Hughes interjected, offering a reassuring nod. "Glenraven's actions are for the protection of all involved."

Lady Aurington glared at Hughes. "You know who our son married."

He nodded. "Yes, I do. And I took the necessary actions to ensure its legality. We spoke about this when His Grace gave me power of attorney. It was to facilitate securing the continuation of the line while maintaining the illusion of His Grace's grave condition. In that, we have been successful."

"Was there a marriage settlement?" his mother asked. "There must have been." She sat back, proud of her approach to sleuthing.

"I assure you the young lady is a peer of the realm, smart, witty, and quite charming. Yes, there is a marriage settlement.

Glenraven has been generous. And before you ask, as your solicitor with power of attorney, I have signed the agreement. And as for the Glenraven inheritance stipulation, I have also submitted the papers signed by the archbishop who performed the weddings to attest to it all."

"How do you plan to keep your marriage a secret? You're the most eligible bachelor in London. Won't it seem strange that you and the young lady are missing from events or attending together?" He had to admit his mother tried every ploy to get his wife's name.

"We've agreed to attend the social events separately. We will both be attending Lady Gladstone's Soiree this evening. Will you and Father be joining me?"

"Of course not." His mother's defiant answer didn't surprise him, although it did make his father chuckle. "How can you be in the same place together but apart, and no one deduce what you two are about?"

"Rest assured, no one will be aware of our marriage until we choose to reveal it. The secret will remain intact." He took a seat next to his father. "I have another matter to discuss with you, the Ace of Hearts you left for me. Was that part of the deception as well?" Ewan's question loomed over them, heavy with implications.

His father's response came with a slow shake of the head, his gaze never wavering from his son's. "I wish it were,"

THE EVENING AIR was crisp as carriages lined the cobbled street leading to Gladstone Hall in Berkeley Square. The coaches drew up to the entrance one by one, where footmen waited to hand down the passengers. Among the arrivals were two carriages bearing the crests of the houses of Rosefield and Glenraven.

Ewan, his coach fourth in line, waited with Barrington as

footmen assisted Aunt Geraldine and Juliet from the Rosefield coach, shook their skirts, and went inside. His gaze lingered on the entrance to the hall long after Juliet and Aunt Geraldine had disappeared into the house. He reclined in his seat, turning to Barrington with a quizzical look. "What?" His friend could barely contain his amusement.

Barrington's eyes twinkled as he composed himself. "Just be mindful of your expression when you look at Miss Hayward," he said with a chuckle. "The whole of London needn't know your heart's been stolen."

As the carriage door swung open, the footman unfolded the steps. Ewan stepped out first, then turned to assist Barrington. With subtle but unmistakable pride, he said, "And I will remind you, my friend, that is not Miss Hayward. That is Lady Glenraven—my wife."

"Let's hope you keep that information close to your chest this evening. Tonight, you are still an eligible bachelor. Come, it won't be too bad. You don't even have to stay long." Barrington's words carried a note of caution, along with the fellowship shared between close friends. The two men entered the busy hall, ready to face the evening's charade.

The ballroom was elegant, with candles and spring flowers. Couples danced gracefully across the polished floor. The soft strains of a string quartet filled the air, complementing the murmur of conversations and the subtle rustling of silk gowns.

In the midst of the revelry, Juliet, in a lavender gown that made her eyes sparkle like stars, moved gracefully among the guests. Her smile was courteous, yet he wondered if her heart ached as his heart did with the secret they kept hidden. From his place across the room, drinking wine with Barrington, Glenraven glanced at her over the rim of the glass as he brought it to his lips. He waited patiently for the right moment.

As the Master of Ceremonies stepped forward, Glenraven put down his glass and made his way to Juliet.

"Ladies and gentlemen," the room fell into a hush. The next

dance will be a waltz. I invite you to find your partners as the musicians prepare." A murmur of excitement filled every corner of the ballroom.

"May I have this dance?" Glenraven extended his hand to Juliet, his voice barely above a whisper.

"With pleasure, my lord." Juliet put her hand in his, and they took their place on the dance floor. For a brief moment, as they moved in perfect harmony, they were not marquess and lady but simply two souls intertwined.

"I don't see Lady Rosefield." He scanned the room but didn't see the woman. "I'll stay here until she returns."

"No, you will not. That is certain to begin tongues wagging. I am quite safe here." She nodded. "Thank you, Lord Glenraven. It was a pleasure dancing with you."

He nodded. "Thank you, Miss Hayward, for a most enjoyable waltz."

Juliet nodded, and Glenraven turned on his heel and headed to Barrington, who was speaking to a group of men.

Lady Madeline Ashfield, resplendent in her emerald silks, approached Juliet with the eagerness of one bearing exciting news.

"My dear Juliet," Lady Ashfield began, her eyes twinkling with mischief, "I must introduce you to a gentleman of considerable interest. Mr. Sebastian Morgrave, a man whose fortunes have been most… intriguing lately."

As if summoned by the very mention of his name, Sebastian appeared beside Lady Ashfield, his smile practiced and his bow flawless.

"Allow me to present Miss Juliet Hayward, the daughter of the Baron of Fairmont." Lady Ashfield faced Juliet. "Miss Hayward, may I introduce Mr. Sebastian Morgrave?"

"Lady Juliet Hayward," he said, his voice smooth as velvet, "it is a pleasure to make your acquaintance finally."

Juliet politely nodded. "Mr. Morgrave," she replied, her voice steady, "the pleasure is mine."

Lady Ashfield d the exchange with the satisfaction of a chess master moving her pieces into place. "I shall leave you to converse." Her mission accomplished, she drifted away and disappeared into the crowd.

"Lady Juliet, your beauty outshines the grandeur of this ball." Morgrave gave a slight bow. "I was a friend of your brothers. I was sad to hear of his passing. He confided in me. If there is anything I can do," He placed his hand on hers. "Do not hesitate to contact me."

Juliet maintained her composure, her smile polite yet distant. "Mr. Morgrave, I appreciate your offer of support." She kept her tone gracious but firm while she gently withdrew her hand from his grasp and set a subtle but clear boundary. "Should the need arise, I shall keep your kindness in mind." Juliet's smile did not reach her eyes.

Juliet was overcome with a surge of relief when Glenraven approached. His presence was a welcome interruption to Sebastian's overtures. Though she and Glenraven were little more than acquaintances in the eyes of society, his timely arrival felt like a silent pledge of protection.

"Morgrave, Miss Hayward," Glenraven greeted them, his tone effortlessly polite. "I trust the evening finds you well?"

The subtle shift in his stance, placing himself slightly closer to Juliet, was all the reassurance she needed. Her pulse steadied, and the knot of worry in her stomach unwound. She offered him a small but sincere smile, her eyes conveying a silent message of gratitude for his timely intervention.

Sebastian's gaze shifted to Glenraven, a preceptive glint in his eye. "Ah, Glenraven, celebrating another year, I hear? A man of your stature should be careful not to let time slip by," he teased.

As Sebastian's words drew attention, Glenraven's concern was not for the barbs he threw but for Juliet's comfort. With a discreet glance, he sought assurance in her eyes that she remained untroubled by the exchange. "Time will tell, Mr. Morgrave. Now, let's return our attention to the festivities."

"Mr. Morgrave." They turned to see Lady Ashfield approach. "There is someone I must introduce you to." She glanced at Glenraven and Juliet with a weak smile and guided Morgrave away.

In the quiet wake of Lady Ashfield's intervention, Juliet and Glenraven found themselves alone amidst the throng of the ballroom. Their eyes met, a silent conversation filled with words they dared not speak aloud. Aunt Geraldine's soft, deliberate cough pierced their silent reverie, her presence a gentle reminder of the night's progression.

"I believe it's time we retired for the evening," Aunt Geraldine suggested, her voice low but firm, her eyes reflecting a mix of empathy and subtle urgency.

Juliet nodded. "Of course." As she drew closer to Ewan, her breath a whisper against his ear, she imparted words meant solely for him.

He straightened. Their gazes met, and he offered her a slight nod, acknowledging their shared secret.

He stood at the library window as the two women prepared to leave. The echo of Juliet's whisper remained a silent pledge that bound them together even as they parted. "Time will tell," he whispered to himself.

Chapter Twenty-Four

April 23, 1820

THE FAIRMONT DRAWING room was abuzz with the refined activity of the afternoon's callers. Each gentleman, from Mr. Hargrove with his pristine bouquet of white roses to Viscount Mandeville and his box of fine chocolates, vied for a moment of Juliet's favor, their friendly rivalry underscored by an unspoken competition.

"Mr. Hargrove, Viscount Mandeville," Juliet greeted each man with a nod, her smile gracious yet reserved. "Your gifts are as lovely as they are thoughtful. I am truly honored."

Mr. Hargrove inclined his head. "The honor is ours, Miss Hayward. Your presence brightens even the dreariest of London days."

Viscount Mandeville, not to be outdone, added with a charming smile, "And we hope that these small tokens might add a measure of enjoyment to your afternoon."

"That is very kind of you, both." She glanced at the men. The conversation would be very dull if she didn't take action. "Gentlemen, have you heard about the latest developments in the Vauxhall Gardens? Considering your shared interest in architecture, I'd love to hear your thoughts on the matter."

Mr. Hargrove leaned forward. "Miss Hayward, you know this subject is dear to me. The proposed designs are indeed a topic of great interest. The vision for the gardens is quite remarkable."

"Absolutely," Viscount Mandeville chimed in with enthusiasm. "The blend of nature and innovation could transform our experience of the gardens. It's a thrilling prospect."

"Miss Hayward." Sebastian Morgrave stood at the drawing room door. He carried no flowers nor sweets. He walked in with an air that his presence alone was gift enough. His eyes swept the room with an air of superiority, a silent challenge to the assembled suitors.

Morgrave sat stoically, his eyes occasionally narrowing, adding an air of discomfort to the room. His silence was a cloud that dimmed the lively discussion. The other gentlemen shifted uneasily. Their animated conversation was now subdued.

Juliet sensed the need to dispel the unease and turned to Mr. Hargrove with an encouraging smile. "You were sharing your insights on the use of natural light in design. Please, do continue," she urged, her voice bright and inviting.

Grateful for the redirection, Mr. Hargrove cleared his throat and resumed, though he cast a wary glance at Morgrave. "Yes, as I was saying, the strategic placement of windows can truly transform a space."

The conversation picked up again, although more cautiously, as the men navigated around Morgrave's brooding presence. Juliet skillfully handled the situation, guiding the dialogue with grace and ensuring the afternoon retained its charm despite the undercurrents of tension.

"Mr. Morgrave, have you nothing to add to the conversation?" Juliet posed.

"Well, as long as the structures don't crumble and the ladies find the gardens agreeable, what's there to fuss about?" he quipped, a smirk playing on his lips.

The other men exchanged brief, knowing glances, their polite smiles not quite reaching their eyes. Hargrove stood, and Viscount Mandeville followed. "Thank you for tea, Miss Hayward, and your lovely company." They turned to Sebastian and nodded. "Morgrave."

As they reached the door, Morgrave's voice cut through the

quiet that had settled. "Gentlemen, always a pleasure to see the competition." His tone dripped with condescension.

Mr. Hargrove, pausing at the threshold, turned back with a look of disdain. "Mr. Morgrave, in matters of the heart, the truest competition is the grace with which one conducts oneself. Something for you to ponder."

The room held its breath as Morgrave's confident smirk faltered, the subtle rebuke landing with the precision of a well-aimed arrow. Juliet, from her seat by the window, allowed herself a small smile of satisfaction. At that moment, the balance of power subtly shifted, and the drawing room's atmosphere lightened once more, but not for long.

With Mr. Hargrove's and Mandeville's departure, tension gradually returned. Morgrave's earlier bravado seemed to wane after Mr. Hargrove's pointed words, leaving him momentarily adrift.

Juliet rose to the occasion. "Mr. Morgrave," she said, her voice a soothing balm to the prickled atmosphere, "I trust you've come with news or conversation to brighten the afternoon?"

Morgrave, rallying his composure, offered a tight smile. "Indeed, Miss Hayward. I've come to discuss a matter of some importance," he replied, his tone now tempered with a hint of humility.

He took a moment to ensure they were alone, his eyes scanning the room before returning to Juliet with a self-assured gleam. "Miss Hayward," he began, his voice carrying the importance of the moment, "it seems the fates have conspired in my favor. The suitor your family has been so eager to find for you," he paused, allowing the words to hang in the air, "is none other than myself."

Juliet's reaction was a delicate balance of surprise and composure, her mind racing to align this new information with her secret marriage to Ewan. Sebastian, a smug satisfaction settling over his features as he awaited her response.

Juliet's response was measured, her demeanor calm as she

absorbed the implications. "Mr. Morgrave," she replied, her tone betraying none of the surprise or elation he might have expected, "that is indeed a development. I trust my family believes this to be a prudent match." She noted a flicker of surprise—and perhaps disappointment—at her composed reaction. Clearly, he had anticipated a different response, one of gratitude or excitement, but Juliet was neither overwhelmed nor relieved. She was resolute, her stance an unspoken declaration that she would not be so easily won over.

Sebastian's initial calmness gave way to controlled irritation as he processed Juliet's lack of enthusiasm. "Miss Hayward," he began, his voice smooth but with an undercurrent of irritation, "I had hoped for a more… favorable reception. Your family's decision is not one to be taken lightly."

Juliet met Sebastian's gaze with an unyielding expression. "Mr. Morgrave, while I respect my family's wishes, I believe matters of the heart require more than mere compliance."

Sebastian's composure wavered, his lips pressing into a tight line. The subtle shift in his appearance didn't escape her either. She witnessed a silent admission of his disappointment, a criticism left unvoiced yet clearly felt. Outwardly, she showed no reaction. However, she couldn't help but feel a bit of satisfaction at her small victory.

"Indeed, Miss Hayward. I had not anticipated such… restraint. It is a rare quality, one that your brother, God rest his soul, could have benefited from at the gaming tables."

Sebastian's words, with its barb, were designed to unsettle. Yet, as he prepared to leave, he paused, turning back to Juliet with a calculated casualness. "One does hope, Miss Hayward, that the beauty of Fairmont remains unmarred by misfortune," he remarked, his tone light but the implication clear.

Juliet's heart skipped a beat, not from fear but from the recognition of the phrase. The anonymous letters she'd received were the threat that had been haunting her. She held his gaze, her composure unbroken, even as the realization dawned that

Sebastian may be more involved in her troubles than a suitor.

Juliet's hands trembled, not with fear, but with a cold decisiveness as she faced Sebastian. "Your games end here," she stated, her voice a low hiss. "I will not be intimidated in my own home."

Sebastian's smirk wavered, the gravity of her stance piercing his arrogance. "My dear, I merely—"

"Enough," she interrupted sharply, pivoting away from him with a swish of her skirts. "Mr. Wilcox," she called out firmly as she strode down the hall, "please see Mr. Morgrave out."

In the kitchen, Juliet's emotions were a tempest. How dare he assume she'd welcome his proposal? The memory of their exchange played over and over in her mind, each word, each glance examined for missed clues, for the true intentions behind his threats. And yet, amidst the anger, she felt a surge of empowerment, a newfound strength from standing her ground. By the time she reached Aunt Geraldine and Mr. Wilcox, who confirmed Sebastian's departure, she was ready to tell them everything.

Juliet related the encounter to Aunt Geraldine, her words tumbling out in a rush. She made it clear she did not doubt that the written threat she received was from Sebastian. After sharing everything, she paused, hands folded on the table, as she decided what to do next.

"You must speak with Ewan. He needs to know all this." Her aunt was insistent.

Juliet hesitated. "We can take care of ourselves."

Aunt Geraldine stared her down. "Can we? Who is here to help us? Mrs. Murthy and Mr. Wilcox. No, my dear. He is not the type of man we turn our back on. We'll send for your husband at once. Be prepared. His arrival may draw attention and reveal your secret."

At that moment, the servant's door creaked open. Mrs. Murthy entered, shedding her cloak and placing her basket on the table. In that moment, an idea struck both Juliet and Aunt Geraldine simultaneously.

"Perfect," Juliet breathed out, a plan forming in her mind.

Without a word, she excused herself and hurried upstairs. She quickly changed into a plain brown day dress, retrieved the box containing her brother's effects and the threatening letter, then returned downstairs.

She slipped into Mrs. Murthy's cloak, stashed the box and letter she held into the basket, and donned the housekeeper's hat.

"Perhaps I should go with you or Mr. Wilcox?"

Juliet patted her aunt's hand. "That won't be necessary. I dare not go directly to Ewan. Instead, I'm going to Lord Barrington's house. It is only fifteen minutes away. I'll return as soon as I can."

With her aunt's reluctant agreement, she left the house in the same manner that Mrs. Murthy had entered, her identity hidden beneath the guise of an ordinary errand.

⊁⊱⊰⊀

BARRINGTON'S VOICE CUT through the quiet of his drawing room, his query directed at the butler. "Sanderson, what's all the commotion?"

The butler's reply was prompt, though with a hint of confusion. "A tradeswoman, my lord. I directed her to the servant's entrance," the butler replied promptly, a hint of confusion in his voice.

Sitting comfortably with his parents having tea, Ewan caught Barrington's curious look. "Tradespeople know their place. Are you expecting a delivery?" Ewan asked his host.

Before Barrington could respond, Duncan stood decisively. "I'll see what this is about," he announced, striding out of the room.

Moments later, Duncan returned, escorting a cloaked figure whose bearing struck a chord of familiarity in Ewan. He rose swiftly, a mix of concern and recognition in his eyes. "What's the matter? What brings you here?" he asked, moving closer to the mysterious visitor.

As the woman faced him, her hat slipped away, unveiling Juliet's unwavering expression. "Thank goodness you are here. Ewan, I'm here on an urgent matter. I need to speak with you," she whispered, her plea barely audible yet laden with importance.

Lord and Lady Aurington looked on, bewildered by their son's alarm at the appearance of a seemingly ordinary woman. "Ewan, who is this?" his mother's hand paused mid-gesture, her teacup forgotten.

A smile threatened to break through Ewan's composed facade as he assisted Juliet out of the cloak and bonnet. Together, they faced his parents, "Mother, Father, please meet Juliet Hayward— my wife, the Marchioness Glenraven." His voice was filled with a touch of pride.

The room fell into stunned silence, broken only by Lord Aurington's chuckle. "Well, that's a surprise worth waiting for!"

❦

Chapter Twenty-Five

April 23, 1820 Late Afternoon

T HE DRAWING ROOM fell still, like the silence following a sudden thunderclap. The grandfather clock ticking a solitary sound amidst the quiet.

Lord Aurington's chuckle, still warm with humor, softened into a smile of realization as he stared at Juliet for several heartbeats. "Bradley's sister, is it? He was a fine young man, full of life, not one to... well, it's a tragedy indeed. The lad was always so guarded about his private life, a stark contrast to his... let's say, more exuberant social endeavors. We all felt for the lad's untimely passing." He let out a deep breath and glanced at Juliet. "We are, indeed, sorry for your loss."

Ewan met his father's gaze with a solemn nod, drawing strength from Juliet beside him. "Father, the circumstances surrounding Bradley's death are complex, with hidden truths yet to be uncovered. Juliet and her family have been through a great ordeal since his passing," his voice carrying a gravity that matched the seriousness of his words. "Our marriage is a mutual decision, borne out of necessity and understanding, protecting her family and ensuring our safety."

Lord and Lady Aurington exchanged a glance, as the revelation of a marriage of convenience settled over them. Lady Aurington's hand found her husband's, their fingers intertwining in a wordless gesture of solidarity.

Lady Aurington nodded, her eyes softening as she looked at

Juliet. "My dear, life presents us with many challenges, and we must face them as best we can. If your marriage brings stability and happiness to you both, then you shall have our blessing." She glanced at her husband with a knowing look in her eyes. "Love blooms in many ways, but often the most enduring love is that which grows from friendship."

"Such arrangements as yours are not unheard of," Lord Aurington finally said. "It is not for us to judge. You, indeed, have our blessing."

Comforted by his parent's support, he noted the subtle shift in Juliet's stand as the tension appeared to drain from her shoulders. His parents' acceptance was not just a formality. They genuinely welcomed Juliet into the Aurington family, and for that, he and Juliet were grateful.

Juliet had allowed him to assist her with her cloak. However, when Ewan reached out to take the forgotten basket out of Juliet's hands, she drew it back firmly and gently pushed his hand away. In the process, a note slipped out and fluttered to the floor.

"No, Ewan. It is one of the reasons why I am here." She fished out a small, worn box. "This contains what was in Bradley's possession when we found him."

Juliet opened the box and revealed the items. On top was the single playing card, the ace of hearts.

Lord Aurington's hand shot out, plucking the card from the box with a sudden sharp intake of breath.

Ewan's attention was drawn to a fine leather glove with a distinctive monogram under the card. He removed the glove and at once saw that it bore the initials 'S.M.' intricately stitched over a small, embroidered raven, a symbol that Sebastian had made his own. He stared at it for several long heartbeats.

"Juliet," he glanced at her, a crease forming between his brows. "Where was this glove found?"

Juliet's eyes met Ewan's with a flicker of sorrow as she recounted the grim discovery. "It was under Bradley." Her voice was barely above a whisper. "Mr. Wilcox found the leather glove pressed into the earth beneath him, in the garden where he…" Juliet took a deep, steadying breath, lifting her chin with a resilience that belied the turmoil within. "We must find the truth behind this, for Bradley's sake and our own," she declared, her resolve firming like steel.

Ewan stepped closer, gently cupping her cheek in a comforting caress. "And we shall." His touch conveyed the support and solidarity that words alone could not.

With a lingering touch to Juliet's cheek, Ewan's expression hardened as he turned his attention to the glove in his other hand. The scent of woodsy cologne wafted from the leather, igniting a spark of recognition. "This belongs to Sebastian Morgrave." His disbelief quickly turned to understanding. "The raven, his chosen emblem, it's all too fitting. He thinks himself wise when he is really dark, cunning, and ominous."

Lord Aurington looked up, he glanced at Barrington then his gaze met Ewan's. "Sebastian's glove, in Bradley's possession? The raven, the Order of Shadows. And this card…" He flipped it over. "Order of Shadows. What game is this?"

Ewan's mind raced as he pieced together the implications. "A game that ended in tragedy."

Juliet's breath hitched, her mind reeling with the implications. "Sebastian Morgrave?" she echoed, her voice barely audible. "Then… then the marriage settlement he claims to have…"

Ewan swung her around. "What marriage settlement?" The room went quiet.

"Ewan," she paused, her breath coming in spurts as she tried to put the pieces in place. "Sebastian Morgrave came to me with a marriage settlement, claiming my mother sanctioned it." Her eyes, wide with the gravity of her realization, sought his. "He walked into my drawing room as if it was his. He spoke of my brother's gaming. But when his words echoed the very threats from the note I received, I had Mr. Wilcox show him out. It was then I knew I had to come to you and bring these," she gestured to her brother's effects.

Lord Aurington's eyes widened, a realization dawning. "Sebastian, at the gambling table, was laying claim to Juliet's hand… It's a calculated move."

Juliet's fingers brushed Ewan's arm. "How is Bradley, my family, caught in this web? What can I do to shield them?"

Ewan covered her hand with his own, a silent pledge of unity. "Together, we'll guard them. This I promise you."

Ewan turned to the others. "We must act quickly. Sebastian's ambitions are far-reaching, but this," he held up the glove, "may be the key to stopping him."

Lord Aurington, still holding the ace of hearts, raised it for all to see. "This card—it's a taunt. If Sebastian were playing a shadow quest, there would be four aces of hearts. We have the one by my bed, the one in the vault, and now the one that Bradley carried. There's one more. We need to find what he is planning for his end game."

The room fell into a contemplative silence, each person considering the implications. Barrington broke the quiet, his tone thoughtful. "Perhaps it's not about preventing the marriage but creating chaos within the family. Disrupting the line of inheritance, perhaps?"

Ewan's expression darkened, a storm brewing in his gaze. "It's all connected, isn't it? Sebastian's been weaving a web around the family this entire time."

"That's impossible," Juliet pulled on his arm. "We only truly began to know each other a fortnight ago. There must be a deeper reason. He knows of your inheritance and your need to marry, but he knows nothing of our marriage."

"I find it more than coincidence that of the five men at a weekly card game, three are deceased or injured." Aurington nodded at Barrington, who had been quiet.

"Who else was at the table besides Quinto, Bradley, and Father?" Ewan asked.

"When Quinto and I played, only Ashfield and Morgrave," his father answered.

"It is something that has bothered me as well." Barrington rose and went to the cellaret. He returned to a round of sherry for everyone.

Lord Aurington moved forward on his chair. "It took me a while to realize it, but every man at the table has something Morgrave wants."

"What could Ashfield give him? He has funds, but nothing overly substantial. He certainly doesn't have property." Ewan said.

"Lady Ashfield," Juliet said. "Lady Ashfield introduced Morgrave to me at Lady Gladstone's party. She and her family are well-connected. Thank goodness she pulled him away from me and brought him to meet someone else."

"Enrico Quinto was an excellent horseman with connections at various racetracks. I suspect Sebastian wanted him to guarantee the winners at select horseraces." Barrington sipped his sherry.

Lord Aurington looked up, his gaze meeting Ewan's. "After I learned of Hayward's death, I received the ace of hearts in the post from Quinto's widow. It's a matter of timing. Enrico, Bradley, then my accident happened on my way to see her. There are lingering questions about Bradley's final days... about the game that took everything from him.

"After the game, he came to see me. He was sure that Sebastian was cheating. He told me how he called him out, but Sebastian just laughed at him. He said Sebastian wanted him to sign vowels for money he hadn't lost. He refused and left."

"That's impossible." Juliet began to seethe. "I'm being hounded with demands to pay Bradley's vowels."

A hush descended upon the room, every whisper and rustle ceased as if in collective anticipation. Ewan's jaw set firmly, his decision to uncover the truth burning fiercely. "This is why Barrington called me back from Paris, to get to the bottom of this. I wish I had returned sooner. I may have been able to prevent some of Sebastian's plans from succeeding."

"Have you found it strange that you never received the letters

Hughes sent to you, but you received my pouch?" Barrington put his glass down and took a seat. "Aurington, how did you communicate with Ewan while he was gone? How did you send the messages?"

"I gave them to my estate manager, Robert Fletcher, to handle."

Ewan shot out of his seat. "Fletcher told me Sebastian has been helping him with matters recently." Curses dropped out of his mouth. "He could have sabotaged the messages. No wonder he was surprised when he first saw me."

"What would he gain by doing that?" Juliet turned to Glenraven.

"The inheritance documents state that the heir must be married by his thirtieth birthday or forfeit to the next in line. While Sebastian is a distant cousin, he is the next male in line."

"Sebastian? I had no idea." Juliet's mouth dropped. "Then, his game to be introduced to the *ton*, his need for wealth all revolves around his intention of becoming the next Marquess of Glenraven."

"No, my dear," Lady Aurington interrupted. "The next Duke of Aurington."

"I think Juliet may be correct." Aurington drummed his fingers on the table. "Morgrave needed money to keep up with the game, someone who could introduce him to wealthy targets, and someone who would ensure he won every horserace."

"Are you saying he targeted my brother for his money?" Juliet asked, aghast.

"Yes," Aurington looked at Ewan and was breathing hard. "But he also wanted the property your family owns on Chapel Street and Lowndes Place." He glanced at Ewan and waited for him to respond.

"Why that's…Do you mean the property behind Aurington Hall?" Sebastian's intent dawned on Ewan. "Sebastian wanted to own the Fairmont Property adjacent to Aurington Hall ever since he was a boy. He would brag about how one day it would all be his."

Lord Aurington, still holding the ace of hearts, raised it for all to see. "This card... it's a taunt, using my mark as if it was already his."

Ewan pondered the pattern of the aces, finding it as puzzling as the complex chess move, the King's Gambit—a daring ploy that risked everything for the promise of a greater victory. Just as in the gambit, where White offers a pawn to gain control, the shadow quest seemed to lure its players into a trap, sacrificing them one by one for a grander scheme.

"The final ace," Ewan mused, "must be the key to the gambit, the piece that completes the attack. It's hidden, yet pivotal, much like the move after the pawn sacrifice, leading to a fierce battle for dominance."

Ewan saw the parallel—the last ace of hearts was not just another card. The last ace of hearts was the move that would expose the true orchestrator of this deadly game. And perhaps, it was hidden in plain sight, waiting for the right player to make the decisive move.

"Come, dear," Lady Aurington rose and reached out to her husband. "We've imposed on Lord Barrington's hospitality long enough. Besides, you no longer have the luxury of lingering as an invalid. You're needed. It will be very interesting to see what Morgrave does when we announce and celebrate Ewan and Juliet's marriage."

"Mother," Ewan glanced at Juliet and caught the flicker of panic in her gaze. "We cannot—"

Lady Aurington's voice carried the finality of a gavel's fall. "We shall make our stand at Aurington Hall come the first of May. Let's see what Morgrave does." Her gaze swept over Ewan, pride and challenge mingling in her eyes. "You, Ewan James Alasdair Glenraven, have never been one to avoid a battle. Do what you do best."

With a nod of agreement, Lord Aurington stood, his smile broad and defiant. "I'm glad you've returned, Ewan." A smile of quiet rebellion played on his lips. He extended his arm to Lady Aurington. "Come, dear. It's time for us to go home."

Before his departure, Lord Aurington handed Ewan a slender folio he had brought to Barrington's home for safekeeping. "These pages do not hold all of our family's history. But inside, you'll find everything related to the gambling scheme and its entanglements with our name. It's important that you add the new evidence we've uncovered. It may very well unravel Morgrave's plot," he glanced at Juliet, "and clear your wife's family's honor. And son, your mother didn't tell you the entire truth when you arrived. While I argued otherwise, there were some who truly believed my life was in jeopardy—not from the accident itself, but from the person who orchestrated it," With those parting words, Lord Aurington rejoined his wife.

Barrington and Ewan glanced through the folio. "Barrington." Ewan's voice betrayed a hint of trepidation, "I've found something." He handed the man a stack of letters, their seals broken, the handwriting elegant but hurried. "These were among my father's papers—correspondence with several known gamblers, including some we've suspected."

Barrington's eyes flicked across the page, absorbing the words that wove a narrative far more intricate than they had imagined. He met Ewan's gaze, a silent question hanging between them.

Ewan continued, "It seems our suspicions barely scratched the surface. There's a network, the Order of Shadows, and it's entangled with not only our family's legacy but others as well. This goes more deeply than I feared."

Barrington glanced at Ewan. "There is a great deal going on here. I agree with your mother. The time has come to draw Morgrave out." He stood and nodded to Juliet. "Congratulations, Lady Glenraven. I'm looking forward to the big birthday celebration. Please excuse me. Based on what I've seen here, I have matters to attend to."

As the room emptied, Juliet felt the graveness of the situation. She turned to Ewan and hesitated a moment. "I'm not certain that announcing our marriage is the best course of action."

Ewan, absorbed in his notes, barely glanced up. "It will be all right," he assured her absentmindedly.

She picked up the monogrammed glove and put it in the box with the ace of hearts and Bradley's other effects.

She bit her lip, her mind racing with potential consequences. "No. I disagree," she shook her head. "Morgrave has gone too far to turn back now. He can almost taste victory, and it's blinded him."

Ewan was absorbed in a leather-bound folio, its contents strewn across the mahogany desk. The pages contained family records and confidential correspondence, each a step deeper into the maze of intrigue surrounding his family.

Juliet watched from the doorway, a pang of exclusion tightening in her chest as she observed Ewan's unwavering dedication to the task.

Juliet quietly slipped away with both Mrs. Murthy's cloak and basket. Her departure went unnoticed in the commotion of plans and strategies.

Hours later, Barrington re-entered the room and glanced around. "Where's Juliet? I thought she'd be with you for tea. Have you lost your wife so soon?" he teased with a light chuckle.

The words hung in the air as Ewan's gaze swept the room, the papers in his hand forgotten. A sense of unease settled over him and grew heavier as he noted the empty chair where her cloak and basket had been. "She was just here…" he murmured, the sinking feeling in his stomach intensifying. He glanced at his friend.

Barrington summoned his butler with a sense of urgency.

"Mr. Sanderson. Have you seen Lady Glenraven?"

"She left several hours ago. I inquired if she would like the carriage, but she said she preferred to walk."

Ewan was already gathering his things, his heart racing with worry.

Chapter Twenty-Six

J ULIET STOOD AT the threshold of Bradley's room and took a deep breath to steady herself before she stepped inside. The air was thick with the dust of disuse, and the silence seemed to hold its breath. A faint, unfamiliar scent teased her senses, almost as if the room itself held onto the memory of its occupant. She hadn't entered his room since…his death. She closed her eyes, fighting against the overwhelming tug that wanted to bring her back to that day. Letting out a breath, she stepped inside.

It was strange. As she approached his desk, she half-expected him to walk in, sit down, and begin his correspondence. Her fingers brushed over his crystal inkwell, his quill, and his blotter. She opened the single desk drawer, and her heart skipped a beat. She found his leather-bound diary.

Lifting it out, she chuckled softly. It was an old one from 1813. She knew Bradley kept a diary for each year. This was just one piece of his meticulous record-keeping.

"Bradley, what secrets have you kept?" she murmured, flipping through the pages filled with his elegant script.

1 January 1813

The Collingwood soiree was as grand as expected, though I confess I would have much preferred a day of hunting with my friends. I wore my finest navy tailcoat with silver buttons, a crisp white cravat, and freshly polished black boots.

The evening began with a dance with Celeste Collingwood. She looked lovely in her emerald gown, but I found her company rather dull. I suspect our conversation will not be one I'll re-member.

I was fortunate to find a chess game in the game room, where I spent most of the evening. It provided the stimulation I craved. Lord Aurington had remarkable luck at the card table, earning my admiration for his skill and composure.

Dinner was a feast. The menu included:

- *Roasted pheasant with chestnut stuffing*
- *Creamed carrots and peas*
- *A rich beef consommé*
- *Freshly baked bread rolls*
- *Plum pudding for dessert*

As the evening draws to a close, I reflect on the festivities with a mixture of satisfaction and longing for simpler pleasures. Tomorrow, perhaps, there will be time for more invigorating pursuits.

She chuckled at his description of Celeste Collingwood and his preference for chess over dancing. It was so very Bradley—reserved, thoughtful, and always seeking intellectual stimulation. Yet, beneath the lightheartedness, she felt a pang of sorrow. This was a window into a time when he was alive, when their family wasn't shrouded in disaster and grief. She traced her fingers over the ink, imagining him sitting at his desk, writing these words, unaware of the dark shadows that would envelop their lives.

Reading his thoughts brought him closer, even if just for a moment. She sighed, closing the book with care. There were so many questions left unanswered, and she wondered if the pages of his other diaries might hold the key to understanding his secrets—and perhaps even her own.

Beneath the diary, a stack of letters caught her attention. Each was folded meticulously, bound not with ribbon but with the precision of a man who valued order even in chaos, but with twine. She untied them, her heart aching with each crease she smoothed out. There were several condolence messages, but others spoke of debts, of desperation, of a man cornered by his own folly.

Determined to find his current diary, she searched his wardrobe, under the cushions of his armchair, and even the window seat. Juliet pulled back the carpet and looked for signs of loose floorboards. She found nothing there. Her hands searched for loose bricks along the hearth but found none.

A small, carved chess piece, a black king, rested on the mantle. She picked it up, the wood warm from the sun that filtered through the window. "You were always the protector, weren't you?" she said to the figure as if it were a channel to her brother. "Always rushing headlong into battle."

With the diary, the letters, and the king as her talismans in hand, she glanced around the room to ensure everything was in order. She closed the door behind her and heard a familiar voice from downstairs. A moment of panic came over her before she hurried to her room and quietly closed the door.

⫸⫷

"LORD GLENRAVEN, WELCOME." Mr. Wilcox greeted him and led him into the drawing room, where he found Mrs. Murthy serving tea to Aunt Geraldine.

"Good afternoon." He was in a hurry and not his usual casual self. "Please tell Juliet that I'm here."

Aunt Geraldine glanced at Mrs. Murthy and then at him. "We thought she was with you?"

He asked them questions, but they could offer no answers, heightening his anxiety. "Please inform me immediately when she returns," he implored them before he rushed out.

As the sound of Ewan's coach departing, Juliet came down the stairs, a small bag in hand filled with some essential items, including Bradley's diary, correspondence, and the chess piece.

Mrs. Murthy and Aunt Geraldine exchanged a glance before turning to her.

"Are you certain this is necessary? What will you do?" they asked, their voices filled with worry.

Juliet accepted Mrs. Murthy's basket of food. "I must handle my family's troubles without risking Glenraven's future. He has much more to lose."

"But he has so much more to gain with you by his side." Both women protested.

Juliet smiled and hugged her aunt. "I wouldn't expect you to say anything else, but don't you see, he cannot announce our marriage without me. It's safer this way." She could see they weren't convinced. "If he announced our marriage, what would stop Sebastian from making Glenraven his next target?"

"And where will you go?" They pressed, their eyes searching hers for a hint of her plan.

"To a place where no one will find me," Juliet replied, "I will not tell you and make you an accomplice. I love you both too much. I will be at a secret place where I can think and breathe."

Before she left, Juliet paused. "Did anyone find Bradley's diary?"

Mrs. Murthy shook her head. "No, miss. But there was something strange about his room after Mr. Wilcox and the coroner finished. The fireplace…"

"The fireplace?" Juliet echoed, puzzled.

"Yes," Mrs. Murthy confirmed. "We found what looked like a burned leather binding but no pages. Bradley had burned papers."

Juliet was taken aback. Her brother kept every paper and never destroyed any. For him to burn papers meant something significant.

Mrs. Murthy then retrieved a small wooden box. "I kept the binding in here for safekeeping."

Juliet opened the box, expecting the acrid smell of smoke even after two months. Instead, a faint, unfamiliar fragrance, musky and rich with a touch of lemon, wafted out and lingered in the air. She put the scorched binding back into the box.

"Please, keep this safe. The Bradley we knew would never destroy his diary. But the more I find out, the more I think I didn't know the Bradley we buried."

Wearing Mrs. Murthy's cloak and hat, she left by the servant's door. Her steps were firm as she made her way through the busy streets, her decision never in question. No one took notice of her as she entered The Penny Post. She paused at the entrance, her heart heavy with what she was about to do.

The clerk's voice interrupted her thoughts. "Miss?" he inquired, reaching out for her letter.

With a deep breath, Juliet handed over the letter and the fee. The sound of the coin hitting the counter echoed in her ears, sealing the finality of her decision.

She turned away and let the door close softly behind her. She was on her own now, on a path that would challenge her courage and conviction, but she would not fail.

April 23, 1820 Dusk

EWAN PACED THE length of the library, his boots echoing against the polished wood floor. Each report from his men came back the same. There was no sign of Juliet anywhere. His hands, flexing into fists, betrayed his growing frustration.

The door opened, and the archbishop entered. "My lord," he began, his voice somber. "I'm here to see your father, but I find I have troubling news for you. I've received this," he held up the Glenraven circlet, "along with a message from Lady Glenraven. She mentioned there may be a prior settlement that could threaten your marriage. She asked that I return this to you." He placed the circlet on the desk.

The room stilled. The gravity of his words and Juliet's actions settled over the family. Ewan's mother stared at the Glenraven treasure, trying to hide the worry in her eyes. "Nonsense! Juliet is Ewan's lawful wife. There can be no truth to such a claim."

Ewan's father rose from his chair, his stature commanding. "Juliet is overreacting. We must see this alleged settlement. Without proof, it's mere tittle-tattle."

The archbishop nodded, his gaze meeting Ewan's. "I, too, want to see the document. This is a serious allegation."

Duncan entered carrying a letter. "This just arrived for you." He extended it toward Ewan.

The familiar script struck him like a lightning bolt. Without hesitation, he broke the wax seal and unfolded the letter. The parchment trembled as he silently read the message.

Ewan,

As I pen this letter, I find myself reflecting on our vows. Though our marriage was born of necessity, it now leaves me questioning our haste.

I am stepping away, not out of a lack of affection but from a deep-seated care that compels me to protect you from my family's misfortune. I must find clarity and a way forward that does not endanger you or your family's legacy.

I hope that we can both find the answers we seek and perhaps, in time, a way back to each other.

Juliet

The archbishop, his expression one of compassion and concern, gently placed a hand on Ewan's shoulder.

Ewan's breath hitched, each inhale sharp and erratic as the reality of Juliet's absence settled like a weight upon his chest. "She's gone," he whispered, the words barely making sense to him. He shook his head slowly. "No, it can't be true. There must be a mistake," as if saying the words out loud could change the truth.

His mind raced, thoughts tumbling over one another—how

could she leave, how could she question the sincerity of his feelings? He had to find her, make sure she was safe, and above all, assure her of the truth. He loved her. "I'll turn London inside out if I have to." His voice rose with a fierce tenacity. "I will find her, and I will bring her home."

Duncan looked up, having read the message. "I'll go to Barrington at once. He has men throughout London who can aid in the search."

Ewan glanced at his batman and nodded. Duncan turned toward the door.

"Wait." Ewan caught Duncan's arm as he turned to leave. "Sebastian is unaware of our marriage. To him, Juliet merely questioned his proposal." A plan began to form in Ewan's mind. "While you speak to Barrington, I'll consult with Lady Rosefield. With Juliet's parents away, she's the one to address this claim." He refolded Juliet's letter and tucked it in his pocket. "I'll go and speak to her now."

The archbishop interjected, "Be cautious, Ewan. If you challenge the legality of a marriage settlement, you'll need irrefutable evidence."

"So will Sebastian." With a mutual nod of understanding, Duncan departed, and Ewan prepared to follow.

"Go," the archbishop urged, turning to sit beside Lord Aurington. "Your father and I will manage here."

With a final glance at the circlet, Ewan turned on his heel and strode from the room. The archbishop's words fueled his mission to uncover the truth and find the woman he loved.

Chapter Twenty-Seven

April 27, 1820

J ULIET HAD NO difficulty locating the key in the statue of Artemis and unlocking the door. Now, four days after leaving Fairmont Hall, she sat in the dimly lit summerhouse, with the stack of letters to the side, she stroked the diary's leather cover cool under her fingertips, finally finding the courage to read it. She flipped through the pages, smiling at the familiar handwriting and chuckling at some of the aliases her brother had created for his friends.

"Always so clever," she murmured, feeling a bittersweet pang of nostalgia.

As she neared the end of the year, her smile faded. The entries did not stop at December 31st. Instead, there were more entries dated this year for the months leading up to his death.

Her heart quickened as she turned the pages, reading Bradley's words. These entries were different. They were less about daily life and more about his fears and suspicions. He wrote of strange occurrences, and people he thought might be watching him. There were cryptic notes and mentions of the "Order."

Juliet's fingers trembled slightly as she read on, piecing together the fragments of Bradley's final months. Her brother had been in trouble, and she hadn't known the extent of it. She read on.

"The Rookery and The Gilded Lily," she read aloud. The names were probably the private residences where the gambling stakes were high and the company secretive. She let her mind dwell on deciphering whose homes these could be and went on. Her finger traced the dates on the calendar, each marked with a list of secret names.

She turned the pages, her pulse quickening as the last four months listed only The Gilded Lily—Fray, Eclipse, Anchor, Key, and Gentry, in attendance. But where Shadow once stood, there was now an angry black spot, a violent scribble obliterating the name. And above it, scrawled in a hand driven by emotion, the word VIPER in all capital letters.

Then there were numbers. They didn't lie. His winnings had turned to disastrous losses, and while the IOUs payable to VIPER had piled up like autumn leaves, each was crossed out and marked paid in full.

She whispered to the room, "Bradley, what were you thinking?" She gazed at the small black wooden king she perched on the mantelpiece. "Viper. No one can be that fortunate," she whispered. "He must have been cheating."

She turned the page and found Bradley's script tight and hurried. *"Arrived early at The Gilded Lily and sat in Viper's seat, the one that faced the door. No matter where the game was, his chair always faced the door. He was furious. No one wins that often. Must be more than luck."*

With a sudden movement, she snapped the diary shut with a booming thud, the sound slicing through the silence. "You knew there was cheating." She glared at the wooden king as if Bradley was in front of her. "What were you planning to do?"

A slow moaning of the door hinges shattered the stillness and sent a shock of fear through her. She spun around. Her heart pounded. A silhouette filled the doorway, ominous yet familiar.

He stepped through the doorway, the soft light revealing... "Duncan!" She let out a breath she didn't realize she was holding. "You gave me a fright. How did you find me?"

Duncan's concerned expression softened, relief in his eyes. "I'm sorry. I took a shortcut through the estate and saw the light from the window. I hoped it was you. Ewan has had everyone in London searching for you these last four days."

"Here I am." She opened her arms wide. "Would you like some tea?"

"Ewan keeps something stronger at hand." He went to the cabinet and retrieved two glasses and a bottle of brandy. "He's been worried sick about you." He poured them each a glass.

"I've kept this with me," he handed her a letter, "in case I found you. You dropped it at Barrington's."

Juliet took it from him. "And yes, I read it. Whoever this bastard is, I canna wait to get my hands around his throat. He can't even spell. Ach, all the more reason, Lass for you to—"

"I am sorry I've upset you and Ewan, but it cannot be helped." She put the letter on top of the stack she took from Bradley's desk. "I've always fought my own battles. I am not going to stop now." She sat, took the filled glass from him, and sipped her drink. "All these months, I thought Bradley had taken his own life." She glanced at Duncan and his understanding gaze. "When all along he had been murdered. And probably by the man who stole everything from him. This man, Viper, not only took his money, but he also took his life."

Duncan slowly lowered himself into the seat next to her. "What makes you so certain?"

"Bradley told me." She smiled at him and took another, bigger sip of the amber liquid. She opened the book and told him about the aliases for the houses and the men with whom he gambled. "We used code names when we were children to prevent anyone from knowing who we spoke about or where we went."

"Clever," he smiled.

"I dubbed him Scribe since he kept meticulous details of everything he did and spent. He called me Starling. His reasoning was I talked a great deal."

"What code names would you give me and Ewan?" He leaned back, swishing the branding in the glass.

"For your strength and warrior appearance, you would be Highlander and Ewan…" She thought a bit. With a smile, she said, "Falcon, for his keen insight and strategic mind. Bradley had other thoughts. He dubbed him the tall yew tree."

Duncan gave her a wide smile. "Bradley's secret is safe with me. Although, it is quite fitting. Now, you said your brother gave you the aliases for the location of the games, but where exactly are they? I don't see how the names can help…" He stared at the smirk that brightened her face. She had the answer.

She scooted closer to the table and pointed to the first name, "The Rookery. Birds. Who do you know that has a bird fascination or collection?"

"Justin Rockwood," Duncan said. "I see him in the bookshop researching different species."

"They live on Mayfair Square. Are you certain you've never done this before?" she teased.

He chuckled and shook his head.

"The Gilded Lily, the place Bradley attended the night he died, hints a fine gardens," she said. "Sir Giles has an extensive garden. His residence is on St. James Place. In addition, they were both Bradley's friends."

"How very clever." Duncan browsed through the pages, searching for more coded names. "You two were thick as thieves, eh?" Duncan's lips twitched into a smile. His Scottish lilt added a warmth to his words.

Juliet chuckled, remembering simpler times. "Oh, we were. Partners in crime and champions of hide-and-seek. Bradley always had the best hiding spots."

Duncan's eyes held a distant look as he reminisced. "Ewan and I share a similar history. Our friendship is rooted in more than just shared experiences. It's woven into our very upbringing. Being the sixth son of Baron Blair meant that my path was never going to be at Blair Castle. In Scotland, that meant I had to carve out my own destiny, for the land and title would pass to my eldest brother."

He leaned back, his gaze returning to the present. "My mother and Ewan's, bless them, were as close as sisters, and when it came time, it was Ewan's parents who opened their home to me. They fostered me and gave me opportunities I might not have had otherwise. That's why my loyalty to Ewan is unbreakable—it's built on gratitude and respect as solid as the ancient stones of the highlands."

A shadow came over Duncan's expression. "Sebastian was different, though. Two years our junior, he always saw himself as the rightful kin, and me? I was the intruder in his eyes. Ewan and I bonded quickly, thick as thieves, you might say. We tried to include Sebastian, but there was always an edge to him, a sort of... attitude. He played a good game of chess, although he always took unnecessary chances."

Juliet listened with care, piecing together the nuances of the past that painted a picture of the present. "And Sebastian's jealousy?"

"It was always there, simmering beneath the surface. Ewan might not have seen it, always giving his cousin the benefit of the doubt, but I did. There were signs, little things that hinted at a deeper resentment. Sebastian was careful, though, and kept it well hidden from Ewan. But not from me."

Juliet absorbed Duncan's words, the pieces of a long-unseen puzzle coming into place. The undercurrents of jealousy and rivalry that had always been part of Sebastian's interactions with Ewan now made chilling sense.

Her eyes softened with understanding. "I never knew the depth of the bond you share with Ewan nor the strength of the ties that bind you both."

Duncan sighed, a hint of frustration in his voice. "Ewan always knew, deep down, the envy Sebastian harbored. But he chose to overlook it, to discount it as mere family rivalry. He never let it affect their relationship, always hoping for the best."

He paused, a smile slowly replacing the frustration as he reminisced. "Since we were lads," Duncan continued, leaning forward, his elbows resting on his knees, the glass in both his hands. "Ewan and I have had our share of capers too. Did he ever tell you about the time we 'borrowed' Lord Aurington's carriage for a midnight escapade?"

Her laughter rang out, clear and bright. "He failed to mention that to me. I can only imagine the mischief you two have managed. It must have been quite the adventure."

"Aye, well, we were young and daft. But those days forged a bond stronger than the steel of my claymore." Duncan's expression softened. "And when Ewan was called to war, I stood by him as his batman. We faced more than our share of narrow escapes."

Juliet's eyes widened. "You were with him in the Peninsula?"

"Every step of the way." He gave her a glance that said he remembered every nuance of what they went through. "That's where we met Barrington. Now there's a chess player. Between you and me, I think Ewan's still trying to best him at chess."

She couldn't help but smile. Duncan's easy grin was infectious. The warmth of the moment pushed back the shadows. "I can imagine them now, hunched over a chessboard, the fate of the empire hanging on the next move."

Duncan's amusement filled the space. "Oh, the empire's safe enough. It's Ewan's pride that's in peril. The man has a rather... spirited aversion to losing."

Their laughter intertwined into a shared rhythm that warmed the room, drawing them closer into a comfortable friendship.

As the laughter subsided, Duncan's gaze wandered around the room. His eyes fell upon a small stack of letters on the side table next to him. Absentmindedly, he picked up the top one, his fingers lightly tracing the edge of the paper.

"Why don't you come back to Glenraven Hall with me?" he asked, glancing at the letter without really reading it.

Juliet's eyes met Duncan's, a depth of understanding passing between them. "You care for him deeply, perhaps as much as I do. That's precisely why I cannot do what you ask. If I return now, questions about why we married will linger and cast a shadow over us. He might not think so now, but he is a proud man, a very proud man. Should the slightest doubt that we married for anything less than affection creep into our relationship, it could change us, perhaps, into very different people. I don't want that, and neither do you."

Duncan nodded thoughtfully, still holding the letter loosely. A slight furrow appeared on his brow as his gaze flickered back to the page in his hand. "You know him better than I thought. You're correct." She stood next to him. "I love him. I realize that more now that we are apart. Nothing would make me happier than to return to Ewan. To earn that right, I must take back what is rightfully my brother's honor and our family's good name."

He returned the letter to the table, his momentary curiosity replaced with a warm smile. "You are not a starling. Lass, you're a wee warrior," he said with a smile.

Chapter Twenty-Eight

"THAT IS A compliment coming from you. Others just call me stubborn." Juliet's gaze was unwavering as she faced Duncan in the dim light. "I must go to The Gilded Lily." The playfulness was gone from her voice.

"Absolutely not." Duncan countered his Scottish temper flaring. "A gambling den is no place for a lady."

"That's not what Lady Ashfield believes." Juliet stepped closer, her stubbornness shining through. "We had a lovely conversation at Lady Gladstone's. She mentioned how she enjoys the company of the other ladies in the drawing room while their husbands play. On occasion, she visits the card room to offer her husband encouragement." Juliet's expression shifted. The levity drained away as she locked eyes with Duncan. "Bradley's fate was sealed in that room, and I intend to discover how. That's where the answers are."

Duncan's expression was a tumult of conflict, torn between his loyalty to Ewan and the earnest desperation in Juliet's plea. "Lass, it's not just about walking into a viper's nest. It's about what Ewan would think—"

She interrupted him, her voice rising with a passion that echoed through the summerhouse walls. "Ewan would want the truth as well! He would leave no stone unturned if our roles were reversed." Juliet closed the distance between them. "Help me, Duncan. Help me for my brother's memory and for the peace of Ewan's family. Come with me to The Gilded Lily."

Duncan's resistance crumbled with her plea. His loyalty to Ewan and his family had always been unwavering, but Juliet's determination was infectious. He knew he couldn't let her face this alone.

He conceded with a heavy sigh, "Very well. I will accompany you to The Gilded Lily. But we do this carefully, with every precaution."

A wave of relief washed over her, her gratitude apparent. "You mustn't tell Ewan. He cannot know."

Duncan exhaled deeply. "You have my word. I will not speak of your plans or whereabouts to him."

"Thank you, Duncan. We go this evening."

"That soon? I understand. The anticipation must be unbearable. We'll wait until evening; the game you seek doesn't start until later. Meanwhile, let's examine your brother's diary. We need to be thoroughly prepared."

She handed him the diary with a grateful smile.

Juliet and Duncan studied Bradley's diary. She turned the pages and found a mosaic of thoughts, fears, and cryptic notes that seemed to dance just beyond comprehension.

Duncan's hand suddenly pressed against the page, halting Juliet's fingers mid-turn. "Hold on," he said, his voice low.

"Have you found something?" Juliet leaned in, her eyes scanning the entry. "It's about a chess game. Bradley was an avid player." She gestured toward the mantle where the black king stood. "I've been imploring that piece for answers all day."

Duncan's finger traced the lines of text. "Here, he mentions 'Viper' and a particular opening move." His eyes widened as he read on. "The King's Gambit," he murmured, a spark of realization in his voice. "Sebastian was obsessed with that strategy. He claimed it was the mark of a superior mind."

Juliet met Duncan's gaze, a shiver of apprehension coursing through her. "Are you sure? That it's a signature of Sebastian's?"

Duncan nodded firmly. "Aye, I'm certain. It was a point of pride for him." He leaned back, contemplating the diary before shifting his gaze to Juliet. "Your brother's diary—It's not merely suggesting Viper is a chess enthusiast. It's implicating Sebastian directly."

Juliet's fingers lingered on the page, her thoughts racing. "There must be more to uncover," she murmured and began to examine the pages with renewed purpose. "Here is an entry, the day before he died."

> *February 20, 1820…The air was filled with the Shadow fragrance of citrus and spice that clung to the room like a whisper. It mingled with the thicker scent of tobacco and secrets tonight. The usual suspects gathered, their faces shadowed, their whispers just as veiled. Fray was there, his cuffs more tattered than his fortune, yet he carried himself with an air of undeserved nobility. Eclipse sat opposite, the dimming light in his eyes reflecting the state of his coffers.*
>
> *But it was the clandestine exchange I witnessed that has set my mind racing. They spoke in hushed tones, a language of nods and knowing glances. Fray passed a note to Eclipse, who pocketed it with a surreptitious smile. What pact have they forged in the darkness of this den?*
>
> *I cannot shake the feeling that this meeting was but a piece in a larger game, one that threatens to ensnare us all. I must tread carefully, for the stakes are higher than they've ever been.*

Duncan's amusement faded as he absorbed Bradley's account. "Riddles indeed, but each one could be a piece of this puzzle," he said, his tone turning serious. "This meeting… it could be trivial, or it could be the key to understanding the whole scheme."

Juliet's expression mirrored Duncan's concern. "We can't ignore any clue, no matter how small. Bradley was meticulous. He wouldn't have recorded it if this information wasn't important."

Juliet nodded, more determined than ever. "Let's start with what we know. We'll map out Bradley's movements, cross-reference them with these entries, and see where they lead us."

Her finger lingered on the diary. "Monster's Mound might be a child's tale, but in this context, it could mean something more."

Juliet's half-smile was touched with a fleeting memory of simpler times. "As children, we dared each other to approach the mound at dusk, claiming it was haunted." The smile vanished as quickly as it appeared. "What does he say about it?"

Duncan scanned the entry. He speaks about the area *"The tall yew tree is in danger along with the others in the grove."* He's also exposed your childhood myth. And there's a mention of Aurington Pond, but nothing more." Duncan turned the page, then shook his head. "No, there's nothing else about Monster Mound or Aurington Pond."

"That's not the pond's name." Juliet read the section again and then snapped the diary shut. "We were on Fairmont land. The Aurington estate was on the other side of the fence and had its own pond. Ours was Mirror Pond."

"There isn't anything else in here." Duncan mused. "Perhaps we overlooked something…"

Juliet's eyes suddenly widened, a spark of understanding flickering to life. "Blast!" She flipped back to the entry, his eyes scanning the text until his face broke into a wide smile.

"What is it?" Duncan asked, taking the diary from him.

"Bradley always confused juniper trees with yew trees. There are no yew trees on the property." She stared at Duncan, a chill of disaster stealing her breath away. "Could Bradley be telling us that Ewan and his family are in danger?"

"Or that something is going to happen to the juniper trees," Duncan smirked.

Juliet's intuition flared. "Sebastian's ambitions extend beyond wealth. Sebastian is next in line to the title. He is after Ewan's legacy. Now, it's more important that we go to the Gilded Lily tonight."

They set the diary aside, their focus shifting to the evening's challenge at The Gilded Lily.

Duncan's jaw set, his eyes blazing like a Norse berserker. "I agree with you. We need to attend that card game tonight and witness the truth of his cheating with our own eyes. But it's dangerous. Sebastian is a threat, and he won't hesitate if he senses we're aware of his scheme."

Juliet rose, her decision unwavering. "We'll arrive early. I want to inspect that table to uncover the deceit Bradley suspected and understand how Sebastian is manipulating the game."

Duncan nodded, his eyes blazing with determination yet clouded with worry. "We will. But we must be cautious. If things go awry, we retreat immediately. We can't afford to lose anyone else to Sebastian's schemes."

Juliet's mind was a whirlwind as she sat in the dim light with the diary's revelations before her like a treasure map. "How can we outmaneuver Sebastian?"

"You won't be alone. I will be right there with you," he assured her, his expression grave. "We cannot slip in unnoticed. Sebastian knows us both. Disguises won't help. We'll go as we are. He's unaware of your marriage to Glenraven."

Juliet nodded, her mind working, seeking a way to obtain her goal. "Once there, I'll take Viper's—Sebastian's—seat. I'll assess the dealer and the players for any signs of cheating."

Duncan drummed his fingers on the table. "If you're challenged, if Sebastian confronts you, remain calm. Question his wins, subtly, enough to unsettle him, but not enough to cause an uproar."

"And if he becomes suspicious?" Juliet's voice was steady despite the underlying concern.

"He may question you, but he won't harm you. Should the situation escalate, I'll intervene," Duncan promised. "Remember, our goal is not merely to expose his cheating. It's to unveil his true intentions towards Ewan."

Juliet took a deep breath, her gaze meeting Duncan's. "When the moment arrives, when Sebastian's arrogance betrays him, we'll confront him with the evidence from Bradley's diary and whatever else we uncover."

Duncan's nod was a silent pact. "We'll protect Ewan and vindicate Bradley. Tonight, Sebastian's reign ends."

The plan was bold, even dangerous, but Juliet felt a surge of excitement at the thought. She was no longer Bradley's grieving sister. She was a woman on a mission against a formidable adversary.

"I agree." Duncan rose. "I must leave before I am missed. You've done well. Bradley would be proud. Rest now. I'll return this evening, and we'll head to St. James." He moved toward the door.

"Thank you again, Duncan. Remember, Ewan mustn't know."

"My word is my pledge." He stepped out and gently closed the door behind him.

Chapter Twenty-Nine

D UNCAN'S STEPS WERE heavy as he made his way back to Aurington Hall, the secret of Juliet's whereabouts trapping him like a suit of armor. He had given his word to keep her safe, to honor her request for silence, but the thought of Ewan, his friend and brother in arms, unaware and searching for her, festered like an open wound.

He found Ewan in the same position as Juliet, in the midst of planning, with maps and papers strewn across the table, all to find her. The sight of his friend so consumed with worry struck a chord in Duncan's heart.

Duncan stood by Ewan, his friend's distress etched in the lines of his face and the urgency of his movements. The sight stirred something within Duncan—a sense of duty that transcended his promise to Juliet.

"Ewan," Duncan began, his voice steady despite the turmoil within, "I must speak with you."

Ewan paused, his eyes meeting Duncan's. "What is it?"

"I know where Juliet is," Duncan confessed, his words hanging in the air like a storm cloud, heavy with unspoken consequences. Ewan's eyes widened with relief, his shoulders visibly relaxing for a brief moment.

"Where is she?" Ewan demanded, the edge of desperation in his voice.

Duncan's face hardened with resolve. "I can't tell you that."

The relief drained from Ewan's face, replaced by a fiery anger. He stepped closer, his fists clenching at his sides. "You can't tell me? She's my wife! I have a right to know where she is."

"I swore an oath to her. I feared if I didn't, she would leave, and we'd never find her," Duncan replied, his voice steady but his eyes revealing his conflict. "She's frightened, Ewan. Frightened for you."

Relief washed over Ewan, knowing Juliet was safe, but it warred with a surge of betrayal. How could Duncan, his most trusted friend, have kept Juliet from him? The air crackled with tension, like a storm about to break, as they faced each man locked in a silent battle of wills.

"You knew all along," Ewan's voice was barely a whisper, yet it carried the devastation of a deep trust coming undone. "How could you?" The betrayal stung, not just because of the secret kept from him, but because it came from Duncan, his most trusted confidant.

Duncan stood his ground, his loyalty to Juliet clashing with his fealty to Ewan. "I found her today. I had to protect her, Ewan. You know I—"

"No!" Ewan's shout cut through the tension. He advanced on Duncan, his hands clenched at his sides. "You had no right!"

The tension between Ewan and Duncan was clear and undeniable, a reflection of their long-standing camaraderie now strained by recent events. Ewan's hand shot out, grabbing Duncan by the collar, pulling him close. "Best for who, Duncan? For Juliet? For you? What about me?"

The question hung between them, heavy with implications. Duncan's eyes never left Ewan's, his own conflict evident. "For all of us, Ewan. For all of us."

Ewan's grip tightened, his other hand raised, poised to strike. But as he looked into Duncan's eyes, he saw not defiance but an unwavering commitment. With a ragged breath, Ewan released him, his arm dropping to his side.

"I trusted you." The hurt in Ewan's voice was more impactful than any physical blow could be.

Duncan straightened his collar, his voice soft. "And you can still trust me, Ewan. To protect her, to protect you, to protect the family you're building."

He paused, his gaze shifting to the floor for a moment as he gathered his thoughts. His jaw tightened, and he took a deep breath, clearly weighing his next words carefully.

He paused, his gaze flickering as if weighing the consequences. Then, with a firm nod, he decided. "There's something else you need to know. It's about the anonymous letters you and Juliet have been receiving."

Ewan's eyes narrowed, a mix of confusion and apprehension. "What about them?"

"I've discovered who has been sending them," Duncan revealed. "It's Sebastian."

Ewan's expression shifted to disbelief. "Sebastian? How can you be certain?"

A wry smile lit Duncan's face. "Aside from his handwriting matching a letter he sent to Juliet's family offering condolences for their son's loss, the bastard can't spell. He consistently misspells 'unbearable' as 'unbareable'—in both the anonymous threats and his own letters."

Ewan stared at him, the weight of the revelation sinking in. "He's been behind this all along," he muttered, anger and realization mingling in his eyes. he turned away, his anger spent, replaced by an aching sense of betrayal. "Just... make sure she's safe, Duncan. That's all I ask."

A fragile truce hung between them, the understanding clear and yet fraught with unspoken fears. They were in uncharted waters, but their course was set—to protect Juliet, no matter the cost.

As Ewan's anger subsided, the memories of Paris crept into his mind—the assignment that had ended in tragedy, the life he couldn't save. It was a failure that haunted him, a shadow that loomed over his every decision. Now, faced with the possible loss of Juliet, the fear of failing her as he had failed before was unbearable.

"I cannot fail her, Duncan. Not like I did in Paris," Ewan confessed, his voice breaking with the admission.

Duncan's hand found Ewan's shoulder. "You won't, Ewan. We won't let that happen."

⟫⟪

THE CARRIAGE WHEELS crunched on the gravel as it rolled to a stop before Sir Giles' grand estate. Juliet's heart was a drumbeat in her chest, a mix of anticipation and nerves for the card game she expected to witness—and unravel. Aunt Geraldine patted her hand reassuringly as they stepped out into the cool evening air.

"Thank you ever so much for extending your hospitality at such short notice," Aunt Geraldine nodded with a gracious smile. Her words struck the correct note of gratitude to Lady Giles, who greeted them with open arms. "My niece and I are most grateful."

Lady Giles welcomed them with an unaffected warmth. "It's our pleasure, Lady Rosefield. We're always delighted to have new company." Her smile was a beacon of genuine friendship.

As they entered the parlor, the expected sounds of shuffling cards and hushed wagers were conspicuously absent. Instead, a small gathering of guests mingled quietly.

Juliet's pulse quickened with disappointment. "I thought there was to be a game tonight," she whispered to Duncan, who had accompanied them as a silent guardian.

Duncan's sharp and assessing eyes scanned the room, taking in the scene. "It seems plans have changed," he murmured back.

Juliet excused herself with a polite nod to Aunt Geraldine and made her way to the card room. As she moved through the crowd, the mingled scents of perfumes and fresh flowers enveloped her. Suddenly, a sharp aroma cut through the sweetness—a peculiar blend of lemon's crispness entwined with the smoky undertone of extinguished embers. She paused, the unfamiliar scent sending a faint chill down her spine, though she couldn't quite place why.

Reaching the card room, the door opened to reveal a room shrouded in shadows, save for the flicker of a lone sconce.

Juliet's eyes swept across the room, landing on the card table in the center of the room. It stood abandoned, an island of green baize in a sea of uncertainty.

"Seems we're too late," Geraldine murmured, disappointment filling her words.

"Not necessarily," Juliet replied, her gaze fixed on the table. Her fingers searched under the table for any sign of trickery, but the smooth underside offered no secrets. The green baize of the table was unremarkable, untouched by hidden devices or marks. She moved from chair to chair, her eyes sharp, her mind racing to uncover the slightest clue.

Juliet sank into the chair that faced the door. She had been so certain she would see how he ensnared his victims, but her efforts were all in vain. Ready to claim defeat, a flicker of the candle caught her attention. The mirror behind the sconce revealed the back of a chair and the table in front of it. She went to the door and motioned to Duncan.

He slipped into the room with her.

"Sit here, please." She showed him to the Viper's chair, and then she sat in the chair in front of the candle, took her calling card out, and held it as if it were a playing card.

"Look at the mirror behind the candle and tell me what you see."

She followed Duncan's gaze as he glanced at the candle, but when he focused on the mirror, he nearly jumped out of his seat. She rose and lit each candle then sat in the seat in front of each one. Duncan nodded. He could see her calling card in the mirror.

"I found it—a subtle vantage point from each seat, a cheater's paradise."

Juliet's fingers trailed along the edge and brushed against a small, uneven section. Her curiosity piqued, she pressed gently, and a hidden drawer popped open with a soft click.

Inside lay a stack of papers. Juliet's heart quickened as she scanned the records, recognizing the handwriting that had doctored the figures—it wasn't Sebastian's.

Duncan leaned over her shoulder, his eyes narrowing. His keen eye for detail caught the irregularity as he sifted through the papers. "Look here," he said, his finger tracing a column of numbers. "The sums don't add up. These tallies are off—someone's been altering the records to skew the winnings and losses." He straightened up. "But by whom?"

Juliet gathered the papers and folded them carefully. "Someone has been manipulating the outcomes, and it's not just Sebastian we're dealing with."

With a triumphant yet silent cheer, Juliet extinguished the candles and, along with Duncan, slipped from the room, her discovery a precious secret.

"I've seen enough," she whispered to Aunt Geraldine. "We can leave now."

As they prepared to leave, Lady Ashfield approached. "I agree with you. Without the card game, there really isn't any reason to be here. It was a disappointment. Lord Aurington has made a swift recovery and is hosting a gala as well as a private game this Monday. Will you be there?"

"Perhaps." She felt a jolt when she realized Monday was Ewan's birthday. Juliet exchanged a glance with Duncan, but he remained unmoved and stoic. "It was good seeing you again, Lady Ashfield." The small party made their way to their waiting carriage.

As they left The Gilded Lily, the records tucked safely in Juliet's reticule, the night air felt charged with possibility. The game had changed, and with it, the rules. Now, they were playing for higher stakes than ever before.

THEY WALKED UP the steps to Fairmont Hall. "Good evening," Wilcox greeted them as they entered and directed them to the drawing room. Two messages sat in the silver salver, one for Lady Rosefield and one for Lady Glenraven. Juliet's hands trembled as she opened her invitation, her anger rising like a crescendo with each word she read.

"It seems we've been invited to your husband's parents for a gala," Aunt Geraldine's tone was icy with disapproval.

"Yes, and I've been extended an additional invitation to a private card game." She went up to Duncan, her eyes blazing.

"You promised you wouldn't tell Ewan what we planned. 'My word is my pledge,' you told me." She brandished the invitation like a weapon before she tossed it on the table.

"I told him nothing," Duncan's defense was swift and firm. "Other than I had seen you and that I knew where you were. Nothing more."

"How did he know we would be at the Gilded Lily? And this? Laughing at me. Is that what—"

Her accusations were met with Duncan's unwavering honesty. "No. Lass, we didn't laugh at you. Ewan demanded to know where you were I told him I could not tell him. We almost came to blows, but I wouldn't raise my hands to him. Instead, he asked that I keep you safe, and we parted ways."

"Parted ways? That's not possible," Juliet whispered. The revelation that Ewan and Duncan's friendship had been tested to its limits left her reeling.

"You gave me little choice. I knew what I was doing when I made my pledge to you. I couldn't let you and Aunt Geraldine go to the Gilded Lily alone."

"Come, Juliet. I'll help you change while Duncan waits here for you."

Behind the closed bedroom door, Aunt Geraldine's anger mirrored Ewan's—a reflection of the trust Juliet had shattered. "How could you demand such secrecy from him?" she demanded.

"I never meant to—" Juliet's protest died on her lips as she faced the results of her actions.

"I've never thought you selfish, but this quest you're on isn't about Bradley. This is all about you. Why else would you make such a demand of Duncan? This isn't a game with your brother who you had to best at every turn."

Juliet stepped back in horror. "No. That's not true." Her voice was a whisper.

"Isn't it? Think about it when you're alone, hiding from everyone," Aunt Geraldine challenged.

"I left to protect Ewan." Juliet insisted, clinging to the justification she had woven around her actions.

"Do you really believe that? He is more capable of dealing with this than you are. All you've done is abandon him," Aunt Geraldine countered. "You are still his wife. I know. I was there when you spoke your vows in front of the archbishop. Your leaving and hiding doesn't change that. All you've done is leave him to face everything by himself. You even took Duncan away from him. It will be a miracle if Ewan speaks to the man again."

Juliet sank onto the edge of her bed. "What should I do?"

"That is for you to decide." Aunt Geraldine's advice was clear and unyielding. "Neither Ewan nor Duncan deserve what you've done."

Aunt Geraldine headed to the door and spun around to face her. "Your brother didn't run away. I never believed he committed suicide. He died trying to save his family."

Juliet followed Aunt Geraldine down the stairs and into the drawing room. Duncan stood as she entered. She glanced at the invitation to Aurington Hall she had tossed onto the table, a mocking reminder of the challenge and the choice to be made.

The carriage ride back to the summerhouse was shrouded in silence, a tangible reflection of the turmoil within Juliet. Aunt Geraldine's scolding words still echoed in her ears, a stinging reminder of the rift she had caused. Duncan sat opposite her, his presence a silent comfort despite everything.

As the horses trotted along the familiar path, Juliet gazed out the window, the landscape a blur of shadows and moonlight. She wanted to speak, to fill the void with apologies and promises of change, but the words eluded her, caught in the web of her own making.

Finally, as the summerhouse came into view, a sanctuary and a prison all at once, Juliet found her voice, though it was barely a whisper. "Duncan, I am so sorry."

Duncan's eyes met hers, but they were unreadable. He saw her going inside and left without saying a word.

Chapter Thirty

April 28, 1820

THE MORNING LIGHT filtered through the windows of Fairmont Abbey. Aunt Geraldine, Mrs. Murthy, and Juliet sat together, the remnants of last night's discord hanging silently between them. Yet, there was work to be done and plans to be made. They could not afford the luxury of dwelling on regret.

With a collective breath, the three women leaned in, their voices a hushed murmur against the stillness of the room. The plan was simple yet bold. They would spread rumors of an impending announcement at the Aurington Gala. These whispers would not only draw the curious and the concerned but would also serve to unsettle Sebastian, ensuring his attendance.

Aunt Geraldine's gaze was steady, her voice firm. "You're doing the right thing, Juliet. It's time the truth came to light."

Juliet nodded, "I'm glad you agree. We only need a spark to ignite the curiosity of the *ton*." Her mind raced with a variety of scenarios. "A carefully dropped hint here, a veiled suggestion there, and the gossip will circulate rapidly."

"There is no time to lose. Monday isn't far away." Aunt Geraldine had paper and pencil ready in front of her.

"There are several less obvious places we could use to move the rumors quickly," Mrs. Murthy offered. "The grocer's wife is a reliable source. I could speak with her when I go to the market. She has nine children who are all in service. We won't even have to ask for their help. Tell their mother the rumor, and the offspring will take care of the rest."

"Do you know anyone in service for Lady Ashfield?" Juliet looked hopefully at Mrs. Murthy.

"Yes. Her housekeep makes a particularly tasty punch."

Juliet tilted her head and tried not to smile, although she was quickly losing that battle.

"Would you like me to pass a particular rumor to that house?"

"Yes. I will share information with Lady Ashfield that there is something afoot at the gala, and her staff will give her more information."

Aunt Geraldine glanced at Juliet. "That is a very good idea. A tease with additional information. Two sources will give the gossip more credibility."

"Could we ask Duncan to make a mention to the Aurington staff?" Mrs. Murthy asked.

Aunt Geraldine stopped writing and glanced at her over the rim of her reading glasses.

"No. I think not. We'll take care of this ourselves." Juliet let out a breath. A dull ache still rose every time she thought about what she'd done. "We need to decide on the rumors and where we will plant our little gems."

Juliet paced the room. She couldn't be rash. She needed to think this through. "We need to be cautious," she said to Aunt Geraldine and Mrs. Murthy. "We keep the rumor vague but enticing." And consider Ewan and Duncan's acceptance of what she writes.

Aunt Geraldine nodded. "I understand. This needs to be a delicate balance. What do you have in mind?"

"An unexpected event," Juliet mused. "Something that promises intrigue but keeps the details shrouded in mystery. It needs to draw Sebastian out, make him believe he stands to gain."

Mrs. Murthy's eyes twinkled with a hint of mischief. "And where shall we plant this seed of curiosity?"

Juliet took a deep breath, her smile widening with her decision made. "The London Chronicle's gossip column. It reaches the eyes of everyone, including Sebastian." She turned to her aunt. "Do you agree?"

"One minute." The woman dipped her quill and wrote furiously. She crossed out a word or two and continued on. Finally, she put down the quill and blotted the paper. "Now, I'm ready."

Juliet positioned herself in a chair. Mrs. Murthy next to her. Aunt Geraldine lifted the parchment.

Dear Reader,

Prepare your carriages and your finest attire, for the whispers on the wind speak of an event not to be missed at Aurington Park. It is said that a revelation will take flight like a dove and will grace the halls of the Aurington estate, promising to leave the ton abuzz with anticipation.

Aunt Geraldine glanced up as Juliet and Mrs. Murthy nodded, encouraging her to go on.

"Please change dove to starling, if you will. The change will not go unnoticed. Duncan will know we're involved in the rumor."

Aunt Geraldine made the change and continued.

Dear Reader,

Prepare your carriages and your finest attire, for the whispers on the wind speak of an event not to be missed at Aurington Park. It is said that a revelation will take flight like a ~~dove~~ starling and will grace the halls of the Aurington estate, promising to leave the ton abuzz with anticipation.

The nature of this revelation remains shrouded in mystery, but one cannot help but wonder if it will shine a light on the shadows that have long danced at the edges of high society. Will it be a scandal unveiled or a triumph declared? Only the night of the gala will tell.

One thing is certain, my dear readers: every eye will be turned to Aurington Park, every ear straining to hear the secrets it might spill. Even the matriarch of the Glenraven family has been overheard expressing her intent to witness what promises to be the talk of the season.

So mark your calendars and prepare your whispers, for this spectacle promises to be as enchanting as it is enigmatic.

Yours in anticipation, The London Chronicle's Society Scribe

"That's brilliant. You have a real talent for gossip." Juliet teased. "Next, I think one for Mrs. Murthy to help circulate would be good."

"It should be about gems or something valuable that's been found," Aunt Geraldine said. "Possibly an heirloom. Everyone likes a mystery. What do you think, Mrs. Murthy?"

The housekeeper didn't write anything down. She beckoned the others to come round her. They huddled in close. "Have you heard? A treasure once thought lost has been rediscovered. An item of no small significance, I heard, and it's set to make quite a stir at the Aurington Gala." She straightened up. "But, oh, don't mind me. I'm just sharing a bit of harmless chatter."

Juliet and Aunt Geraldine straightened, their jaw open. They glanced at each other and started laughing.

"You have your own talent, Mrs. Murthy. That is exactly what we need." Juliet let out a heavy sigh. "We have one more."

"Excuse me, Miss Juliet." Mr. Wilcox entered the room. "This came for Lady Rosefield." He handed Aunt Geraldine a message.

"Mr. Wilcox, have you heard? There is talk that an announcement of great consequences concerning the future of the Aurington estate will be made at the Aurington Gala. It's all very hush-hush, but this revelation could shift the very foundations of London society. Why, anyone who's anyone will want to be at Aurington Park on Monday to see what unfolds!"

"Indeed, Miss Juliet?" His eyebrow raised ever so slightly. "Such news is most…intriguing. It shall be interesting to see what transpires at the gala." His tone remained neutral and gave away nothing of his personal thoughts as he left the women.

Aunt Geraldine rose putting the note in her pocket. "Your mother sends you her love. It's a lovely day, and while we have attended to much-needed business, it would do us good to make our afternoon calls. Juliet, will you join me?"

Juliet glanced at Mrs. Murthy. "I have some errands to run. There's the grocer, first on my list, then the modiste to gather your gown. I think the baker, too. And I'll bring your article to the London Chronicle office. I best me on my way."

THEIR STRATEGY UNFOLDED as they mingled among the guests at various social calls. Juliet's casual remark to Lady Ashfield about an upcoming 'surprise' at the gala was met with a raised eyebrow and a knowing smile. "Oh, what do you know?" Lady Ashfield urged, her interest piqued.

Juliet's smile was mysterious. "Let's just say that surprises may be afoot."

After an afternoon of calls, Juliet and her aunt returned to Fairmont Abbey.

Mrs. Murthy brought the tea service into the drawing room.

"Thank you, Mrs. Murthy." Aunt Geraldine glanced at the housekeeper as she poured tea. "How was your afternoon?"

"It was very interesting indeed. I handed in the article at the London Chronicle, and the clerk took it from me. I stopped for a moment when a gentleman rushed out of his office and demanded to know who gave him the note. The clerk looked around. 'The woman must have left,' he said. They were putting it into the next edition of the paper."

Juliet and Aunt Geraldine smiled and sipped their tea.

"I made my stops along the way." Mrs. Murthy poured herself a cup and joined them. "I think the Aurington Gala will be the talk of the dinner table above and below stairs."

>>><<<

"MY LORD," SANDERSON stood at the library door. "Mr. Herbert from the London Chronicle to see you."

Aurington glanced at Ewan and Duncan. "Are you expecting someone from the newspaper?" The two men shook their heads. Aurington turned to his butler. "Send him in."

Mr. Herbert, a man of sharp eyes and sharper wit, entered the Aurington library with a respectful bow. "Your Grace, gentlemen," he greeted.

"It is good to see you, Mr. Herbert. I may be a bit late, but I understand congratulations are in order. You've left the London Gazette for the Chronicle."

"Thank you, my lord." He bowed again. "That is very kind of you."

"What brings you here?"

"We've received a curious note regarding your upcoming gala, and we seek your comment before publication." He passed the note to Aurington, who read it and passed it on to Ewan.

Ewan took the note from the editor, his eyes scanning the words. The message spoke of an unexpected event, a revelation that would captivate all who attended the Aurington Gala. Yet, as he read, his brow furrowed in confusion.

Duncan, who had been silent, suddenly let out a hearty laugh, drawing curious glances from Ewan, Aurington, and Mr. Herbert. "What amuses you so, Duncan?" Ewan asked, a hint of irritation evident.

Duncan pointed to the word 'starling' within the note. "She's telling you this is her work," he explained quietly, still chuckling. "Who else but Lady Glenraven, your wife, would be so clever?"

Ewan's eyes widened in realization, and he re-read the message with newfound understanding. "Clever indeed," he murmured. "She wants to ensure the gala is well attended."

The editor shifted uncomfortably, unsure of his role in this private revelation. "Shall I wait for your response, my lord?"

Ewan nodded, lost in thought. "Yes, wait, please." He pondered aloud, "How will she know it's me responding? I don't want it to be obvious to everyone…"

Duncan, quick to offer a solution, suggested, "Refer to yourself as Falcon. She'll know it's you."

Ewan nodded, a plan forming. He took up his quill and began to draft a response to be included in the morning edition of the Chronicle. When he was done, he shared it with Duncan and his father. They returned it to him, and he gave it to Mr. Herbert.

"To the Starling with secrets aplenty,

What game do you play with whispers so many?

The Falcon watches with keenest of eyes,

Awaiting the moment when surprise flies.

At the gala, amidst the grand scene,

Will the Starling reveal what her murmurs mean?"

"I would appreciate it if you had this in the morning paper."

Mr. Herbert took the new article, a knowing smile on his face as he left to prepare it for publication.

"Do you want to tell me what that is all about?" his father asked.

"Have I told you, Father, that I'm married to a very clever woman?" Ewan and Duncan exchanged a look of shared conspiracy, united once more in their quest.

⤜⤜⤜✦⤛⤛⤛

JULIET SAT AT the table with her breakfast, reading the morning edition of the London Chronicle. Their gossip had been posted in last night's edition, and now they were eager to see if there was any mention of her rumors.

"What?" Tea splashed over her teacup that almost fell from

her hand.

Aunt Geraldine lifted her head.

Juliet was still staring at the paper. "Have you seen the paper?"

"Are you speaking of the very well-written poem your husband had published just for you? If that's what you're referencing, then yes." Aunt Geraldine stopped putting raspberry jam on her toast and glanced across the table at Juliet. "I did." She tried not to smile and returned to her toast. "Well written and definitely romantic," she said, biting into her toast.

Juliet re-read the poem. She could almost see his smile and mischievous eyes. "Yes. It is romantic."

Chapter Thirty-One

May 1, 1820

I T WAS EARLY afternoon. Juliet sat in her bedroom window seat, staring out at the garden. Over the days, whispers through London's high society swirled around Juliet like leaves in an autumn wind. Each conversation she overheard was filled with speculation, each theory more elaborate than the last. The mysterious event she had hinted at had taken on a life of its own, and the *ton* buzzed with anticipation.

The world around her was alive with speculation and anticipation, yet she stood apart, a solitary figure on the edge of the excitement she had herself orchestrated. It was as if she were observing the whirlwind from a distance, untouched by the fervor that she had ignited.

The anticipation for the Aurington Gala had woven itself into the very fabric of London's high society, and Juliet could feel its pulse in every corner of the city. The rumors she had set in motion had done their work well, stirring curiosity and excitement in equal measure. Yet, despite the success of her plan, Juliet had kept her distance from Ewan and Duncan, her heart torn between the desire for reconciliation and the fear of rejection.

"There you are." Aunt Geraldine crossed the room and sat beside her. "You've created quite the spectacle for tonight. The entire city is eager to witness what happens. You'll stand and see what you created."

"Will Ewan want to be with me?" Juliet's concerns tumbled

out of her mouth as she clutched her aunt's hand. "The thought of facing Ewan's coldness, or Duncan's… I'm not sure I can bear it."

"You belong there as much as anyone, Juliet." Aunt Geraldine's response was a comforting embrace. "You have an invitation, and you won't be alone."

"Lady Glenraven, your presence has been specifically requested." Mrs. Murthy nodded, reminded her. "And there's a special invitation for the card game. It's clear you're expected at Aurington Park."

Juliet allowed a smile to break through her doubts. "I hadn't considered it quite like that."

Aunt Geraldine handed her a note, its seal bearing the Aurington crest. "There's more reason for you to attend." She gestured for Juliet to read it.

"Lady Aurington requests our presence this afternoon before the gala begins. There will be room for us to prepare for the evening." She handed the note back. "It will provide an opportunity to come to an understanding with Ewan. This must be fate playing games with me."

"Like fate did the afternoon at the Punch and Judy theater?" Aunt Geraldine asked.

"'*Together, we'll find the strength to conquer all.*' That's what we vowed. How quickly I forgot." Juliet lifted her head, a serene smile on her lips. "I cannot avoid Ewan forever. The words my falcon offered publicly were a silent olive branch. And another thing. I love him. With all my heart. And I intend to fight for him."

Aunt Geraldine threw her arms around her and held her close. "Welcome back, Juliet. I've been waiting to hear that strength."

Her Aunt's hug was a welcome anchor: "Come, my dear. We shouldn't keep Lady Aurington waiting."

Mrs. Murthy packed what she needed for the evening while Juliet slipped Bradley's diary into her reticule. It contained the precious evidence of Sebastian's duplicity. He was at Sir Giles, but he would be at the Aurington Gala tonight. She hurried into Aunt Geraldine's room.

"Do you think it's too early for us to arrive? She didn't provide a time, but it isn't even noon."

"No, this is not too early." Aunt Geraldine looked around one more time as Mr. Wilcox came in and took her baggage, as Mrs. Murthy entered.

"I've seen to your things. They're being packed in the carriage now." Mrs. Murthy, her job done, turned and left the room.

They went down the stairs and faced Duncan, who stood at the door with Mr. Wilcox.

"Duncan? Why are you here?" Juliet asked. Her heart skipped a beat at the sight of Ewan's carriage outside.

"I was sent to bring you and Lady Rosefield to Aurington Park." He said nothing else. And she didn't pry but gave him a warm, welcoming smile.

"Ach, Lass." His stance eased. "You've been sorely missed by all of us, everyone,"

Juliet's smile turned into a combination of nerves and delight. "I've missed you all as well."

Still chuckling, Duncan offered an arm to both ladies and handed them up into the carriage.

As they rode towards Aurington Park, Juliet's thoughts were a whirlwind, but at their center was Ewan—her husband, her love.

The coach approached Aurington Park, the afternoon sun casting a warmth over the grand estate. The manor's chief gardener and his team were in a flurry of activity, putting the final touches on the gardens in preparation for the evening's gala.

They came to a halt, and the door opened. Ewan stood there with his hand stretched out to help them descend. Juliet was the last to step out of the carriage. She placed her hand in his and, at his touch, realized how much she had missed him. She steeled herself and said nothing as she stepped down.

Ewan nodded to Duncan as he released Juliet's hand.

"This way, Lady Rosefield." He gestured toward the manor entrance.

"I appreciate the formality, but I am Aunt Geraldine to you." Aunt Geraldine's smile was infectious as Duncan chuckled and tucked her hand on his arm.

Juliet waited as the footman took their boxes, then began to follow Duncan and Aunt Geraldine.

"Lady Glenraven," he called.

She looked over her shoulder. "Yes."

He offered a small, reassuring smile and gestured towards the garden's secluded path. "Walk with me?" His voice was a gentle invitation. "The footman will see to your things. There's much we need to discuss, and the garden offers a quiet, private place."

Ewan led Juliet into the garden. The air was filled with the scent of roses and the distant sound of preparations for the evening's gala. They walked in silence until they reached a secluded bench, a private place amidst the sprawling estate.

"I sent for you because I wasn't sure you'd come on your own," Ewan said, his voice betraying a hint of vulnerability. "I thought it best we talk away from the crowd."

Juliet's heart was a mix of emotions. "I considered staying away," she admitted. "I feared you might reject me, given the last days."

Ewan's eyes held hers, but he was a master of controlling how much people saw of him. At the moment, he showed her nothing. "Juliet, I would never turn you away."

Ewan led Juliet to a stone bench nestled among the roses, their petals a vivid reminder of the beauty that can arise from thorny situations. He took a moment before speaking, choosing his words with care.

"The recent weeks have been a journey of sorts." Again, he stopped to choose his words with care. "A journey we've navigated together, albeit apart."

"Indeed," she paused for a moment to take stock. "It has

allowed us to reflect, to perhaps understand one another in ways we hadn't anticipated. It is humbling. Please know I never meant to hurt you or Duncan. I was so certain I was protecting you."

Ewan listened, understanding and regretting his actions. "I never doubted your intentions. I was determined to make everyone do things my way without thinking whether it was correct or not." He gave her a sideways glance. "Duncan has a way of making me see the truth of things. You and I, we both have learned."

"And, here we are." Juliet nodded, her hands clasped in her lap.

"Yes, here we are," he echoed. "And I believe we're the stronger for it. We married in haste to help each other as well as ourselves," Ewan continued. "Now, I find myself curious about the woman you are beyond the obligations."

Juliet considered his words and longed for the warmth of his voice. Perhaps it was too soon to hope for that. "And I wish to know the man behind the Marquess." She turned in her seat to face him squarely. "Do you think we can build a friendship, a foundation for a good future together?"

Ewan's hand hovered near hers, a silent offer of companionship. "Take my hand, and as friends who share a name and a home, we will find our way." He paused, waiting for her reaction. She didn't move. "Together, Lady Glenraven, we can conquer anything."

A shadow crossed his face, and his voice dropped to a whisper. "There's something I haven't shared. In Paris, I was tasked with a duty I failed to fulfill and cost a person their life. It's a mistake that haunts me, one that I will not repeat. The memory of that failure drives me to keep control over everything around me, to ensure I never make the same mistake again."

Juliet's eyes softened, understanding the depth of his confession. "We all carry burdens, Ewan. What matters is how we move forward."

Lady Glenraven, he called her, not Juliet or even Starling. She found it curious that she fought the idea of marrying without affection, yet here she was. Fate had played a dirty trick on her. She married someone whom she had great affection for, but by her own doing, it is no longer reciprocated. However, she swallowed around the hot knot in her throat. Juliet placed her hand in his.

Chapter Thirty-Two

THEY SAT QUIETLY on the bench, each in their own thoughts. The gentle breeze and the warmth of his hand gave her hope.

She focused on the garden and the land on the other side of the far wall. "It all looks the same."

"What does?" Ewan followed her gaze.

"The Fairmont land on the other side of your garden wall. Monster Mound isn't far."

"Monster Mount? You'll have to explain."

"My brother and I visited the Fairmont property when we were younger. Father forbade us from coming here. We were not to intrude on the Auringtons."

"Shall we walk? You can get a closer look at your Monster Mount." He rose and held out his hand.

She gave him her hand, and they walked through the garden.

"Of course, the two of you came here anyway," he said as he led her under the wisteria arches.

"Of course. Forbidden fruit is always the sweetest kind." She couldn't keep the smile out of her voice. They walked around the small pond.

"We reasoned by renaming the property Monster Mound, and we were not disobeying Father."

He chuckled, and the strain between them seemed to ease.

"We explored the land and groves of trees, pretending we were the first ones to ever set foot on it. And, of course, we climbed the base of the mound."

"Monster Mound," he interjected.

"Are you laughing at me?" she teased.

"Oh, no. Simply enjoying your story."

"As I was saying, we climbed up the mound and found an ancient oak tree with gnarled roots twisted through the earth. Its branches stretched out like the arms of an old friend. It became the keeper of our secrets and the silent witness to our games. Bradley found a deep crevice in its bark, a hidden hollow where we hid things." She peeked over the modest stone wall at the field beyond and then turned to Ewan. "I hadn't thought about the mound until I read Bradley's diary and found his mention of Monster Mound and the old tree amid his ramblings."

"Ramblings? Did you find anything else of interest?"

Her heart pounded. She had assumed Duncan told him what they found. Glancing at his beautiful, penetrating gray eyes, she didn't know if she was going to laugh or cry. Duncan had kept her confidence.

"Yes, a great deal…about his card games. It had the aliases he had given the players and the places where their games were held."

She removed the worn leather diary from her reticule, opened it to a specific page, and handed it to Ewan.

"Arrived early at The Gilded Lily and sat in Viper's seat. He was furious. No one wins that often. Must be more than luck."

When he lifted his head and stared at her, she said, "That is why I decided to go to The Gilded Lily." There was nothing playful in her voice.

Ewan held her stare. "You were that determined."

"Single purposed." She nodded.

"And Duncan—"

"I didn't ask him to come with me," she interrupted. "If that is your question."

"He would never let you go there alone." His gaze was unwavering. "Neither would I."

She sucked in a breath and let it out slowly at his unspoken promise, the deep commitment to protect her. Juliet felt a surge of determination to address the issue. It was now or never.

"When Duncan found me, he asked me to return to Glenraven Manor with him. I told him I couldn't until I took back my brother's honor and my family's good name. I refused to bring you or your family shame."

"I wouldn't expect anything less from you." They were both quiet for several minutes. The gentle rustle of leaves and the distant chirping of birds filled the silence, creating a moment of reflection.

Ewan finally broke the silence, his voice gentle. "What else did you find in the diary?"

She took the diary from him, found the page she wanted to share with him, and then handed him the book. "Duncan mentioned that you play chess."

He gazed at her, and she saw his mind working. He read the pages, and she waited as Ewan realized what Bradley had given them.

"Sebastian is Viper as well as the author of threatening letters."

"I thought Duncan found something in that letter. I laughed when I found the spelling error."

"He must be stopped." His anger boiled. "I'll walk you to the house." He looked past the wall. "I want to go to the tree and see what Bradley left there."

"I'm going with you." She took the diary back from him. "You'll never find the tree by yourself."

He smiled that smile that made her heart thump. "Why am I not surprised?"

"There are no yew trees on the Fairmont property. As a boy, I searched everywhere for the oldest tree. I know each tree there." Ewan led her through the small maze.

"Bradley knew there were no yew trees there. '*Tall yew tree*' was his alias for you." She said nothing else, her eyes searching his, waiting for the moment he understood the meaning.

Ewan stopped and studied her face, his expression turning serious. "He was warning—"

"That Viper wanted to destroy you and your family," she finished for him. Her hand tightened around his, her heart pounding. Tears welled in her eyes, but she blinked them away, meeting Ewan's gaze with determination.

Ewan's eyes darkened with anger and a flash of protectiveness. He gently cupped her face, his thumb brushing away a stray tear. "I won't let that happen. We'll stop him, together."

They walked to the garden door, where Ewan pulled on the bolt, swung the door open, and gestured for her to go before him.

They ventured into the Fairmont property, their steps taking them across the field and into the forest. Juliet led him to the mound, and they quickly climbed to the top.

"Here it is, Ewan." Juliet's voice was soft and reverent. "This is where we hid our treasures."

Ewan looked from her to the tree, his eyes widening in surprise. "This is your tree?"

She nodded.

He laughed, a sound of genuine amazement. "Do you remember my quest to find the oldest oak?"

"This is your tree?" Her surprise was as great as his.

Her surprise was as great as his. "It appears this tree played an important part in your youth as well as mine."

They stood back and looked at their old friend. "There, by the second branch." Juliet pointed to the place where the treasures would be. Ewan climbed the knotted roots, found the crevice, and reached into the hidden hollow. His hand brushed against the rough interior until he found what he was searching for. He pulled out a leather pouch, climbed down, and gave it to Juliet.

Her fingers traced Bradley's embossed initials. She opened the pouch and found the fourth ace of hearts and a note in Bradley's handwriting. *Starling, Guard this with your life.*

Chapter Thirty-Three

EWAN TOOK THE card from her and examined it. "It's the same as all the others, but I want to see them side by side. We may see more."

With the precious pouch in hand, they turned back to the manor.

"What was Bradley afraid of that he had to hide this for me here? He didn't even call me by name."

"He's protecting you yet giving you a mission. We will have a better idea once we can see the cards together."

They entered the house, and Ewan led them to the drawing room where the others had gathered.

"We found the fourth ace of hearts," Ewan said as Juliet placed it on the table. "Bradley left Juliet a message in his diary." He opened a drawer in the writing table and took out the three cards he had.

He laid all the cards side by side. When arranged, the cards revealed a deliberate and telling pattern. Each card bore a unique mark, a subtle difference in the filigree design around the border that, when placed together, formed a coherent message—a map.

Ewan, Juliet, Lord Aurington, and Duncan gathered around the table. The intricate lines created the familiar outline of Aurington Park, leading to a destination none had expected. "That's the estate office."

"It's almost time to prepare for the gala," Lady Aurington said. "Perhaps we can do this in the morning. The office is only used to store documents. Your father conducts his business in his study."

"No, dear. We cannot." Lord Aurington was adamant.

"Father's correct, Mother. If anything, we must uncover whatever Bradley left before the gala begins."

The group moved with purpose, their footsteps echoing through the halls as they made their way to the estate office. The door creaked open to reveal a room steeped in the musty scent of paper and leather. There were shelves stacked with the annual estate ledgers. What light they had come through a shuttered window.

Ewan looked through the drawers while the others started to examine the ledgers.

"Here it is." Ewan stood at the desk, holding a folded and sealed message bearing his name.

"You've worked hard to find this," Ewan said to Juliet. "You open it." He handed her the package.

Juliet carefully unfolded the paper, its edges creased from being meticulously folded into a compact shape. The wax seal bore the distinct impression of Bradley's signet.

With hands that trembled ever so slightly, she broke the seal, It was addressed to her and dated the day of Bradley's death, the handwriting unmistakably his.

My Dearest Juliet,

As I pen this letter, as evening draws near, and a chill that I fear may not be solely from the night. Today, I stumbled upon a truth that has shaken me to my core, and I must confide in you for your safety and the future of our family. The fear that grips me as I write these words is real, Juliet. I implore you to heed my warning.

It began harmlessly enough with the discovery of letters in our estate office—correspondence addressed to Ewan Glenraven among our accountant's papers. When I questioned Reynolds, he assured me they were but exchanges between him and Ewan, another client. Wanting to see the best in him, I chose to believe his words. Yet, an invitation to a card game hosted by Sir Giles marked the start of my descent into a world of deception and greed.

You know well of my fortunes at the card table, the good fortune that could only be explained by luck with my every play. But that luck did not last. I soon found myself ensnared in losses that far outweighed my wins. Today, the man known as the Viper laid bare his demands for Monster Mound and the lands held by our family, and he would wipe out my debt. He was ignorant of the entail that protects them. His threats did not cease there. He produced vowels in my name that I never signed. Of course, I denounced them. He said Wickham did a good enough job in creating the documents that it would stand up. But there is more. I am ashamed, Juliet, to tell you that he spoke of you, of claiming your hand in marriage as a means to seize the Fairmont property. I implore you to stay away from him.

It seems that the viper's venomous plans are not just aimed at our family's holdings but are part of a grander scheme to bring about Ewan Glenraven's downfall. This revelation came to light when he unwittingly revealed his intentions, speaking of Glenraven with a malice that could not be mistaken. The viper will stop at nothing, and his reach is limitless. I found evidence that he arranged to have Ewan assassinated while he was on assignment in Paris.

I made a further discovery. He is a member of the Order of Shadows, an elusive and dangerous organization known for its manipulation and deceit. Their influence stretches far and wide, and their intentions are shrouded in mystery, but make no mistake, their intent is to disrupt and gain power.

Today, in the quiet of our estate office, I have uncovered further evidence—messages from Mr. Hughes to Glenraven, urging him to return home to fulfill the obligations of his inheritance and to marry before the first of May. I have no idea what hold the viper has over Reynolds or why these messages are in his possession.

I cannot sit idly by with this knowledge. Tonight, I plan to *confront the Viper with everything I have learned. I have the Ace of Hearts and sent them to those who need to know. I've kept one. The others have been sent to Enrico Quinto and Lord Aurington. This one is for you. If I am not here to see the dawn, know that I acted to protect our family and to expose the betrayal that threatens to consume us.*

Be vigilant, Juliet. The path ahead is fraught with danger, and I trust you to navigate it with the strength and grace that have always been your nature.

With all my love and a brother's concern,
Bradley

Still reeling from Bradley's words, she lowered the letter and handed it to Ewan. The silence was deafening.

"We must act." Those weren't just words. In her heart, they were a vow. "Bradley's last wish was to protect us and expose the viper's treachery. I owe it to him to see this through."

Ewan's eyes met hers, filled with determination. "Juliet. This fight is ours now, yours and mine. Together, we will bring the viper to justice and protect our families." Ewan folded the letter and handed it to her. "We have what we need. I'll ask Barrington to speak to Reynolds. Now, let's see this through—for Bradley."

As she turned to leave the room, she paused. "What confuses me is what part Fray and Eclipse played in all this?"

"Do you mean Whitby and Gray?" Lord Aurington asked.

Juliet and the others stood and waited.

"Whitby or Fray was deeply in debt. Gray, or Eclipse, was helping him. They were trying to gather information to help me to protect Ewan and expose Sebastian. They were allies, not enemies. Bradley misunderstood their intentions."

"There is no doubt." Lord Aurington stood firm. "Sebastian has been behind the crooked games, the thievery, and even the deaths. Your brother saw it. I read a few more pages in his diary. Are you familiar with the King's Gambit? It's a chess opening where a pawn is sacrificed to gain a stronger position."

Juliet nodded, her curiosity piqued. "Yes, Duncan has explained it to me. But how does that relate to our situation?"

Aurington leaned forward. His voice was filled with urgency. "Sebastian's moves have been calculated and bold, much like the King's Gambit. He's sacrificed pawns—Bradley, Quinto, and he tried to sacrifice me—to position himself for a greater gain. But just like in chess, his arrogance will be his downfall. He believes he's outmaneuvered us, but we've seen through his strategy."

Juliet's eyes widened as the metaphor clicked into place. "Sebastian's been playing a dangerous game, thinking he's always one step ahead. But now, we have the advantage."

Aurington nodded, a determined glint in his eyes. "Exactly."

"Lady Glenraven,"

"Yes, my lord?" Her heart skipped a beat as her husband's words resonated deeply. The title felt like a promise, a declaration of their bond.

A warm smile lit Ewan's face. "Go with Aunt Geraldine and get ready for the evening. I'm looking forward to seeing the look on Sebastian's face when we announce our marriage."

Chapter Thirty-Four

THE GRAND BALLROOM of Aurington Park was spectacular. The air was thick with the murmurs of the elite and the subtle fragrance of opulence.

"I made my husband change his plans to attend this evening. I had no intention of missing this event." Ewan stifled a grin as he nodded at Lady Campbell as he slipped by. He was confident Lord Campbell would rather be at his country house fishing.

Juliet deserved credit for the overwhelming attendance, which gave him a degree of satisfaction, but his sights were still on the rest of the evening. The room was a sea of finery and whispered speculations—rumors of royalty attending the event sent ripples of excitement through the crowd.

Juliet had yet to enter, and her absence was as conspicuous to him as the glittering chandeliers above. The archbishop mingled with dignitaries, his presence lending a solemn grace to the evening. The Ashfields surveyed the room with keen eyes. Sebastian's arrival, marked by a certain pompous air, drew the attention of many, his confidence bordering on arrogance. With Duncan's skillful help, Ewan was able to avoid him.

With all but one of the necessary players in place, Ewan needed a moment. He excused himself from the conversation with his friend Mr. Thomas and made his way to the library. The promise of solitude and brandy seemed a welcome reprieve.

When he entered the room, he found neither solitude nor the need for a drink. Instead, he was met with a vision that arrested his every sense.

Juliet stood by the window, the soft candlelight creating an enticing image. She wore her dark green gown, the fabric hugging her form in a silent echo of their wedding day. The sight of her, poised and magnificent, had him speechless.

Regaining his composure, he approached her. "Lady Glen-raven, you look ravishing this evening." His voice carried a gentle formality. His words were sincere yet tempered by the reserve that had grown between them.

Juliet turned, her eyes meeting his, and in them, he saw a reflection of the same complex emotions he felt. "Thank you, my lord."

Rather than reach for the decanter, Ewan extended his arm in a silent invitation. "Shall we join the others?" The simplicity of the gesture contradicted the significance of the moment. "Your plan has worked better than you could have expected. We will be fortunate if there is room to walk and greet the guests. Everyone is here, including Sebastian."

"Of course." She placed her hand on his arm, accepting their tenuous truce, and together, they stepped into the ballroom.

The ballroom was abuzz with anticipation as the gala reached its height.

"Glenraven." Sebastian nodded at them with a smug air of triumph. The air around him seemed to shift, and Lora caught that now-familiar scent—lemon intertwined with the smoky residue of burnt wood. Realization struck her like a bolt; the fragrance was no mere coincidence.

"Pardon me, Sebastian." Lady Aurington walked past him, almost pushing him out of her way. "You'll have to wait." She nodded to Duncan, who was in the middle of the room.

"Ladies and Gentlemen," Duncan called out, his voice ringing with command. "May I have your attention, please?" He waited several moments for the center of the dance floor to clear and for the guests to quiet down.

"Thank you. Your hosts, Lord and Lady Aurington."

Duncan stepped away as Ewan's parents took his place.

"My wife and I would like to welcome you all to Aurington Park. We hope you enjoy the evening. It has come to our attention that rumors are circulating about an announcement this evening. I understand there is a great deal of activity in the betting book at White's." He took out a piece of parchment.

"One entry reads: I wager that the announcement will reveal a new political alliance, one that could shift the balance of power in Parliament." He looked up. "Before you take sides, that is not our announcement. Another entry reads; I'll bet you two to one that they've discovered a new continent. Yes, right beyond the Americas, and they'll name it after our illustrious host."

"I read one of the entries."

Aurington looked up. "Is that you, Sir Haroldson? What did you read?"

"I've heard you're going to announce an expedition to the moon. They say you're funding a flying contraption made of silk and dreams!"

A burst of laughter rolled through the room. When it quieted, Aurington wiped his eyes. Laughing had brought him to tears.

"That is very good, but my dreams are more down to earth."

"If I were allowed to bet," came Aunt Geraldine's voice from the back of the room. Everyone turned. "My money's on the declaration of an engagement for the Duke's heir. It's high time the young lord settled down, and what better occasion to announce it than tonight, his thirtieth birthday."

All eyes turned to Ewan, who had Juliet on his arm.

"Well, Glenraven?" As the room reached its peak of anticipation, with murmurs and the clinking of glasses filling the air, Ewan prepared to make his announcement. It was then that Sebastian stepped forward, a document clutched in his hand and a gleam of triumph in his eye.

"Ladies and gentlemen, if I may," Sebastian's voice rang out, clear and confident, cutting through the din of the crowd. "Before Lord Glenraven makes his undoubtedly erroneous announcement about himself and Miss Hayward, I have a matter of utmost importance to share."

He unfurled the document with a flourish, holding it high for all to see. "Behold, the true marriage settlement with Miss Juliet, the daughter of Baron Fairmont. So you see." He gazed out at the crowd as they all listened to his every word. "He has not met the requirements of the Aurington inheritance legacy, which will put to rest any claims the young former Marquess here might have."

His smile was wide, almost predatory, as he turned to Ewan. "It seems, my dear Ewan, that your time of playing lord of the manor is coming to an end. And what a spectacle it is to have all of society as witnesses to your downfall. And with the legal contract, I will spirit Lady Juliet to Gretna Green this very evening."

The room fell into a stunned silence at the gravity of Sebastian's words. Ewan maintained his composure, his eyes never leaving Sebastian's face.

"Let me see that document." Aunt Geraldine called out as the crowd parted, giving her room.

"Of course, dear Auntie." Ewan wanted to wipe the smirk from his face. Instead, his thumb made small circles on Juliet's hand to help her stay calm.

"I think there is something wrong with this document." Aunt Geraldine looked up and out at the crowd. "Cecilie," she called out. "Sister, you're needed here."

Chapter Thirty-Five

E WAN NUDGED JULIET and nodded toward Sebastian, whose face had gone pale.

The room's murmur hushed to silence when Juliet's parents made an unexpected entrance. With a grace that gave no indication of their mission, they approached the gathering around Sebastian and the archbishop.

Aunt Geraldine and her sister stood side by side. Cecilie took the document and scanned it with a practiced gaze. A frown creased her brow as she turned to face the onlookers. "I did not sign this." Her voice resonated with authority. "And even if I had the power to do so, which I assure you I do not, I would have at least spelled my own name correctly."

A collective gasp rippled through the room as she pointed to the signature at the bottom of the page. "This says 'Cecily,' with a y but I am Cecilie, with an ie and I have always been so." She turned, glaring at Sebastian. "This document is a forgery."

Sebastian's earlier confidence evaporated like mist under the warm morning sun. His face paled, and his eyes darted around the room, searching for an escape. The crowd's murmurs grew louder, a wave of indignation and disbelief crashed over him.

Two men, Bow Street Runners, stepped forward and positioned themselves on either side of Sebastian. He attempted to step back, but their firm grips on his arms halted his retreat.

"Unhand me!" Sebastian demanded, his voice cracking with desperation. "This is a misunderstanding!"

Ewan stepped forward, his expression resolute. "There is no misunderstanding, Sebastian. You forged Lady Fairmont's signature and threatened to abduct Lady Juliet. All by your own words. Your deceit ends here."

Sebastian's eyes flickered with a mix of fear and anger. "You cannot do this! I have powerful friends—"

"Your friends will not save you now," Ewan interrupted, his voice cold and unwavering. "You will answer for your crimes."

"Lord Barrington, if you please." The archbishop motioned to his friend, who stood close by.

"It would be best to take Sebastian into the library and address this there. We don't need the entire *ton* involved."

Barrington nodded, his expression serious. "That is a wise move," he agreed, glancing around to gauge the mood of the room.

The archbishop stepped forward with a reassuring smile. "I'll see to your guests."

Ewan inclined his head, gratitude in his eyes. "Thank you, Your Excellency."

Barrington nodded, understanding the need to control the situation. He turned to the Bow Street Runners holding Sebastian. "Come with me. We'll take Mr. Morgrave to the library." As Barrington and his men moved swiftly across the room. Sebastian's protests grew louder, his face twisted with panic. "You can't do this! It's an outrage!" But his words fell on deaf ears as the Bow Street Runners firmly guided him out of the ballroom.

Ewan turned to the others. "Come with me, please. There is still much to discuss. For all our sakes, we will do it in the library." Juliet, Aunt Geraldine, her parents, Dr. Manning, Duncan, and Ewan's parents followed.

The tension in the ballroom began to ease. The musicians resumed playing with calming music.

"I don't think this was what Lord Aurington had in mind as a surprise." The archbishop stood near several matrons of the *ton*.

"Your Excellency, do you have any idea what they plan?"

asked one of the women.

"I can assure you this was not the evening's entertainment. I have it on very good authority you will be very glad you stayed." He gave a knowing smile and made his way to the next gaggle of women while others kept an eye on the library doors, awaiting further developments.

ONCE INSIDE THE library, the door was closed, ensuring privacy. The room, lined with rows of leather-bound books and a warm fire crackling in the hearth, starkly contrasted the tension that filled it.

Ewan turned to Dr. Manning. "Dr. Manning's examination of Bradley Hayward's body revealed signs of a struggle and injuries consistent with being pushed from the balcony."

Juliet's gasp echoed through the room. Her grip tightened on Ewan's arm, and her heart pounded. Ewan gave her a reassuring nod. She glanced at her parents, holding each other tightly.

Her mother, eyes brimming with tears, clutched her father's arm. "I knew it," she whispered, her voice breaking. "I always knew our Bradley wouldn't leave us like that."

Her father, usually stoic, had a rare, visible tremor in his hands. He pulled his wife closer, his voice rough with emotion. "Justice for our boy. Finally."

Dr. Manning nodded solemnly. "The bruises and the angle of the injuries clearly support this conclusion."

Sebastian's face blanched. "This is preposterous!" he blustered. "Sheer fabrication!"

"We are not done." Barrington held up a sealed letter. "Through the diligent efforts of our associates abroad, we have obtained a confession from a man in France—a hired assassin who was responsible for the tragic death of Duke Berry. In his confession, he reveals that the true target was not the Duke." He turned to Ewan. "But Lord Glenraven."

Sebastian sneered, his bravado slipping. "These are mere allegations with no solid proof."

Ignoring the outburst, Barrington pressed on. "We have further evidence of Mr. Morgrave's illicit activities." He continued, "Mr. Reynolds, Lord Fairmont's accountant, has come forward with a confession. He admits to 'adjusting' the Fairmont books under the direction and duress of Sebastian Morgrave. He was coerced into manipulating the ledgers to conceal funds being funneled to… unsavory parties. He feared for his livelihood and his life if he refused."

Juliet's heart pounded with a whirlwind of emotions: grief, anger, and a fierce sense of relief. She released Ewan's hand and glanced at him. He gave her the silent encouragement she needed. Juliet stepped forward, her voice trembling yet strong. "We've been living in a nightmare, but now, now, the truth is finally out." Tears welled in her eyes, but she held her head high. "You will pay for the pain you've caused us. For Bradley's sake and for all of us, you will answer for your crimes."

Sebastian sneered, his veneer of charm slipping. "You have no proof of anything. Accusations, that is all you have. That and the word of a cowardly accountant means nothing."

Barrington's eyes narrowed. "On the contrary, we have tangible evidence." He produced a small vial. "Duncan found this among your possessions. It's a concoction of Bergamot and birch tar, the scent the Order of Shadows uses in their rituals."

He handed it to Lord Aurington, who took a whiff. His face turned crimson with fury.

"Moreover," Barrington continued, "the stain of this same scent was detected on the fragment of cloth found at the scene of Bradley's death and the binding of his diary."

"And my carriage!" Aurington shouted, his voice shaking with rage. "By God, you have the nerve to tamper with my property and smear my name with your vile schemes!" He turned to Barrington. "And I owe Watts an apology." He shook his head.

Sebastian's eyes darted around, seeking an escape or an ally, but found none. Desperation etched lines across his face. "You cannot prove any of this! You're all against me!"

"It's over, Sebastian," Ewan said coldly.

Chapter Thirty-Six

"S EBASTIAN MORGRAVE," ONE of the Bow Street Runners announced, "you are under arrest for conspiracy, fraud, and the murders of Bradley Hayward and others."

"You think you've won?" he spat out the words. "The Order of Shadows reaches further than you know!"

Barrington met his gaze evenly. "Perhaps. But justice must start somewhere.

As the Bow Street Runners escorted Sebastian out of the library, his protests faded into the distance. The small group left behind in the library took a moment to gather themselves, the magnitude of what happened fully understood.

Ewan turned to the others, his voice calm but resolute. "We should return to the ballroom. People are waiting for us."

Together, they made their way back to the ballroom. As they entered, the guests, who had been anxiously awaiting news, turned their attention to the group. Conversations hushed, and all eyes were on Ewan, Juliet, and Barrington.

The archbishop came forward. "It is good to know that we are once again safe. Let us also remember the joy and celebration that brought us together tonight. In moments like these, we must hold fast to the bonds of community and fellowship. Sadly, I must tell you that no one had the winning wager at White's."

A collective chuckle, as well as disappointment, went around the room.

"I do have a joyous announcement to make."

The room fell silent, every ear tuned to the archbishop's words.

"On the twenty-first of April, in the sanctity of my private chapel, I had the honor of joining Lord and Lady Glenraven in holy matrimony. Tonight, they wish to recommit to those sacred vows before you, their family, and friends. Please find your seats, and we will begin."

In the stillness of the ballroom, with the soft rustle of her gown, Glenraven knew that this image of Juliet, splendid, unadorned, and wholly his, would be etched upon his heart forever.

Ewan's surge of emotion, a blend of joy, gratitude, and something he could not define, threatened to overwhelm him. Whatever this unknown thing was, it filled him to the brim and spilled over in a single tear.

Juliet stood before him, and his heart pounded in a silent thunderous drumbeat. His hand reached for hers, and as their fingers entwined, a sense of rightness settled over him. "You are a vision," he murmured for her alone. With a gentle squeeze of her fingers, they turned to face the archbishop.

They both turned and stood before the archbishop. In a gentle voice that resonated through the chamber, he began, "We are gathered here to join this man and this woman in matrimony, witnessed by those they hold dear."

As the archbishop's words echoed through the stillness, Juliet and Ewan listened, each understanding the full meaning of their commitment. The archbishop paused with a silent invitation to Ewan.

Glenraven took a deep breath, his gaze never leaving Juliet's. "Juliet, with you, I find the courage to face any challenge, the joy in every moment, and the peace I've longed for. I vow to cherish our bond, to support and respect you, to laugh with you in joy, and to comfort you in sorrow. Together, we will create our own destiny."

Tears shimmered in Juliet's eyes as an overwhelming sense of completeness filled her as she gazed into Ewan's eyes. "Ewan, you are my heart's true companion, my strength when I falter, and my light in the darkest times." Her voice was a soft but firm declaration of her commitment. "I vow to stand by your side with unwavering support and share the endless adventures that are before us. Together, nothing and no one can come between us."

Glenraven turned to Duncan, who placed an etched gold band in his hand. He faced Juliet and took her hand. He placed the ring on her finger and stared into her bright hazel eyes. "With this ring I thee wed, with my body I thee worship, and with all my worldly goods I thee endow."

The archbishop cleared his throat softly, a smile dancing on his lips as he drew the couple's attention. "By the sacred trust placed in me, I declare you husband and wife. May your journey be rich with love, steeped in understanding, and abundant in joy."

The vows had been spoken, echoing through the grand hall, binding Ewan and Juliet once more.

Ewan's gaze shifted to Duncan, who stood proudly in his kilt with Baron and Lady Fairmont. Duncan came forward and handed him Glenraven Circlet.

With the heirloom in hand, he turned to Juliet. Ewan gently placed the circlet upon Juliet's head. He leaned in close, his breath a whisper against her ear. "Juliet, my starling. Try to keep it this time," he murmured.

Juliet's eyes closed for a brief moment, the passionate overtones in his voice curling her toes. Her eyes glowed with a mischievous glint. "Oh, I fully intend to, Ewan," she whispered back, her lips curving into a teasing smile. "But if I return it again, just know you'll have to win me back all over."

"Ladies and Gentlemen, Lord and Lady Glenraven."

The applause that followed was heartfelt and thunderous, a celebration of love's triumph. Juliet's eyes met Ewan's, and in them, she saw not just her husband but her partner, her champion, and her dearest friend.

Juliet and Ewan found a quiet moment to slip away from the

festivities as the gala continued. In a small, dimly lit anteroom, they finally saw her parents. Her mother's eyes were bright with unshed tears, and her father's usual stoic manner softened as he saw her.

"Mother, Father," Juliet said, her voice catching with emotion. "This is Ewan, Marquess Glenraven." Juliet stared at him, a smile broadening on her lips. "My husband."

"We arrived last night. Ewan was waiting for us. He remembered flitching tarts from Mrs. Murthy with Bradley. We had a lovely time getting reacquainted," her mother said.

"I cannot believe a coincidence brought you home," Juliet said.

Her father placed a hand on her shoulder, his touch reassuring. "Barrington and Aunt Geraldine sent word of what was happening. Your mother and I were distraught to think that Sebastian would go to such extremes. We would move heaven and earth to protect you."

"Let's go back to your party. You and your husband should be celebrating." Her mother adjusted Juliet's skirt and glanced up at her with tears in her eyes. "Lady Aurington asked to see your father and I."

"I have one more thing to do," Ewan said as the four returned to the ballroom.

"I'm going to miss you." Her mother dabbed a handkerchief at her tears.

"Mother, don't cry." Juliet glanced at Ewan. "We are taking up residence at Glenraven Manor. I won't be far away. Don't keep Lady Aurington waiting."

"Come with me. I must speak to Barrington." He took her hand and led her to the far corner of the ballroom.

He found Barrington near the entrance, overseeing the final arrangements with the Bow Street Runners and Sebastian. Ewan approached him, the gold coin held firmly in his hand. "Barrington," he called, his voice steady.

Barrington turned, his eyes meeting Ewan's with a knowing

look.

"Is it done?" Ewan asked, even though Barrington's expression made the answer clear. He extended his hand, the gold coin twinkling in the candlelight.

"The job is done. The culprit is captured, and justice will be served. Edward sent word that Bradley's information about Paris was correct. The assassin provided all the information." Barrington took the coin, a rare smile breaking across his stern features. "Well done, Ewan."

Ewan felt a sense of pride and relief wash over him. "Thank you, Barrington. Your guidance were invaluable." He turned to Juliet. "As was Juliet's."

Barrington nodded, pocketing the coin. "This is just the beginning. Bradley provided more information about the Order of Shadows. There will be more work to do, but tonight, we celebrate a victory."

"Why don't you both celebrate your victory," Juliet said. "I need to speak to someone."

As she moved through the room, glancing into several quiet corners, she finally found Duncan standing alone by the grand windows. His gaze was lost in the night sky. She approached him hesitantly.

"Duncan," she began, her voice barely above a whisper. "I owe you an apology."

Duncan faced her, his expression unreadable. Silent, his stoic gaze was fixed on her. Her heart raced, and her mind grappled with the possibility that things could not be repaired or forgiven.

She took a deep breath, steadying herself. "I was wrong," Juliet continued, her eyes meeting his. "I let my own needs and fears blind me. I put you in an impossible position, and I am truly sorry."

The rigid lines of his posture eased as he listened. She waited. Finally, Duncan spoke in a low voice. "It takes courage to admit when you're wrong. Your apology is accepted."

Duncan's expression lightened, a chuckle escaping him as he

regarded Juliet. "The rumors had your touch. It was a clever plan. And when Ewan heard them, he spun his own to bring Sebastian into the open. It seems you're both quite the strategists." With a playful nod, he added, "It was a good plan. Just try not to set our hearts racing next time, eh?"

A smile lit her face. "No racing hearts. I am glad you both approved of the plan."

Chapter Thirty-Seven

"Do you think they mind that we're gone?" Lady Glenraven asked as they walked through the garden and out the gate to their enchanted cottage.

"Not at all, my lady. They would wonder if we weren't." He smiled one of those smiles that could charm a bird off a tree.

Ewan retrieved the key from Artemis, and they entered the cottage. A large bouquet of flowers and a bottle of wine were on the table next to a hamper.

He opened the wine and poured them each a glass. "To Punch and Judy." He raised his glass.

"Yes, to Punch and Judy," she laughed as they sipped their wine cuddled on the sofa.

"Until now, our efforts have been centered on safeguarding one another." He paused, his gaze meeting hers with true curiosity, "We haven't spoken about what we want for ourselves, for our own future. What are your hopes and dreams?"

Juliet's eyes met his, and in them, she saw the spark of shared aspirations. "A home filled with laughter and warmth," her words were a breathy echo in the hushed space. "Children, perhaps, running through the gardens without the worry of the world beyond these walls."

Silence settled between them, the air thick with unspoken dreams and hopes. Finally, Juliet tilted her head, her smile soft and tender. "You have a way of making the ordinary feel extraordinary."

Glenraven raised an eyebrow playfully as he refilled her glass with wine. "Juliet, in your presence, even this humble wine seems as though it should be savored in a royal chalice." His tone was light, the corners of his mouth twitching with the hint of a smile.

Juliet sipped her wine, the rich aroma complementing the bouquet of scents from the garden that filled the room. She let the silence stretch between them, a comfortable lull in their conversation. "Ewan, I've always admired the loyalty and friendship between men." Her gaze met his, reflecting the flickering candlelight.

Juliet nestled against Glenraven's shoulder with ease. Their conversation flowed naturally, meandering like the garden paths outside. They spoke of their favorite books, revealing a shared love for the classics and an appreciation for poetry that surprised them both. They discussed the changing seasons and how each preferred the crispness of autumn to the heat of summer. Glenraven expressed an interest in horticulture, which Juliet matched with her fondness for painting. She confessed a desire to capture the beauty of the summerhouse garden on canvas. They even touched upon lighter subjects, such as childhood escapades, how he played chess with his cousin, and the simple pleasures of a well-brewed cup of tea.

She lifted her head and caught her breath as his smile danced across his lips. More than charm and confidence, she saw his promise of passionate encounters and thrilling adventures.

"I thought you were beautiful when you approached me in the chapel. You were even more radiant this evening."

She closed her eyes as his deep, rich voice flowed over her. He awakened a deep longing in her, a craving so fierce that she forgot all caution and restraint.

"But now—"

She reached up and kissed his lips softly, tentatively not allowing him to finish what he was saying. Hesitantly, she broke the kiss. Their eyes connected, holding for a moment that went on and on.

He stared at her eyes and hair, but when he focused on her lips, he pulled her close and claimed them. His kiss, first tender and sweet, grew more demanding.

She was lost to the storm, to sensations she had never experienced, sensations to which she surrendered and hoped he wouldn't stop.

He drew back slowly, the warmth of their kiss lingering as their lips parted. A soft sigh filled the space between them, a silent echo of their tenderness.

"I'll be your Abigail, Madame." His voice was deep and husky, and he pulled out one of her hairpins.

She glanced at his eyes and saw the laughter and couldn't help but laugh with him. "Then I must be your valet, my lord." The twinkle in her eye had him chuckling.

He gently lifted the circlet from her hair and placed it on the nearby table. Then, one by one, he removed the rest of her hairpins, letting them scatter without concern. Once her hair fell loose, he ran his fingers through the soft strands, massaging her scalp with a soothing rhythm.

Her eyes closed in response, a serene smile spreading across her face. He was captivated by the simple joy that played upon her features.

He stepped closer to her, her chest nearly against his, reached around, and pulled the bow loose at the top of her gown.

Her eyes flew open. She stared at him for a heartbeat as the corners of her lips tipped up. She undid his cravat and then his waistcoat. He didn't move. Her fingers worked unbuttoning his shirt. After she pulled the linen back over his shoulders and helped him shrug out of it, she ran her fingers down his chest.

"Your gown, my lady. It's a beautiful shade of green." He unlaced the ribbon as she held the bodice in place. When he had the ribbon free, he tossed it to the side, gently took the gown from her hand, and let it fall to the floor.

Ewan stood awestruck.

Nothing. Juliet stood without anything on. Her chestnut hair cascaded, flowing down over her shoulders, modestly covering her breasts. In Glenraven's eyes, she was his own Botticelli's Birth of Venus.

"I thought women—" he stammered.

"It was Aunt Geraldine's idea," she whispered, never looking away from him.

"I will thank her—"

"You will do no such thing," her voice louder than she planned, "Ewan James Alasdair Danford Glenraven."

He began to laugh but quickly sucked in his breath as she began to work him free of his trousers. When she was done, he guided her onto the bed amidst the plush pillows and the soft fabric. He held her close, her breasts against his chest, and felt her heart beating quickly like a timid sparrow.

"What did I do to deserve you?" he murmured, cradled her. "I love you."

"I know," she sighed.

He gazed at her, a bit of mischief in his eyes. "How did you know, Juliet Anne Glenraven?"

"The way you look at me, touch me, care about me, and even listen to me. It makes me love you even more."

They held each other close, and together, in their secret summerhouse, they explored each other, each touch, each kiss a revelation, and each revelation binding them closer. Her shallow breathing had her heart racing as if she had run up five flights of stairs. Her eyelids fluttered shut as she anticipated what was to come. A warmth spread through her chest, grounding her. Unease was replaced with safety. Need was replaced with passion.

Her eyes fluttered open to find his gray eyes sparkled like lightning, their intensity holding her spellbound. He drew closer, never taking his eyes from hers. Closer. She could see his firm, soft lips. Closer. She reached out—needing to touch him.

She nestled against them. The mere touch of his hand, his knuckles stroking her face, sent a warming shiver through her. His eyes focused on her mouth, and she instinctively wet her parched lips. He ran his thumb gently over her lower lip, sending a tingle through her with each gentle stroke. She kissed his finger, feeling the warmth of his skin against her lips. His quick intake of breath sent a thrill through her, a silent acknowledgement of their shared desire. As he eased closer, wrapping her in his arms, a sense of urgency began to burn inside her. Her heart raced, and there was this deep, insistent need to be closer to him, to feel his touch and warmth. Every part of her responded to his embrace, driving her to press against him, seeking to be closer, but it wasn't enough.

He lowered his head, and she felt the warmth of his lips on hers. She lifted her trembling hand and caressed his cheek. The thought of him sent her to places she could only find in her dreams. He left her lips and kissed her along her cheek. *Juliet*, he whispered in her ear. His arms cradled her, feeling the steady rise and fall of his chest. She wanted him to let her go. Then, he tenderly kissed her forehead, his lips lingering for a moment. With a gentle touch, he lifted her chin with the crook of his finger and captured her lips once more. Liquid heat roared through her veins. Every nerve was alive. Every touch of his lips made her dizzy with delight. A hushed moan escaped her lips, the sound meant only for him.

He kissed her lips and she sank further into his arms as he left a trail of velvety, warm kisses down her neck. Another moan, ragged, wavering on the edge of surrender, escaped her lips.

Outside, the rising wind matched her growing desire. He pressed his manhood against her while his lips seared a path across the top of her breasts. She gasped at the sensations and held him tighter lest he stop.

His hand covered her breast, She was going to die, the sensation was exquisite joy. His mouth advanced in a warm, steady march across her collarbone and down the soft incline of her breast. He hesitated, and she panicked. "Please, don't stop."

His gaze was intense and unwavering, filled with deep emotion and passion. His eyes, locked on her, conveyed a silent promise and yearning that words could never capture. And she felt cherished, the only person in his world.

A sense of urgency began to build. She attempted halfheartedly to control the dizzying current racing through her but quickly gave up. He dipped his head. His mouth found the softness of her breast. Slowly, he licked her hardened nipple, the sensation pure and explosive.

Her soft curves molded into the hard planes of his body. He raised his head, and she closed her eyes, feeling his breath on her neck as began to trail kisses down her body once more. His hot breath against her stomach, her thigh, and…places, secret places she suddenly felt compelled to share with him. His hands stroked and caressed her, but it wasn't enough. He was tender, coaxing, kissing, stroking and soothing until she craved more from him. He began slowly at first, still cooing and comforting, and he moved inside her.

The wind picked up—slowly at first. The faster her heart beat, the wilder the wind blew, and the more insistent she became, the deeper he went. Juliet was lost in her desire and Ewan's passion, but she didn't care. Slowly, they found a rhythm that brought her to an edge she had never been to before.

"Forever, my Juliet," he murmured.

A delightful demanding sensation kept building inside her. When she could no longer contain it, she surrendered, her resistance shattered into a million pieces. How would she ever be the same? Her hands raked his back as her heartbeat slowed. She soothed him, until a long, low groan escaped his lips, ending with her name, *Juliet*.

The wind had calmed. Ewan pulled away, his eyes glistening with contentment. He tucked her head against his chest. "My wife," he whispered. He kissed the top of her head.

She let out a soft sigh. "Forever, my husband," she said softly as they fell asleep in each other's arms.

In their shared journey of discovery, they told each other they were loved, showed each other they were loved, and in the quiet sanctity of their wedding night, they forged a bond that was unbreakable.

Outside the walls of the summerhouse, the world, the ace of hearts, Order of Shadows, and intrigue beyond the gate ceased to exist. In each other's embrace, they found what they hadn't realized they had been searching for all along—each other.

Epilogue

May 2, 1820

EWAN AND DUNCAN strolled through the park, their conversation a mix of estate matters and lighter musings. Ewan's attention drifted from time to time. Duncan clapped a hand on Ewan's shoulder. "She'll be back shortly."

Their walk was interrupted by the familiar voice of Percival Thimbleby, the puppeteer.

"Lord Glenraven, it is you. How fortunate to see you and your friend."

"Good day," Ewan touched the brim of his hat, "to you."

"Ladies and gentlemen. This is Lord Glenraven, a most excellent hero for our poor Judy." The puppeteer turned to Ewan. "My lord, I beseech you, your heroics are needed once more!"

About to turn wave off the man, Ewan spotted a pair of small feet peeking out from under the curtain where Juliet once stood. Somewhat disappointed, he leaned toward Duncan. "You don't have to stay."

"Oh, I will not miss this." Duncan took a seat with the rest of the audience.

"Very well, Mr. Thimbleby. Your Punch has returned from a long journey."

"Excellent, my lord. We have missed you. You are one of our best lords. No one else plays a lord like Lord Glenraven."

"I've had good practice."

The audience laughed as Ewan took his place behind the

curtain on the far side of the theater.

The puppeteer set the scene for the audience, his voice booming. "Punch has returned with a treasure most rare, and now he must convince his dear Judy of its worth!"

Ewan embraced the moment and began with gusto. "Oh, Judy, my heart, I've braved dangers untold to bring back this prize, a treasure beyond measure!"

Juliet's voice, sweet and clear, responded from behind the screen. "But Punch, my love, we must tread with care, for envious eyes are everywhere."

Ewan felt a warmth spread through him, the words they exchanged transcending the play. Juliet: "Fear not, for together we are a force formidable, our love shielding us against all woes."

The puppeteer, with deft hands, brought Punch and Judy together on the stage. "Then let us stand united, our bond unbreakable, our future a canvas awaiting our strokes."

Ewan's gaze was fixed on the far curtain where Juliet stood, his voice tender. "And should the morrow bring trials anew, know that my heart beats only for you."

Juliet emerged from behind the curtain. "And mine for you, dear Punch. Together, let us embrace the love that is our right."

The audience erupted in applause, but for Ewan and Juliet, the applause faded into the background. Ewan came out from behind his curtain and extended his hand, his voice barely above a whisper. "I love you, Juliet. With every fiber of my being."

Juliet's eyes met his, her own love shining through. "And I, you, Ewan. Always."

"We've faced more than our share of difficulties," he said.

"But you taught me together, we'll find the strength to conquer all," Juliet declared.

She delicately touched Ewan's face. "And what of commitment, Ewan? Will your flames endure, or will they be snuffed out?"

"Fear not, dear Juliet," even the audience could hear the smile in Ewan's voice. For desire may kindle our passion, but it's a commitment that fuels our eternal flame."

"Then let our love burn brighter than the stars, Ewan, for both desire and commitment bind us."

He enjoyed this little game the first time. Once again, it excited him in ways he hadn't anticipated. The sincerity in Juliet's voice warmed him.

Once a game, this puppet performance became his opportunity to right something that had been bothering him since Juliet left after the gala.

"So, my love," Ewan said tenderly, "let us dance through the pages and write our own story, bound by fate and love."

"Forever entwined, together we'll craft our own destiny. It awaits, Ewan, my dearest." There was a pause. "Forever," was Juliet's breathless reply.

He reached out, his hands gently cradling her face. His thumbs softly traced the contours of her cheeks. As Ewan's hands tenderly framed Juliet's face, the audience collectively held their breath. And then, as if moved by a single heartstring, a soft sigh rippled through the crowd.

The world seemed to stand still as he leaned in, the promise of a kiss. "Juliet, with you, I find the courage to face any challenge, the joy in every moment, and the peace I've longed for. I love you." He kissed her lips softly.

He lifted his head and stared into her eyes.

"Ewan, you are my heart's true companion, my strength when I falter, and my light in the darkest of times. I love you," she said. "Together, we can conquer anything.

"Lady Glenraven, shall we? It is a good day to explore the secret room at Aurington Park, find a map, and make some plans." He turned to her. "Would you like that?"

Juliet took his hand, her smile radiant. "Yes, my lord, I would."

Together, they left the puppeteer's stage behind, their hearts full, their path forward clear. They were Punch and Judy, Ewan and Juliet, Lord and Lady Glenraven. They were partners in life and love.

DUNCAN ENTERED THE drawing room at Fairmont Abbey, the air filled with the relief and excitement of recent events. Lord and Lady Aurington, Aunt Geraldine, and Baron and Lady Fairmont rose to greet him, their eyes full of curiosity. "Well, what happened?"

Duncan's lips curled into a knowing smile. "They may have found their calling. Ewan and Juliet were quite the Punch and Judy," he mused, his tone playful. He paused as a thoughtful look crossed his face. "Unless they weren't acting, which, I suspect, is the more likely true."

Mrs. Murthy wagged a finger at him, her eyes twinkling despite her feigned sternness. "You stop your teasing this minute, Duncan MacAlister."

Duncan chuckled, undeterred. "Mr. Thimbleby played his part well. When he asked Ewan to reprise his role as Punch, I thought he would decline, but he changed his mind. Who knew a simple puppet show could hold such a mirror to life?"

"I knew they would be perfect together," Lady Fairmont remarked, her voice soft with sentiment.

"Not just as Punch and Judy," Lady Aurington said, "but as Lord and Lady Glenraven. It seems the trials they've faced have only strengthened their bond."

Lady Fairmont leaned in, her curiosity piqued. "About the Ace of Hearts."

"What would you like to know, Lady Fairmont?" Ewan's father asked.

"Ewan and Juliet told us all about the game, but they never mentioned how the game ended."

Ewan's father took a deep breath, his gaze steady. "The ace of hearts wasn't just a game. It was a reflection of Sebastian's strategy to play with our hearts and trust. It symbolized his deceitful hold over us, and now, it stands as a reminder of the love and loyalty that ultimately triumphed."

The room settled into a comfortable silence, each person reflecting on the journey that had led to this moment. Duncan looked out the window, where the setting sun cast a golden hue over the estate. "They've come a long way," he said, more to himself than to the others. He turned back, his eyes meeting those of the gathered family and friends.

"In the Punch and Judy show," Duncan said softly, "Love and laughter wins in the end. Ewan and Juliet have shown that no matter the trials they face, their love will always prevail."

He smiled, a sense of peace and contentment settling over the room. "And now, their story, like a beautifully told play, concludes not with an end but with a new beginning."

The End

About the Author

There was never a time when *USA Today* Bestseller, RUTH A. CASIE hasn't had a story in her head. When she was little, she and her older sister would dress up and act out the ones Ruth creative. Today, Ruth writes exciting and beautifully told legendary historical romances that are both rich and engaging. Her stories feature strong women and the men who deserve them, endearing flaws and all. Her stories are full of, 'edge of your seat' suspense, mind-boggling drama, and a forever-after romance.

She lives in New Jersey with her hero, three empty bedrooms and a growing number of incomplete counted cross-stitch projects. Before she found her voice, she was a speech therapist (pun intended), client liaison for a corrugated manufacturer, and vice president at an international bank where she was a product/ marketing manager, but her favorite job is the one she's doing now—writing romance. Ruth hopes her stories become your favorite adventure.

Fun facts about Ruth:

1. She filled her passport up in one year.
2. She has three series. The Druid Knight is a time travel romance. The Stelton Legacy is a historical fantasy about the seven sons of a seventh son. Havenport Romances are contemporary romantic suspense stories. She also writes for the Pirates of Britannia connected world.
3. She did a rap with her son to "How Many Trucks Can a Tow Truck Tow If a Tow Truck Could Tow Trucks."

4. When she cooks she dances around the kitchen.

5. Her sudoku books is in the bathroom and that's all she'll say about that!

Social Media Links:

Website:
ruthacasie.com

Instagram:
instagram.com/ruthacasie

Facebook private reader's page, Casie Café:
facebook.com/groups/963711677128537

Facebook Author Page:
facebook.com/RuthACasie

Twitter:
twitter.com/RuthACasie

BookBub:
bookbub.com/authors/ruth-a-casie

Amazon:
amazon.com/author/ruthacasie

Goodreads:
goodreads.com/author/show/4792909.Ruth_A_Casie

YouTube:
bit.ly/3hI5eQr